THE WEDDING RANCH

Also by Nancy Naigle

Christmas Joy

Hope at Christmas

Dear Santa

The Christmas Shop (mass market paperback)

Christmas Angels

A Heartfelt Christmas Promise

Visit www.NancyNaigle.com for a list of all Nancy's novels.

THE
WEDDING
RANCH

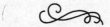

Nancy Naigle

ST. MARTIN'S GRIFFIN
NEW YORK

First published in the United States by St. Martin's Griffin, an imprint of St. Martin's Publishing Group

THE WEDDING RANCH. Copyright © 2022 by Nancy Naigle. All rights reserved. Printed in the United States of America. For information, address St. Martin's Publishing Group, 120 Broadway, New York, NY 10271.

www.stmartins.com

Library of Congress Cataloging-in-Publication Data (TK)

ISBN 978-1-250-79413-0 (trade paperback)
ISBN 978-1-250-79414-7 (ebook)

Our books may be purchased in bulk for promotional, educational, or business use. Please contact your local bookseller or the Macmillan Corporate and Premium Sales Department at 1-800-221-7945, extension 5442, or by email at MacmillanSpecialMarkets@macmillan.com.

First Edition: 2022

10 9 8 7 6 5 4 3 2 1

Beyond every difficulty is an opportunity
to forgive yourself or someone else. Move forward
and shine on!

THE
WEDDING
RANCH

Prologue

Valentine's Day was a sore spot for Lorri this year, and being stuck in the office surrounded by co-workers' flowers and shiny foil heart boxes made it worse.

For her it was more than just Cupid's big day. It was also the one-year anniversary of the day she was convinced Craig was cheating on her. The last-minute business trip had been a disappointment for them both, or she'd thought at the time. He'd said it would be a late night, so she'd decided to arrange delivery of a charcuterie tray and a bottle of their favorite wine to his room. Only when she called the hotel, he wasn't registered.

That weird swirling that had hung in her stomach as she ended the call that day made a repeat performance.

She'd have sworn on her life that Craig would never be unfaithful.

But when he returned, he ran down the events of his business trip like he always did, and when she asked about his stay at the hotel, he lied right to her face. Had she not known for certain that he hadn't been there, she would've believed him too.

Confronting him had ended in a nasty argument about lack of trust, and her apologizing for doubting him. He'd said the hotel he usually stayed at was full, and he was rebooked somewhere else at the last minute. Lorri still had her doubts.

This year his business trip over Valentine's Day had been planned for so long that she'd considered ways to track him to catch him in the act.

But if their marriage had come to that, did it matter? Guilty or not, the damage was done. Which is why she'd finally talked to a divorce lawyer.

Her phone rang, bringing her focus back on work. "Lorri Walker. Can I help you?"

"Happy Valentine's Day!" Pam's voice sang out.

"For you maybe. I should've sent myself flowers to the office today. I think I might be the only one without them."

"They just die anyway," Pam said. "Took me years to get Bobby to understand that. Finally, I get what I really want. He cooks for me, then rubs my feet. My toes are going to be so happy tonight."

"I guess Craig is still a work in progress on that."

"Well, I just wanted to check on you."

"I'm fine. With him out of town I'm picking up Chinese food, and I'm going to eat it right out of the container. I might even crank up the air conditioner and turn on the fireplace—which Craig would never allow—and just relax."

"Sounds like a perfect night to me." Pam's laugh eased the tightness in Lorri's chest.

A new email pinged on her phone. "Oh, great." Lorri sighed as she read the message. "I just got an alert that we're over the limit on our credit card. Again. I hate it when he does that." Lorri logged in to their bank's website to make a payment to the account to cover it.

"Maybe he's going to surprise you with something amazing," Pam said with a laugh.

"Highly unlikely."

"You might want to at least pick up some cheap conversation hearts for him just in case," she teased.

"Definitely not. They don't make a conversation heart with what I have to say to him. Although throwing a box of them at him does hold some appeal." Being a graphic designer, her creative mind conjured up an image of heart-shaped candies dropping in slow motion from the sky all around Craig. As he caught the colorful candies midair, he read them out loud. "Cheater." Tossing it aside, the next read "How Could U" followed by more in pastel colors like, "It's Over," "Bye-Bye," "U R The Ex," and "Half Mine."

"No violence. Never do anything you can't undo." Pam's voice held a hint of laughter.

"One little box wouldn't do *that* much damage." The image made her smile. *Hey, babe,* she'd say. A little shake-shake of the candies, then *wham-o.* He'd yelp and look at her like she was crazy. "It might be just the right kind of wake-up call."

"That would definitely get his attention, but Lorri, you've really got to pick a side on this. You're letting this consume your life. You're losing confidence because of it. I know it's not easy, but you have to make a decision."

"I want him to be faithful. To actively participate in our marriage. What I want is for things to be like they used to be."

"I get it, but we can't control anyone else, we can only control ourselves—so your options are to forgive him and let it go, or if you really can't forgive him then you should leave."

"How do I forgive?"

"I don't know, but as long as you keep focusing on how he's wronged you, you've got one foot out of the marriage."

"Ouch."

"I just want you to be happy. Marriages make it through transgressions sometimes. I can't say how I'd react. But love guides us, and forgiveness is key."

"Seems to me if we were both following the same wedding vows, there wouldn't be anything to forgive. If I just knew the truth it would be so much easier."

"I'm sorry this happened to you," Pam said.

Lorri looked down. With a shake of her head, she said, "Me too. I still love him."

"I know you do. You're hurting, and a year is a long time to hold on to this."

"You're right, it's no way to live, and I know I didn't do anything wrong, but it makes me feel like a failure."

"Honey, you're not."

Lorri scanned the charges on the credit card. "I don't believe this."

"You are *not* a failure. You're wonderful—"

"Not that. I'm looking at the credit card bill. There's a one-hundred-and-twelve-dollar charge for flowers, and last week there was one for three hundred and twenty dollars at a jewelry store." *Jewelry? He's buying her jewelry?* She swallowed back the acrid taste that suddenly filled her mouth.

"Wow," Pam said. "It looks like Craig finally figured out Valentine's Day after all. Maybe it's not too late for him to shape up and be the man of your dreams again."

"Honestly that did not cross my mind." She let out a sigh. "I was thinking he bought someone else jewelry. Or maybe he's feeling guilty."

"Marriage is hard," Pam said. "Especially when trust is broken. It's like a piece of paper you've crumpled. When you smooth it out you can use it, but it's never the same."

Lorri hesitated, almost afraid to say the words out loud. "There is a little flutter of hope in my heart right now." She transferred money to cover the over-credit limit. "You must think I'm an idiot for still feeling that way after all my complaining about him."

"Not at all. You're the only one who can decide when enough is enough. You'll never hear judgment from me. I'm your friend. Your happiness is what matters to me."

Lorri smiled into the phone. "Thank you. Have a wonderful celebration tonight. Hug Bobby for me."

"Will do. Call if you need me."

"I'll be fine. Bye." Lorri hung up. Pam was a true friend. The other women they'd met through neighbors, husbands, and country club events. Dutiful wives, all of them. The social time and girls' lunches were necessary for life balance, but the women weren't the kind of friends you confided in. It was Pam who had convinced Lorri to confide in their friend Kelsey, the best divorce attorney in Raleigh, about her options so she'd know what to expect if it really came down to that.

She didn't know if she'd take the next step. She loved Craig—well, the person he'd been when she married him. For better or worse, but this last year was in the worse column for sure. She strongly suspected, but couldn't prove he'd cheated.

Stop overthinking it.

She dialed her favorite Chinese restaurant. "Order for pickup." She recited the order from memory. "Wait, cancel the General Tso's Chicken." That was Craig's favorite. Tonight was about her, not him.

When she got home, she didn't park her car in the garage like Craig always insisted. Instead she parked in the driveway, carried the takeout inside, and set her keys on the entryway table.

Craig's voice startled her from across the room with a throaty "Surprise!"

She juggled the bag as she spun around. "What are you doing here? I thought you were—" She took two steps into the great room then stopped. Craig sat on the couch petting a dog, which made no sense at all because Craig hated dogs. "Why is there a dog in our house?" The dog's long tongue lolled out of the side of his mouth in a weird grin.

Craig raised the dog's paw. "Happy Valentine's Day!"

"What?"

"You've always wanted one. Right?" He held a shredded red ribbon. "He was wearing a bow, but you're late. It didn't survive the wait."

"I . . ." Part of her was suspicious, but she was genuinely touched by the unselfish gift. "Yes, you know I have."

She knelt to the floor.

Without a moment of hesitation the pup raced across the

hardwood floor toward her. His short tail wagged at such a frantic pace it looked like his rear wasn't attached to his front.

Lorri wrapped her arms around him. With a lap full of dog and a face full of puppy breath she couldn't do anything but laugh.

When she glanced up, Craig stood looking down at them. "What is all this? Why now?" she asked.

"Why not?" Craig shrugged. "He loves you already. See?"

The pup's soft fur tickled her cheek.

"I know things have been off lately, Lorri."

"You've been more than a little distracted."

"And you've been angry for over a year."

"Well, yes, but—"

"I thought the dog would make you happy. That's all I ever wanted to do."

There was hope in his eyes, but could she trust him? It was true. Craig had navigated her through troubled family life since she was a teenager, and as soon as he had a job, he married her. "Things have changed. It's not even polite between us anymore." She stroked the dog. "Sometimes I don't even want to come home."

"We'll fix it. We'll do more things together. The dog's an olive branch. It's my way of letting you know that your happiness is my priority."

The pup lapped at her ear.

"He makes you happy, doesn't he?"

When Craig smiled like that, the lines pulling at the corners of his eyes, it reminded her of days when they laughed more. She pressed her face to the dog's. "You are adorable."

The dog licked her cheek as if he knew what she'd said.

"I can make you happy too," Craig said.

"You've been there at my side through the hardest times in my life." A tear slid down her cheek. She sat back on her heels, and Craig lowered himself beside her.

He moved his hand to her lower back, the way he knew would melt any resistance she had left. He hadn't touched her like that in so long. Before she could calculate the last time, he kissed her with a gentleness she'd never known with him.

She tried to resist all of his efforts.

"You like him, don't you?" Craig's eyes were wide as he waited for her answer.

"He's sweet." *Plan B: Can I take the dog and run?* Why would Craig give in after fifteen years? A red flag waved, but it quickly turned into a cute garden flag with puppies on it.

The dog lapped his tongue up one side of her face, then nuzzled her ear.

"Craig, this doesn't fix our problems. We need to talk about it."

"You're right." He wasn't angry, his voice surprisingly calm. "I'm tired of talking about it, Lor. I hate reliving my mistake over and over and over." He looked away, shaking his head.

She stared at him. He hadn't gotten defensive. It was also the first time he admitted he was at fault. "You *were* seeing someone else." She held her breath.

He stood there quietly for what seemed like forever.

She waited, resisting the urge to lash out and push for answers.

Finally, he lifted his chin. "I'm sorry. It was a mistake."

She pressed her lips together to keep them from trembling. She was wrong, it wasn't better to know for sure.

"Please say something," he pled. "It's Valentine's Day."

"I know you bought flowers and jewelry." Her eyes darted around the room. "I don't see them."

"You're watching the credit card?"

"Over-credit-limit alert," she said.

"Again?" He raised his hand. "I'm so sorry." He closed his eyes and took in a long breath. "This isn't how tonight was supposed to go. I couldn't decide what to get you. I canceled the flowers, and the jewelry has been returned." He shrugged. "I wanted today to be perfect."

"What about the meeting?"

"I took the call remotely. Declined the dinner."

"You love those dinners."

"I do, but I love you more." He hugged her close, pressing his lips to her forehead. "Are we okay?"

She sucked in a stuttered breath. "I love you too. . . ."

He pulled back, looking her in the eye. "But?"

The dog squeezed between them, making them laugh. "Is he house trained?" she asked.

"At eight weeks?" Craig laughed. "Hardly. I've been cleaning up pee for an hour waiting for you to get home."

"He's *huge* for eight weeks old. What kind of dog is he?"

"I know you don't like those froufrou purse-sized dogs. This guy seemed perfect. The breeder said they have a great disposition. Easygoing. Good with kids. He'll be a gentle giant."

She was almost afraid to ask. "How big of a giant?"

"I don't know. Hundred pounds, I guess. Big." He handed her an envelope.

She slid her finger under the edge of the seal. The puppy barked at the sound, then pounced toward the envelope.

"This isn't for you," she said. The Valentine's Day card had a googly-eyed dog on the front, and inside a pedigree. "A mastiff?" She grabbed her phone and googled the breed. "Craig, they can get to be a hundred and eighty to two hundred pounds. That's a miniature horse. I can't handle a dog this big. And he'll need to be trained. I don't have time for that."

"I can handle the puppy training."

"You will?" Craig's charm spilled over her like a spell, like it had so many times since the day they met in high school.

"Sure. It's my slow time of year. It'll be great. I'll take him to classes and then we can all practice together." He tapped his hand on the rug, and the puppy pounced for it. "Look. He's smart. Sit."

The puppy sat. He too was under Craig's spell.

"What will we call him?" It was a rhetorical question. She was already rolling through names in her mind. The puppy was already the size of some adult dogs, but way less coordinated. "How about Mister? If he's going to outweigh me, I better offer him some respect. What do you think?"

"I like it." Craig stood and shoved his hands in his pockets.

The puppy cocked his head, then barked.

"Mister it is." She patted him on the head as she got to her feet.

Craig leaned in and kissed her. Not a peck like they'd become used to, but a slow kiss.

She gave in to the kiss, enjoying it. It's all she'd dreamed of for the past year.

He touched her cheek.

"Wow." She said it like a breathless teenager, even though deep down she doubted this would fix their problems. All those words she'd rehearsed hung in her throat, but none of them made it to the surface. Instead, all she said was "Thank you."

She leaned closer, letting Craig drape his arm around her while the puppy scampered in front of them. Craig's charm was an asset and a big part of why he was such a darn good salesman. No one could resist him, not even her after over fifteen years of marriage. Or maybe it was just easier than starting over.

Chapter One

By the time summer was in full swing, Mister was as tall and gangly as a teenager, and according to the vet he still had a lot of growing to do. Craig had kept his promise, taking Mister to puppy class and on through intermediate training. Mister had more certificates than Lorri and Craig combined, and despite his size Lorri felt that she could handle him.

Lorri had never enjoyed exercise, but she'd grown to love the time she spent walking Mister through their large neighborhood. Her friends had even commissioned a bedazzled pooper scooper from Etsy as a gag gift for her birthday, but the joke was on them, because she carried it proudly.

She was in the best shape of her life, both physically and mentally, and she knew she had Mister to thank. He was a lot of work, but with no kids she didn't mind one bit. Craig had definitely gotten Valentine's Day right this year.

She'd had a long week putting in extra hours to wrap up a project rebranding one of the oldest and most profitable accounts with her company, Brand Creative. The client, a sausage company, was now in its one hundredth year, and the great-great-great-grandson who just stepped into the CEO role wanted a fresh look. It had taken rounds and rounds of redrafting to appease him, but this project had allowed her to get creative, even painting an original scene for the client, and she liked that.

When she got home, Mister met her at the door as he did every night. There was no rambunctious jumping, but rather a very respectable greeting followed by him calmly sitting at her feet to get his head rubbed. Well, he looked calm, but his nub of a tail wiggled like a caffeinated guinea pig with a mind of its own.

"How's my good boy?" She put her things down, and gave him a loving pat. He lifted his chin, pressing it into the palm of her hand. "I missed you too."

She looked up and saw Craig sitting on the couch. "Hey, how was your day?" He looked as worn out as she felt.

"Not great. Lorri, I've got something to tell you." He stood, shifting his weight.

"Are you okay?" She walked into the living room. Craig's eyes darted to his suitcase sitting next to the door. "Ah, another unexpected business trip? That's okay. I can—"

"Not exactly." His face pulled to the left. "I'm leaving."

The word echoed. Not leaving on a business trip. Just leaving. Her stomach dropped as if it had been kicked from the top of a skyscraper. "Leaving?" She almost choked on the word.

"I met someone." He rushed to add, "I wasn't looking. I meant it when I said I was going to make it right. This just happened. I'm sorry."

"*You're* leaving?" How could he? She'd forgiven him. Opened her heart again.

"You know things had been . . ."

"Off." She filled in the blank. *Yes, I know.* "You said that when you said we were going to be okay."

"I want to be with her. It's not like the others."

"The others." She wondered how many there had been, but was afraid he might tell her if she asked. "The 'it'll never happen again' others?"

"They meant nothing. Tiffany is different. I feel alive again with them."

"Them?"

"She has the most precious two-year-old. She calls me 'Popster.' I swear it melts my heart."

The shine in his eyes was undeniable. It pierced her heart. In the past she'd suspected something was going on. In her gut, she'd known. She'd even asked. He'd lied straight to her face and never blinked. How many had there been? And why did it take her by surprise this time?

"I love her."

Which only means you don't love me. Probably never did. Jealousy filled her. "But we've been through so much together." He'd been there for her when her family struggled through her brother Jeff's addiction and all the problems that went along with it. The arrests, rehab, the stealing and lying, and then when he'd died. "It was supposed to be forever."

"You were there for me too," he said.

She'd worked two jobs so he could go to college and made the mortgage when his sales jobs weren't going so well. She'd

been there every step of the way when he had that lung can-
cer scare five years ago. It had been terrifying. Thank goodness
doctors were able to remove it and he'd been cancer-free ever
since.

"I never meant to hurt you, Lorri."

"You're not." She was strangely calm. There were no tears,
and once she pushed aside the bitterness of being beaten to the
punch, she knew the marriage was over. She was happy because
of Mister's companionship, not because of Craig. Nothing had
changed. "There won't be another chance this time. Ever. You
understand that, right?"

He nodded.

"When did you meet her?"

"A year ago. Nothing happened then, I swear."

Why would I believe you now?

"Where did you meet? It doesn't even make sense. When did
you have time?"

"It's Tiffany York. You met her." He paused, but she didn't
place the name. "She's the instructor at the dog training fa-
cility."

*Tiffany? Young, blond, owned a Yorkie that she carried around in her
purse.*

There it was. He'd planned it all along. He'd used her, and
used Mister too, working his way to be with another woman all
along.

"You knew her before you bought Mister." The pieces were
falling together.

"What does it matter?"

"It doesn't." She couldn't believe she'd opened her heart to him only to have this happen. *Tiffany?*

"I'll have my attorney draw up something. I guess we could sell the house and split the profit, unless you would prefer to buy me out," he said.

"We'll sell. I'll have it on the market next week." Better now than later. She didn't want to look at anything that reminded her of him. She might not have even stayed the night tonight if it weren't for having Mister to deal with. Wasn't likely a hotel would allow a dog that big, even a pet-friendly one.

"Okay." He stood, pushing his hands deep in his pockets. "I really am sorry. We had some great years."

More bad times than good for her, but they'd had them together.

He grabbed the handle on his suitcase. "We can figure out who gets what later. I'll call before I come over."

"Good idea." She'd change the locks just in case.

When the door closed, she walked over and sat on the couch.

"So that's that." She looked around the room. Their wedding picture sat on the mantel. That had been nothing more than Craig's first great illusion—like David Copperfield making that jumbo jet disappear. He'd promised her the wedding of her dreams, but when it came down to it, the wedding had been handled like a business lunch. He talked her into a quick ceremony at the courthouse one Wednesday afternoon with two strangers as witnesses. No white dress. No guests. The short version even, because he'd had to get back to a meeting. Her parents had never forgiven her for that.

She picked up her phone and dialed Pam. "You're not going to believe what just happened."

"What?"

"Craig just left me for another woman." The words sounded alien spoken out loud.

"Oh, Lorri. I'm sorry. Are you okay?"

"Yeah. I am. I didn't even see it coming, Pam. How is that?"

"Well, now you can finally start over. Pull out all those wish lists and get started."

"I'm putting the house on the market. Remember the farmhouse-chic neighborhood down in Dalton Mill that I showed you awhile back?"

"I do. Those houses were charming."

"I'm driving down tomorrow to take a look. The sooner I can get out of here the better," she said.

"You don't really want to move, do you?"

"I'm sure half the people in this neighborhood already knew what was going on. He really made me look like a fool."

"No. Lorri, stop it. He's a self-centered jerk. That's what everyone knows."

"Why don't you come with me tomorrow? Do you and Bobby have plans?"

"He'll be golfing. Count me in."

"It's only an hour drive. I'll see if they still have the model homes open, or if anything is for sale down there. Want to plan on leaving around ten?"

"I'll meet you at your house," Pam said. "I'm sorry it worked out this way, but at least there won't be any more wondering."

"Yeah, and I forgive him. I had a happy six months, ever

since Craig brought Mister home. It seemed like he was trying to make things work. It was a relief to feel that way. Maybe that's why I'm so calm. Or maybe I'll fall apart tomorrow. It could happen. Just warning you."

"That's fine," Pam assured her. "I'll be there and we'll get through it."

The next morning, Lorri and Pam drove down to Dalton Mill. "I am still shocked. Every time it replays in my mind, I just shake my head."

"You are remarkably calm. Are you really as at peace with this as you seem?"

"I think I am." She looked over toward Pam. "I guess that year of second-guessing kind of prepared me for this. And Mister took me off that roller coaster and let me get some life balance. At first, I felt so betrayed. Especially after giving him another chance, but then I realized that what had been making me so happy wasn't Craig. It was Mister and the changes that I'd made in my life since Valentine's Day."

"You have found a better balance in your life between work, play, and family."

It was an easy drive right down I-95. They took the exit and drove down a long road with open fields on either side.

"It's not all that far," Pam said.

"Far enough to put the past behind me for a fresh start." She leaned forward, looking at the GPS to get her bearings. "It should be up here to the right."

"Look. A farmers market. That would be nice if it's close by."

There were more cars and people in that one spot than

they'd seen since exiting the highway. Just past it a large sign read MILL CREEK HIGHLANDS.

"This is it." Pam pointed to the sign. The entrance was wide, with extravagant landscaping in the middle making for a grand welcome. "It looks more upscale than I'd expected with it being five-acre lots and all."

Lorri turned the car into the neighborhood. "I love the fancy streetlights." The black poles stretched all the way down the street on both sides. Perfectly edged sidewalks made for a park-like setting.

"This is everything I dreamed of," Lorri said as they slowly drove through the subdivision. The houses sat back off the road, but from here she noticed at least one yard with a horse and small barn in the back.

Pam raised a brow. "Five acres is a lot of grass to mow."

"Mister would love all that space to run. I could have a garden, too."

A few new homes were still under construction in the back.

Pam said, "Let's look at the model home."

Lorri didn't hesitate to turn around. Slowing to a stop in front of the model, she glanced over at Pam. "It's really cute, isn't it?"

"I wouldn't say 'cute.' It's beautiful."

"And the neighborhood is surprisingly affordably priced."

"Yeah, I wonder if that's just because we're out in the middle of nowhere, or they shortcut things on the inside?"

"Good point. We'll know in a minute." Lorri parked her car in the driveway of the model. "Here goes nothing."

As they opened the door a young woman greeted them. "Hi.

Welcome to Dalton Mill." She handed them a brochure. "We only have a couple of lots left here, but we're also starting a project about thirty miles from here with the same concept. Also, breaking news: this model is going on the market tomorrow." She pressed a finger to her lips. "You're the first to hear."

"Thank you."

Pam leaned in as they walked away from the lady. "How about that? Fate, perhaps?"

Lorri shrugged, but she'd been thinking the same thing.

They walked through the model home and neither one of them said much until they walked upstairs to the second level. Expansive windows ushered light into the space.

Lorri stood and turned around. "This would be perfect for a studio."

"You could paint again," Pam said with a nod. "You were so good. You should definitely make that a priority."

"It's been so long I'm not sure where to start, but I did an original piece of art on my last work assignment, and it has me itching to paint again." She walked back downstairs. "This being for sale now couldn't be more perfect timing."

Pam agreed. "There's plenty of room for Mister to run, and if there's decent internet connectivity you could work from home, right?"

Lorri walked to the far end of the living room. "There's great light in this room too. I could set up my desk right here to work from home." The agent was seated at the desk already there and smiled.

"It's a wonderful spot to work with the sun coming through the French doors," the agent said. "I expect this model will go fast. With all the upgrades it's a really good deal." She handed them a sheet of paper with the breakdown of the price that the property was being listed for.

"I love this house. It has such a great vibe." Lorri turned to Pam. "It's perfect for a new beginning. I've been tucking money away for a year just in case. It's all still sitting there." She folded her hands under her chin and closed her eyes. She didn't want to make a rash decision, but this felt so right.

"You can do whatever you want," Pam said.

"I know, and it's so strange to not have to ask anyone for agreement. I'm going to get used to that fast." Lorri took one more walk-through. "If our house doesn't sell for a long time, I'd have to do some side jobs to make it work, but I'm worth it, right?"

"It's your freedom. Of course you're worth it. Better than throwing money away renting a place too."

"Plus, I need distance from Craig and his new girlfriend."

"That's understandable."

"What's the internet situation out here?" Lorri inquired.

The agent spun her laptop screen around toward them. "Great. The farmers market next door is connected to the university and they have great high-speed internet. I'm streaming a movie right now. Look."

"Can't ask for better than that," Pam said.

"Yeah, I've taken online meetings here," the agent said. "Never had a problem. I can't think of one thing to warn you about on this house. Well, except you better be ready for this much land. A few of the new owners didn't realize just how much work it was to keep up five acres. A lot of them are using the same landscape company to take care of their properties instead."

"I'd probably do that too."

The woman reached over and picked up an envelope. "Here's the landscaper's information and pricing. His card is there too."

Lorri looked at the estimate. "Something in my gut says this is where I should be. I'm going to do this." She handed the envelope to Pam and turned to the agent. "What do I need to do to put in an offer?"

Chapter Two

{ornament}

One year later

Lorri wondered if she'd ever get all the moving boxes unpacked. *If I haven't missed what's in these boxes in a year do I even need
to go through them?* She considered putting the rest of the boxes in
her SUV and taking them straight to the landfill.

That was the easy thing to do, but her sensible side won in
favor of possible donations. So, she'd gone through one box
each morning, and that had already made a significant dent in
the pile. She could even see the dresser in the guest room now.

Today, since she'd taken the day off to lunch with her girlfriends in Raleigh, she grabbed a smaller box and carried it to
the living room to sort, toss, or donate.

It wasn't until she set the box on the coffee table and ripped
the tired tape from the top that it registered what was inside.

"Personal" had been written in blue marker that had faded
so much it was hard to read.

The paper on top caught her eye. A third-grade report card. Not her personal things, but rather her brother's. Jeff's. This was the box of things Mom had given her in an attempt to smooth over the rift that had formed between Lorri and her parents the year following Jeff's death.

I'll never see it your way, Mom.

She lowered herself to the couch still clutching the report card, which wasn't a card at all, but rather a folded piece of yellowed paper. *Why didn't I toss this box out before?*

She flipped the paper in her hand. When Jeff was in the third grade they were still as close as two siblings could be. Inseparable. People often asked if they were twins. Mom dressing them alike hadn't helped with that.

Lorri opened the report card. The grades were good, just as she'd remembered. He'd always been a better student than her. The teacher wrote that he was well-liked, cheerful, and had a great aptitude for math. Something she didn't. She remembered shopping for school clothes with Mom and how Jeff could rattle off the sale prices in a snap. Fifty percent off she could do in her head, 10 percent too, but that was the limit. When it came to mathematics Jeff had no limits.

She realized she was smiling as she lifted a stack of school pictures out of the box. Random sizes, misshapen from being cut with kitchen scissors. No teeth in second grade. Football jersey in fifth. Braces in seventh. *If only Mom and Dad had known what a waste of money that would turn out to be.* By junior high Jeff's hair was shaggy, and his smile had faded. There weren't any pictures from high school.

Did any of us notice the subtle changes? Were there warnings that we missed?

Jeff's high school report card recorded the changes. He wasn't focused. Skipped class. Didn't participate. Temperamental. Late. Unapologetic for outbursts. Disrupted class.

He got his first DUI at the age of nineteen.

He went to jail the first time at twenty-two. *Just the on-ramp to years of suffering for all of us.*

Tied with a silky blue ribbon was a stack of letters he'd written from jail to Mom, and one to Dad. The one to Dad had been crumpled up, then smoothed back out. She wondered if Jeff had crumpled it up and then decided to send it, or if Dad had done it.

Why did you give these to me, Mom?

Shuffling through the box, she found receipts from when her parents had put up the house as collateral to post bond to get Jeff out of jail. She'd never known about that. *What else didn't I know?*

She'd hated what his reckless actions did to their family. It was hard to watch. After the car accident, she turned away from him completely.

Unable to push back the curiosity, she opened one of the letters and began to read.

Her thoughts about him needing psychiatric care instead of rehab only grew stronger. The highs and lows. The anger. The apologies.

She dropped her hands into her lap. *Did I ever hear him say he was sorry? Did I give him the chance to say it?*

She now believed he'd suffered from his bad choices and problems too.

Through tears, the words swam in front of her. She wondered how many times her mother had held these letters, cried into her hands over them. Keeping them to herself must have been hard.

Reaching into the box, Lorri took out the last stack of papers and a large envelope.

Mister walked over and laid down in front of the couch, pressing his chin on top of her feet.

Looking into his deep chocolate eyes, she felt comfort. She pressed her hand to his neck. "Thanks, Mister."

The summarized list of all of Jeff's offenses read like a history book. Dates as far back as junior high. Charges as wide and varied as the age range they covered.

The letter Jeff wrote to their mother after he'd been charged with manslaughter was worn. The ink smudged against the soft, faded paper from time. The words were honest, and raw. A sincerity that she'd never seen from her brother.

A tear traced her cheek, settling at her lips. *What a horrible thing to live with, knowing his neglect took another life.*

Her heart hurt for Jeff rather than because of him.

The transcript from the trial shook in her hand. There was a letter from the family that she couldn't bear to read. She'd hated Jeff for this since the day it happened. She hurt for them all now.

She put everything back into the box and folded the top to secure it. She couldn't dispose of this box. Not yet. She carried it upstairs and tucked it in the attic access. She might never open it again, but it had a place.

The large clock on her studio wall showed she was running late. She rushed to her bedroom and pulled out an outfit from the very back of her closet. One that had been a favorite when she lived and worked in Raleigh and had to wear professional clothes.

A dab of makeup and a few twists of a curling iron to snazz up her hair and she was ready to go when the doorbell rang. Mister gave out a security *woof* and positioned himself about six feet from the door.

She raced past him to the front door and opened it. "Tinsley, thank you for watching Mister today. You don't know how much I appreciate this."

Lorri was as nervous about leaving Mister behind as if he were her newborn child. Neighbors for a year now, Tinsley was the first neighbor Lorri met when she moved to Mill Creek Highlands, and that was all because of Mister. Everyone wanted to get an up-close look at the huge dog.

"I've looked forward to this all week. It's like a vacation for me." Tinsley made her way over to Mister and pressed her hands to the sides of his face. "I love this guy. We'll be just fine, won't we?"

Mister's face scrunched into fat wrinkles around her delicate hands.

"If I'm home he's good as gold," Lorri said, "but when I leave him alone for any longer than an hour he chews something up or rearranges the furniture. I don't know if he gets stressed or bored, or if he's punishing me."

Tinsley wrapped her arms around his thick neck. "Are you inviting doggy friends over and throwing parties when Mommy's not home?"

"That explains it," Lorri said with a laugh. "One time he dragged the comforter off of my bed to the middle of the living room so he could sleep on it in the sun. I swear he had a master plan. Seriously, I'd love to be in that dog's head for just one day."

"I think you're going to need a nanny cam to figure this one out. He looks innocent to me." Tinsley gave him a little scratch. "Is someone framing you?"

Mister responded with a head toss that sent his jowls flopping. He shifted his gaze between them as if he knew they were talking about him.

"He's pleading innocent," Tinsley said. "He's totally smiling at me. Look at that."

"That's because you spoil him as much as I do."

Lorri and Tinsley had met the first Sunday Lorri attended the church around the corner. Tinsley had sung a solo that morning and Lorri had stopped her in the parking lot to tell her how much it had moved her. Two days later Lorri crossed paths with Tinsley again while walking Mister through the neighborhood. That's when they realized they were neighbors.

Mister stared up at Lorri. With that black mask framing his face he always looked like a kid dressed up for trick-or-treat—well, mostly treats. "He's still a puppy in so many ways. That's easy to forget with him being so big," Lorri explained.

"As a mastiff, he's still a puppy until he's almost three," Tinsley said. She would know. She was in her last year of veterinary school. "I'll take great care of him," Tinsley promised. "We'll be fine. You get on out of here."

"Oh gosh. I hate to leave him." All 180 pounds of him. He was so tall now that she didn't have to bend down to pet him on the head.

"Don't worry," Tinsley said. "We'll go out back and exert some energy."

Lorri laughed. "Shouldn't take long. He's not much of an athlete."

"I have to know, what made you select this breed?" Tinsley asked. "I love understanding how people pick a dog for their family. It must cost a fortune to feed him."

"I wouldn't have picked a giant breed. My ex-husband surprised me with him on Valentine's Day. I'm glad he did though. He's the best dog and he's huge, but his heart is too. Leaving Craig behind was easy, but I couldn't bear to leave Mister."

"Well, I think you picked the right guy. You go have fun with your friends. You must be going somewhere very nice. I love that dress."

Lorri glanced down at her outfit. Around here she was usually in jeans. This dress had been her last splurge at Kearsy's Boutique before she moved from Raleigh. "It's more for the company than the place."

Tinsley's brows shifted, and Lorri quickly realized she thought she'd meant she was going on a date.

"Not like that. Just an afternoon with old girlfriends. We used to meet up in the same restaurant every week. It's been too long since we've gotten together." Her friends would be dressed nicely, like she used to when she worked from the office. Being home-based had spoiled her. These days yoga pants, comfy tops, and blue jeans were the uniform, and it had turned out to be a nice perk. Only if she showed up for lunch in jeans today, the girls—other than Pam—would think she wasn't doing well after the divorce, and that was one rumor she didn't want spread all over town.

"If you decide to stay overnight, no worries. Just let me know."

"No. I'll be back. It's an easy drive."

"You better go before your little boy here realizes something is up and starts whining," Tinsley teased. "You know how kids can get at this clingy age."

"You're right. I'm gone." Lorri turned her back on them. She had a pang of guilt as she started her car and backed out of her driveway. *This must be what a mother feels leaving their child behind on the first day of school.*

She loved her new little house. What it lacked in square footage it made up for in charm and acreage. It was like living a storybook life.

Every house in Mill Creek Highlands had a southern-style wraparound porch, and a healthy outdoor lifestyle was encouraged with amenities like the clubhouse and sidewalks. From the moment she saw the watercolor rendering of the neighborhood in a spread in *Our State* magazine, she'd daydreamed of living there. Each custom home was unique, but they were all farmhouse chic.

Lorri's house had vertical wood and batten siding in a modern sage green with golden brown cedar shakes that set off the color of the stacked stone. The community had all the twenty-first-century luxuries, including a central solar-panel farm for the eighty-acre neighborhood and a hydroponics program run by students of North Carolina State at the farmers market. The off-campus curriculum yielded stellar results and the residents were rewarded with premium produce.

Tinsley, as a grad student, helped manage the hydroponic farm and market project. Her parents lived in the neighborhood and Tinsley stayed with them fairly often out of convenience.

Lorri fished her sunglasses from the bottom of her purse. She loved her new life and her more relaxed schedule, but her friends acted like she'd moved to another country. To be fair, it was different. A sleepy town with an old-timey Main Street and town square. People in Dalton Mill even had a different accent. It had taken Lorri over a month to get used to it enough to quit asking people to repeat themselves.

Lorri and Craig had lived in their last house for over five years, but she'd be hard-pressed to name more than two or three neighbors who lived on their street. One of them was Charlie Girbons. She only knew his name because he was the head of the HOA. Charlie was always citing someone for a violation. When people mentioned him, it was accented with a groan, sometimes even an eye roll.

There was no HOA in Mill Creek Highlands, and she'd taken full advantage of that by planting a double order of portulaca around her mailbox just like the ones Charlie had made her dig up back in Raleigh. It was a nice housewarming gift to herself. Since she moved in she'd met every person on her block and could name them on sight.

Mister had plenty of room to wander within the fence line of her property, but she liked walking him and stopping to chat with the neighbors, and he was quite the social butterfly. He became so excited when she got the leash out. His short tail wiggled and wagged as he leapt from paw to paw in anticipation. He was such a chill dog, although Miss Kenner's tiny Jack Russell intimidated him. He'd sit and turn away from that yapping dog as it snarled at him, threatening to chew the ears right off of Mister's head. It was comical actually, because Mister could fit the little terrier in his mouth if he wanted to.

Lorri turned her Mercedes G-Wagon onto the main road. She needed a car that was big enough to haul Mister around, and it didn't hurt that it was one teensy step up on Craig since he'd always wanted one.

She'd heard through the grapevine that he and the new girlfriend were on a bit of a budget. She snickered at the notion of Craig watching his pennies. He'd never been good with money. *Good luck with that.*

As she drove, she thought of her new life. Her only regret was not balancing her life and work as well as she'd planned now that she was working from home. If anything, she was working more than ever, but she planned to tackle that.

Step one was transforming the loft into a studio. It had taken a few months, but it was everything she'd dreamed of. The light in that room was perfect for painting, even though she hadn't found the time to make a single brushstroke yet.

Why was it that the promises she made to herself were the easiest to break? *I'm going to sit down and paint something new this week.* She kind of wished she'd used this day off to stay home and paint instead, but it was too late to change plans now.

As she approached the four-way flashing red light, she pressed her foot on the brake and glanced both ways before proceeding, more out of habit than really looking, because no one was ever coming.

A horn wailed out one long blast from her right.

She slammed on her brakes, stopping inches from a pickup truck.

Her fist to her heart, she sucked in several quick breaths before waving an apologetic hand. It was her fault, and she knew it. "I'm so sorry," she said, but there was no way the person driving their truck could hear her. The windows were too dark to make out if the driver was waving back or cursing her. Probably the latter, because the loud diesel swung wide, then sent a puff of black smoke into the air as it sped down the road.

I can't believe that just happened. Her heart pounded. She brushed her sweaty palms against her dress and took a moment before finally crossing the intersection. One mistake. One split second could've changed everything.

Chapter Three

Lorri couldn't remember downtown Raleigh ever being this busy. She hadn't been away that long, but things had changed. She took a ticket at the parking garage gate and began searching for a spot. It made her nervous driving her big SUV, afraid the roof would scrape the top of the garage any minute.

Finally, on the seventh deck, she spotted an open space and was able to eek her vehicle between the lines. *One of these days I'll get used to parking this thing.*

Before she walked into The Blue Hippo she was as nervous as if she were meeting a blind date. There was no cause for all the butterflies; these were her friends. They'd done lunch and listened to each other's problems for years.

Lorri's divorce had just been finalized, which was why Pam had insisted they all get together to celebrate. She stepped inside the restaurant.

"Reservation?" The dapper host of The Blue Hippo flashed her that "answer me" glance.

"Yes. I'm meeting some girlfriends. My last name—"

The maître d' spun and pointed his shiny silver pen toward a booth in the corner. "Must be the group of four in the back."

Four? She leaned forward, her breath escaping like a balloon with a pinhole. Pam, Carmen, Kelsey, as expected, but the fourth was Stacy. Lorri wasn't up for Stacy today. For a brief second she contemplated backing out and sending her regrets, but Carmen was already on her feet waving her napkin.

"Thank you." Lorri muttered the nicety and made her way toward the table. This had been a bad idea. She didn't really understand the whole need to celebrate a divorce anyway. It hadn't been ugly between her and Craig. Just over. She could have done without everyone knowing he'd been cheating on her with Tiffany the dog trainer with the teacup Yorkie, but the end results were the same no matter what.

Tiffany hadn't ruined her marriage. Sure, being replaced by a beautiful young blonde had been a tough pill to swallow. What was it Craig had said when he gave her Mister on Valentine's Day? *I know you don't like those froufrou purse-sized dogs.* Clearly, he was the expert on those.

Lorri wished she'd thought to print up a bumper sticker that read MY DOG COULD EAT YOUR PURSE-SIZED DOG IN ONE BITE and slap it on the back window of the G-Wagon before coming back to Raleigh. It would have been priceless to cruise past Craig and Tiffany's house just to see the look on his face.

She pasted a smile on as proof that her life was perfect in every way.

"Carmen, Kelsey." She hugged them both.

Pam jumped to her feet. "You look beautiful." Pam hugged her then whispered, "Sorry about Stacy. It wasn't my idea."

Lorri shrugged, hoping she pulled off the "it's fine" expression she was faking at the moment. Since Carmen was married to Stacy's brother, Stacy caught wind of their get-togethers more often than they'd like. She was hard to take in large doses, but lack of tact aside, Stacy was one of them. All girls who'd graduated from NC State and stuck around.

Stacy didn't bother getting up, simply waving from her seat. "How's that country living treating you?"

"It's not exactly the country," Lorri said. "I'm only fifteen minutes from a Publix."

Stacy's Botoxed lips puckered. "Well, you need to shop there more often. You're down to skin and bones. Poor thing. The divorce must've been hard on you."

From anyone else sitting at the table that would have been a fair comment, but not from Stacy. Lorri's defenses rose.

"I'm great, and the weight loss is from the exercise I've incorporated into my routines." *Why am I trying so hard?* "Working from home sounds like a real picnic. Pajamas instead of suits, walking the dog between meetings, even tossing in a load of laundry during lunch—it's all great, but there are no sick days, and no one cares what hour it is on the East or West Coast anymore." She slid into the blue leather booth next to Pam.

"Life balance is tricky when you work from home." Pam's dark waves bounced as she pushed her hair over her shoulder. "I finally had to start marking time off on my calendar to be sure I took a lunch break and time to respond to emails. I warned you."

"You did, but I'm still thankful I don't have to make that hour-long commute each day. It's been a real blessing," Lorri said.

"You work too hard." Stacy tossed back the remains of a frothy pink drink. "I guess you're lucky your marriage lasted as many years as it did. Men leave women all the time for being married to their job, but you don't have to worry about that anymore. Here's to your successful career."

Lorri was unsure that was a compliment, but she raised her glass just the same.

Pam flashed Lorri a pained look. They all knew Stacy didn't intentionally mean to be so nasty about things. Her thoughts didn't pass through her brain before exiting her lips.

Stacy's words hit Lorri like little daggers, the same way they had when Craig had said them repeatedly during their marriage.

Since when is being committed to your job a bad thing? she'd say to Craig in response.

Lorri straightened in her chair, silently chanting, *It wasn't my fault. It wasn't my fault*, and wondering when she'd finally start believing it.

They ordered and the initial awkwardness of not being together for so long had passed, thank goodness. Pam ordered the same salad she always did, and Carmen ordered from the appetizer menu. The routine of it made Lorri feel better. She needed normal right now.

Lorri turned the conversation to her friends, getting them to talk to keep them from asking her more questions. No one needed to know that she and Craig had fought over stupid things like the waffle maker.

Pam patted Lorri on the leg while they listened to Stacy go on and on about how great things were. She and her husband had just purchased a winter home in the Cayman Islands.

"You have to come," Stacy said. "It'll be great."

"Yeah, super great," Carmen said. Stacy didn't even seem to catch the mocking tone in Carmen's voice. She rolled her eyes and directed her attention to Lorri. "How's Mister? I can't believe I forgot to ask about him."

"Wait. Mister?" Stacy straightened in her chair. "Lorri, are you seeing someone? Because with Craig announcing that he and Tiffany are getting married I was afraid it would be awkward, but if you're dating then I guess everything worked out just the way it was supposed to. That's awesome."

Carmen dropped her head to her palm.

"Mister is her dog," said Pam.

Stacy looked like she wanted to suck back the words. "Oh. I—"

Lorri wished she could let Stacy wallow in her misstep for a moment, but she didn't have the heart. "It's fine. And Mister is fine, although he is still growing, and he outweighs me already."

"I can't believe you kept the dog. I bet that made Craig mad." Stacy clicked her fingers. "Duh. I guess that's why you kept him."

Kelsey's lips pulled tight. Stacy would trip the invisible line any minute and Kelsey would let her have it in her straight-up Texan accent that would put Stacy in her place. Sort of like a

Clint Eastwood–style "Go ahead, make my day," only from a five-foot-tall pixie of a gal. Lorri loved that about Kelsey.

"He was a gift to me. Why wouldn't I have kept him? If he'd been an Hermès handbag you wouldn't have given it back. Would you?"

"Of course not!"

"So, there you go. My new house is on five acres so he can run." She loved the acreage as much as Mister did though.

Stacy looked genuinely worried. "Do you let Craig have him on weekends? I have friends that have a visitation schedule for their dogs."

"We're not taking a dog back and forth," Lorri snapped, but then started laughing. She glanced over at Kelsey, who was grinning. "If I'm being totally honest here," Lorri went on, "I told Mister his father died. He didn't even seem to care. Is that mean?" She was joking but she knew that would bother Stacy.

"Perfect." Carmen raised her glass. "I'll toast to that. Bye-bye, Craig."

Lorri, Pam, and Kelsey lifted their glasses, and Stacy looked confused, but finally raised hers. "I guess that means you're not going to his wedding," Stacy mumbled.

Beyond the cheerful, silly toast there hung an awkward silence. "Okay, I'm just going to ask," Carmen said. "Had you heard they're getting married?" Carmen glared across the table at Stacy. "I mean before just now?"

Stacy shrugged, mouthing the word "Sorry."

Lorri lifted her gaze to the ceiling. *Even after the divorce he can still find a way to ruin my day.*

That he was marrying Miss Tiffany with the teacup Yorkie

when the ink had barely dried on their divorce papers shouldn't have come as a surprise, but it did. "Um. No, but I wouldn't have expected to be on the guest list either. Maybe they'll have her little doggie be the flower girl in the wedding."

"I heard they bought real pearls from Tiffany's in New York City for her dog to wear in the wedding. Tiffany's two-year-old is going to walk the dog down the aisle. I bet she'll be the cutest little flower girl." Stacy clapped her hands over her mouth. "I'm sorry. Who cares? That's so tacky, right? Subject change. I swear I'm just going to shut up. How is the new house?"

Pam shoved the bowl of bread in front of Stacy. "Have a roll."

"Did all of you get invitations?" Lorri knew Carmen's husband worked with Craig so she wasn't surprised when Carmen nodded.

"I didn't," said Kelsey, "but then I was the lawyer who made sure he didn't get half your stuff, so I'm probably his least favorite person."

"Get in line behind me," Lorri said.

"Probably in front of you," Kelsey said with pride. "Don't mind it either."

Pam placed her hand on Lorri's arm. "I didn't get an invite, but Bobby heard it from one of their golfing buddies. I was going to tell you."

Pam and Bobby got married the same year as Lorri and Craig. They were their first real "couple" friends, and although Bobby had tired of Craig's ego years ago, she and Pam had remained steadfast friends ever since they met in high school.

"We're divorced. What's the difference?" But the words hung in Lorri's heart.

"I'm sure I only got invited because they moved into our neighborhood," Stacy said. "They're at the country club all the time. He and Donald might even be golfing today."

Craig moved into the most expensive neighborhood in town? No wonder they were on a budget. Being house poor had never been something Lorri was willing to be. But Craig was all about the image. "It's fine. We're divorced. He can do whatever he wants."

"So, you wouldn't care if I went to the wedding?" Stacy had no doubt already been planning to go.

"Why would I care?"

"I just thought . . . well, great, because I've been dying to see that wedding venue. It's not that far from where you live. Have you been there? It's called The Wedding Ranch."

Lorri lifted her glass and sipped to the count of three. Heard of it? She'd designed the logo for the business. It was just a few country miles away from her house.

"Oh gosh, it's so gorgeous," Stacy rattled on. "Totally rustic, in this big barn, but with chandeliers and horse-drawn carriages or old antique cars to sweep the bride and groom away. I wish Donald and I had done something like that. Maybe we'll renew our vows. Can anyone just do that?" Stacy shifted her gaze to each woman as if one would ring in to answer like on a game show. "Does anyone know?"

"Don't look at me. I don't know a darn thing about renewing vows," Lorri said.

"Hmmph. Seems like it would be fun," Stacy said. "Maybe

more people should do that. Donald would do anything for me. If The Wedding Ranch is half as beautiful as everyone says, I may just book it and plan the party of the year. You can come too since it's so close to your house. Wouldn't that be great?"

"So great." Lorri worked up yet another fake smile.

Pam kicked her under the table, and they both tried to contain their giggles. Poor Stacy was so clueless sometimes. You just had to love her in that "bless her heart" kind of way.

Chapter Four

Ryder sat down in his usual spot at the counter of Pastrami Joe's, still ticked about the near accident. The red leather stool squeaked beneath him as he read the specials written on the board in colored chalk.

The helix of red, white, and blue stripes out front was original to the first owner of this address, one of the oldest structures in Dalton Mill. Joe had left it as a salute to days gone by even though he could've sold the antique for a nice profit.

Ryder remembered when he was just a kid and this place had been crumbling to the point of danger. Even then Joe used to dream of owning the old Barber Shop building someday. It took Joe years to talk the town into selling it to him for next to nothing so he could bring it up to code. He'd done that and more to stabilize the structure and repurpose it.

Now the corner address had impressive character. All three stories had been completely renovated. On the ground floor, Joe had opened the deli like the one his granddaddy had owned up north, and on the second and third floors he'd built out apartments.

It hadn't taken long for the other merchants on the block to smell the profits. They cleaned up their upper storage levels and turned them into apartments too. The income stream was helping the merchants, and bringing residents to Main Street was breathing new life into the town—an unexpected bonus.

Gladys slid a big plastic cup of sweet tea in front of Ryder. "You look like you're in a mood today." Her eyebrows rose, disappearing behind a heavy fringe of dark bangs, and her lips turned down into a frown full of judgment.

"Just distracted. Some Mill Creek Highlands driver about plowed into the side of my truck on my way over here."

"It wouldn't have bothered you half as much if it had happened somewhere else, right?"

He took off his ball cap and placed it on his knee. She was right, but he didn't have to tell her that. "Thank you." He slid the tea closer and took a sip.

"You never are going to forgive your folks for selling off that land, are you?" Her voice rattled from years of smoking.

"Probably not." He pushed his hand through his hair, one lock defiantly drooping back over his brow. "I could think of better things to do with that hundred acres than build a neighborhood that would do nothing but bring city slickers to our town."

"I'm sure you could have, but none of those things would have funded your parents' golden years. They are living their dream. Traveling the country." Gladys spread her arms out wide, and Ryder wondered if he was getting ready to hear a bellowing version of "America the Beautiful" out of her.

"I for one am living vicariously through them," Gladys said. "Everyone around here is. Can't hate them for that."

If the constant barrage of postcards was any indication, his parents were having the time of their lives seeing America. "I don't hate them. I'm just annoyed with the decision."

He eyed her, hoping she'd give it a rest. He agreed with her. His parents did deserve to live the retired life of their dreams. It was just too bad he and his sister hadn't been consulted prior to breaking up the family farm.

"Well, honey, unless you think you're going to figure out how to turn back time that deal is done and there's no changing it. You being sour about it isn't hurtin' anybody but you. Well, and those of us that have to put up with ya."

Clearly, she counted herself in that group. "I hate change," Ryder said.

"You always did. I remember when you were just six years—"

"Please don't tell me a story. I know you mean well, and I love you for it, but I just need a moment."

Gladys had been a waitress in this town for longer than the forty-some years he'd been alive. When the County Diner shut down she came to work for Joe. Rather than the screen-printed polo shirts he provided his employees, she still wore a dress with a white apron over it. She shouldn't be pointing fingers at Ryder about disliking change.

"What can I get ya to eat then, Ryder?"

"BLT on whole wheat."

"Not *sour*dough?" She pursed her lips, happy with herself over the pun.

He had to laugh too. "Whole wheat will be fine. Thank you. Sorry for my mood."

"That's better. You got it." Gladys pressed an understanding hand to his shoulder before turning away and shouting his order into the kitchen like a drill sergeant.

Reflecting on this morning, it served him right to almost get in an accident being over there by that neighborhood. It was a longer drive the other way, but it kept him from having to face the continued changes on the property that had once been a part of their four-hundred-acre family farm. He and Pop-Pop had ridden those fences every week when he was a kid. Back then Pop-Pop owned it all. He had close to a thousand acres. He ran cattle, and used the rest for hay fields and seasonal crops. It was the multiple revenue streams that had kept the farm going for generations.

Dad wasn't as interested in farming, and he'd split the land a few times after Pop-Pop passed away. Ryder still owned every square inch Pop-Pop had deeded him, and he'd never sell. He didn't raise livestock, just a few feeder cattle to put in the freezer and keep the grass manageable between crop rotations, but he still rode the fence line on horseback out of respect to Pop-Pop's memory. Every time he hit the break where the property had been sold off to build that neighborhood it turned Ryder's gut.

Riding was his way to get right with God each morning. The daily reminder of losing that land humbled him. He worked hard to get the most out of the land he did have. Giving thanks kept him moving in the right direction.

The front door of the deli opened behind him. "Hey, Ryder.

Good to see you, man." Mark, another lifetime resident of Dalton Mill, made his way to the counter.

"Hey. Thought you were hauling NASCAR merch trailers this week."

Mark took a seat next to Ryder. "Off this week. Next week we head up north." He waved to Gladys across the way. "Hey, Gladys. Can I get a patty melt?"

"Sure thing." Gladys scribbled on a ticket, and slapped it on the cook's order wheel, giving it a spin before she shouted the order.

Mark tapped his hands on the Formica countertop. "Did you finish Diane's breakfront? You're running out of time."

"You don't have to tell me, but I'll have it ready." Ryder felt sorry for Mark. The guy had crushed on Diane since Mark and Ryder were in junior high. She was headed to college then. Mark moped for months when Diane got engaged. And when Diane's husband left her, Mark could barely wait to ask her out. Unfortunately, Diane still thought of Mark as her younger brother's irritating school buddy, and Ryder didn't think that would ever change.

"She's going to be surprised. I'd love to see the look on her face." Mark always made himself available when Diane was involved.

"I still need your help moving it over to her house on her birthday," Ryder said.

"Yeah. I'll be there."

"Come by my place around noon. Reece and Ross are bringing her here for lunch so we can move it in while they're out. You'll have to join us for cake. You can bring Caroline if you want."

Mark twisted in his chair. "Broke up with Caroline last week."

"Why?" Ryder wondered if the timing of the breakup had anything to do with Diane's party.

"She's a nice gal. Just not the one."

If Mark was still pining away for Diane, he was gonna die old and lonely.

"I saw that property across the way from yours went on the market," Mark said. "Know anything about it?"

"People from Virginia owned it for years. Pop-Pop said they never took interest in it. Nice piece of land though," Ryder said. "I was thinking about buying it."

"You've got enough land around here. Can't you let me snag that one? You could use a good neighbor like me," Mark said.

"Got that right. Yeah, go for it, but if you change your mind let me know. Don't want any outsiders buying that property." Right now Ryder owned more land than anyone in Leafland County. He could trust Mark to hang on to the property. He was a good old Dalton Mill boy through and through.

Joe brought Ryder's sandwich to the counter himself. "Gladys said you came in mumbling about the new neighbors again."

"Not my fault they keep doing idiot things," Ryder said.

"Hey, those idiots are paying my bills." Joe folded his arms across his black polo. "I'm having my best year ever. I've got more customers, and I'm getting better produce at a cheaper price through the farmers market over there. They are doing their part in this town. I'm happy with how things are shaping up. Could've been so much worse."

That struck a personal chord. Ryder's back teeth ground together. "How do you figure?"

"At least Mill Creek Highlands isn't filled with die-cut Mc-Mansions on postage-stamp lots. Have you seen those neighborhoods? You can't hardly get your mower between them." Joe looked at him dead-on, waiting for Ryder to respond, but Ryder held his tongue. Finally, Joe said, "Did you want fries with that?"

Ryder cocked his head, confused at first. "Is that a McMansion joke?"

Mark almost choked on his cola.

Joe let out a raucous yowl like back in their college days, which were long gone now. "Lighten up, man. Seriously," Joe said. "They could've built a dang Walmart there or a distribution center with big rigs hauling down our streets seven days a week and not spending a single dime in our town. Now if that had happened, I'd grumble right along with you."

"You might not want to hear it, Ryder, but it's a nice neighborhood," Mark said. "At least the five-acre-lot restriction limited the number of houses they could build."

"They all think they're farmers. And the chickens and goats they try to keep don't deserve that level of mishandling." Ryder took a bite of his sandwich and swallowed hard.

"They mean well," Joe said. "It's not any worse than 4-H kids learning their way around animals."

"Yeah, but these adults don't ask for help. And now the feed store is so busy I can hardly get in and out of there."

"My point exactly. Because business is good." Joe shrugged. "Look for the bright side."

"I'm trying."

Joe didn't look convinced. "I know what your problem is, Ryder." Joe pulled out his phone.

"I don't have a problem."

"Yeah, you do. I know what'll fix it too." He swiped his finger down the screen. "I'm going to fix you up on a date. Girl I knew in college just moved out this way. She's real nice."

"Oh no, you don't."

"Take her out to dinner. Flirt a little. That'll lift your mood." He shook his head. "No. Not happening."

"It's been a long time. We're still young," Joe said. "You can't brood forever."

"Who's brooding?"

"Even Gladys said you need to—"

Ryder's mouth dropped open. "Am I suddenly the topic of every conversation around here?"

"Only some of them," Gladys quipped.

"Nothing sudden about it. It's been, like, ten years." Joe leveled his gaze.

Ryder shook his head. "Seven." The word came out sharper than he'd meant.

Mark put a hand on Ryder's shoulder. "Take your time, man."

"It's time," Joe barked. "No one is saying you have to remarry, but you need to get out and have some fun."

"I get out. Look at me." Ryder lifted his hands. "I'm here. That's out."

"Really?"

"Yeah. County fair is next weekend," he said. "I'll be there bidding on 4-H calves."

"Good," said Joe. "I'll see you there. Don't run the price up on our calf though. I plan to have him processed for the restaurant."

"We'll see about that. I'd consider that fun. You want me to have fun, right?" Ryder laughed. He couldn't be angry with Joe. He'd known him a long time and he always meant well. "Maybe I'll buy that calf your kid raised and donate him back to you as payment for the free therapy session, which, by the way, I don't need."

"Bring a big checkbook. I've been counseling your cranky butt for as long as I've known you."

"I wasn't always cranky."

"No. No, you weren't." Joe lifted his chin. "You used to be the happiest guy I knew. We all wanted your life. What you and Valerie had together, that's more than a lot of us will ever have. Be thankful for that." Joe rested his forearms on the counter. "You'll never replace that happiness. I get that, but you *can* find joy again. It'll be different, but it'll be good. You'll see. You have to live your life. She'd have wanted that. We all want that for you, man."

Ryder's jaw clenched. It never got any easier to hear other people tell him what they thought his wife would've wanted for him. What made them think for one second that they knew Valerie better than he did? In this case, Joe was right, but it still irked Ryder. "I hear you. Quit your worrying over me. In fact, I've got plans today."

"Sure you do."

The chime at the door sounded. From the counter stool Ryder watched his niece and nephew parade in. Twins, even in their twenties they were as in sync as they were as toddlers. "There's my plans now. See. I've got a life."

"I meant besides family." Joe looked at Mark and then back to Ryder. "You're one hardheaded somebody."

"Sorry we're late, Uncle Ryder—you're not going to believe what's going on." Reece raced over to him and dropped a kiss on his cheek. She turned to Joe. "Hey, Mr. Joe."

"The usual for you two?" Joe stood.

Ross grabbed a booth, and Reece followed him. "Perfect."

"I'll get that right out." Joe walked back into the kitchen.

Ryder moved his plate to the table and sat down with the twins. Reece had lightened her hair again. He liked it better when it was its natural color, a soft brown that matched Ross's.

Ryder braced himself. Whenever these two wanted to meet for a meal they were up to something. Was he really more amicable on a full stomach? It was possible. Not that he'd ever deny them anything. Funny they hadn't figured that out.

The twins glanced nervously between each other, as if each was hoping for the other to start.

Ryder opened his palms on the table. "What's up?"

Ross bumped his sister's arm, and she spit it out. "Things are going great at the venue. The Wedding Ranch is getting five-star reviews, and we've got more events set up than we projected." She slid a check in front of Ryder. "Here's next month's payment. Early."

"Good job." They'd never been late, not once, even in the first months while they were getting on their feet. They'd secretly worked extra jobs to be sure they could pay him as promised. He never let on that he knew, but he appreciated their tenacity. He took the check without looking at it, folded it, and placed it in the pocket of his shirt. "Thank you. I'm really proud of you both."

He'd had his doubts they could make a living off of planning and hosting weddings in the old barn, but Ross and Reece had proven him wrong. The Wedding Ranch was continually booking events, and these two had been smart about how they spent and reinvested their money.

"We have the best news." Excitement spilled from Reece in a rush. "We just booked the wedding of Cody Tuggle and Kasey Phillips."

He tried to place the names. Was one a relative of someone they knew? By the near tears in his niece's eyes and the gaga grin on Ross's face he knew it was someone he should know.

Reece's smile dropped. "I told you he wouldn't know who they are," she said to her brother.

Ross leaned in toward Ryder. "You know who they are. The country singer? And the photographer that does all the hot rod and motorcycle photographs. You have one of her calendars—"

"In the barn. Yeah, I knew that name sounded familiar," Ryder said. He liked a few of Tuggle's songs too. Valerie had loved his song about a mother's love. He was a big deal. "A celebrity wedding? Here in Dalton Mill?"

"Yes! At The Wedding Ranch." Reece rocked forward in her seat. "This is going to put us on the map. We will be hosting all of the parties leading up to the wedding, and the wedding, of course. It's the biggest project we've ever done."

"Don't overpromise," he warned.

"No. We've got this." She crossed her heart in a promise. "There will be a gathering on Tuesday for the bride's family, a private event for just the wedding party on Wednesday, and a bridesmaid luncheon and a rehearsal dinner on Thursday night. Friday is the ceremony. Reporters will be here and everything."

Ryder leaned back against the bench seat. "Really? Have you spoken to Sheriff Mansfield about that?"

"Yes. I spoke to him right before we came here," Ross said. "He's going to hire a couple of extra people to help with security. We've rolled that into the cost of the event."

"Security?"

"Yeah, the wedding is supposed to be top secret, but if word gets out fans could flock to the area to catch a glimpse of them."

Ryder cocked his head. "I don't have a good feeling about this."

A flash of panic crossed Reece's face. "No, Uncle Ryder, I promise it'll be okay. This is a game changer for our business."

"You said business is already good." He patted his shirt pocket. "I have the check to prove it."

"Yes, but just one event like this every year, or every other year, will set us for a long, long time." Reece looked to the tin ceiling with starry eyes. "Girls will dream of getting married at The Wedding Ranch—but it's not even just that. Cody and Kasey are the nicest people."

Ross chimed in. "It's true. Did you ever hear how they met?"

Ryder shook his. "Don't believe so."

"They met during a photo shoot, and then Cody showed up to help Kasey find her missing son when everyone else had given up."

"Her son? He was okay?" A lump formed in Ryder's throat. A familiar ache.

"Yes. Cody and Kasey became great friends, and now they're getting married," Reece said. "It's like a storybook."

"That song of Cody's, 'A Mother's Love,' it was one of Valerie's favorites." He could still hear her singing to it—off-key—in the truck.

"I know, Uncle Ryder." Ross placed his hand on Ryder's shoulder. "Aunt Valerie would've loved Cody and Kasey. They've put their hearts and money into a foundation to help others find missing children. The PT Foundation took something horrible and turned the focus toward something good. It's their life's work now."

"Such good people," Reece agreed. "We want to do this for them. We *are* ready, Uncle Ryder."

Ross punched the screen on his iPad and opened a spreadsheet. "I've got everything planned out. We're running it as a single project with multiple timelines and checkpoints since many of the activities overlap. See here."

"Impressive," Ryder admitted as he reviewed the spreadsheet. At least those college degrees were being put to good use. Both were business majors, but Reece had a creative side too. She came up with fantastic ways of changing the venue in dramatic ways that didn't take much time. All of the linens were reversible. She'd designed a system to pull sheer fabric along the ceiling that draped down and could be changed out depending on the event's color scheme. Reece designed and Ross built storage space in the rafters to store the heavy rolls of fabric close to where they'd be needed.

Reece reminded him of Valerie like that. Valerie had been the visionary, always coming up with ways to streamline the work that needed to be done, which left him to be the worker bee. Ryder had been known to complain about that a time or two, but it appeared Ross was fine with that role.

Ryder's thoughts were back on what Kasey had gone through and how she and Cody were funneling the tragedy into good works. Valerie would've thought of something like that.

"Hey, do you want some pie, Uncle Ryder?" Reece's dark lashes fluttered over her blue eyes.

"No. I'm good."

"Oh, well there's one thing that we need your help with," she said.

Here we go. "I was wondering what you were buttering me up for."

"We're not buttering you up." She had that wide-eyed innocent look that had twisted his arm a million times over the years. "You're our biggest investor, what's suspicious about that?"

He was their *only* investor. "I know y'all better than you know yourselves. You forget that."

"Okay, well, the one catch is that we've already rented them the cabins at the venue, but that's not enough. We need something bigger." Reece visibly swallowed.

Ross completed his sister's thought. "What we're saying is, we want to rent your house from you for five days."

He could almost feel his eyes bugging out in surprise like a cartoon character's dangling from wobbly springs. That was a big ask.

Before he could open his mouth, Reece interjected. "It's the only place that is gated and sits back off the road so we can guarantee that if word gets out we're prepared. We've really thought this through. We did a whole FMEA on it."

"Failure Mode and Effects Analysis?" If nothing else these kids knew how to speak his language. A short stint working for General Electric straight out of college as a Six Sigma Master Black Belt had armed him with invaluable business sense and he'd ingrained those skills into Reece and Ross from a young age.

"Right," Ross interjected. "And we've already priced a cleaning crew for before and after. We will put all of your valuables in the study and Jimmy John can put a lock on that door, original to the era of the house because we know how funny you are about that. We'll take full responsibility."

"And where am I supposed to stay during all of this?"

"I'm glad you asked," Reece said. "Of course, Mom said you could stay with her, but I know that would make you crazy."

"She knows?" Ryder hated it when his sister kept things from him. She could've at least warned him.

"I came up with the idea that you could pull the horse trailer down to the creek and stay there with Thunder. Like a camping trip on—"

"My own property?"

"Or we could send you somewhere," Ross said. "Where would you want to go? The Bahamas? Mexico? Maybe a cruise."

"You know me better than that." Ryder had to admit, camping here on his own land was about the only vacation he was up for. Traveling to parts unknown had never been appealing to him.

"I told him that's what you'd say." Reece arched her brow that same way his sister did.

"I'm not going anywhere," Ryder said. "What if something went wrong?"

"It won't."

"Famous last words. Have you already signed the contract?"

"No, we wanted to talk with you first. This would be so big for our business. National acclaim. Please, Uncle Ryder . . ."

Who was he kidding asking those questions? He wasn't going to say no to them. When they'd come to him asking to lease five acres and the decaying barn on the lower part of the property, he'd thought they were crazy, but he hadn't said no. And although he thought they'd never be able to renovate that old barn into something beautiful on their shoestring budget, they had. And masterfully so. No, he'd never stand in their way. What they'd built in just a couple of years was remarkable.

"Thunder and I will camp down at the creek during this big week-long shindig. Just a cell phone call away. If something goes wrong, you call me immediately for help. You hear me?"

"Yes! Thank you!" Reece jumped from her seat and practically into his lap.

Ross paused. "You're saying we should go for it."

"I think you two already know you should. I'm behind you all the way," Ryder said.

"Thank you. We are going to make you so proud."

"You always do," he said. "Now, I expect my house to be in the same shape I leave it in."

"We got it," Ross said.

Reece crossed her heart. "I promise."

She did the cleaning there once a week anyway. Had since

Valerie died. Ryder could do it himself, but he liked her feminine touches and she enjoyed the extra cash.

"What can I do to help?" Ryder asked.

"That's all we need from you." She sniffled. "Oh my gosh, Ross. We're doing it. The event of the year right here in Leafland County. Amazing. We'll be famous!" She threw her head back. "We've got to go, Uncle Ryder. There's so much to do." Reece was scooching against her brother, inching him off the edge of the bench to hurry him along. "You understand, right?"

"I do." He winked, loving their enthusiasm for life. Each feeding off the other's strengths, they were a superpower together.

His heart warmed, but then that familiar chill hung over him. *What would my boy be like now?* He'd be eleven, and this conversation would have been so different. Ryder would have been fine getting kicked out of his own house; he and Valerie would have taken Ronnie Dwayne, named after Ryder's dad, camping at the creek together. Or maybe he would've entertained going out of town. They could've gone to SeaWorld to see the dolphins. Ronnie Dwayne loved dolphins. If Valerie had suggested it, he'd have done it. He'd have gone anywhere for her.

Life would have been very different if it hadn't been for a reckless drunk driver one early Sunday morning seven years ago, right after their last goodbye.

Chapter Five

Lorri was glad she'd met her girlfriends for lunch, but she couldn't wait to get back home to Dalton Mill. She loved this time of year when the days were at their longest. Thankfully, it would cool down a little by nine o'clock when the sun finally dipped behind the horizon so she and Mister could take a long walk.

She turned into the neighborhood, looking at it now with a fresh perspective. A year of growth on the landscaping had filled in the bare spots, and the young trees were beginning to make this rolling pastureland look lush and homey. A smile played on her lips as she turned down her street and her house came into view.

In so many ways she was still new in town, having spent most of the past year working from home.

She pulled into the driveway and parked. With her doggy bag in hand she got out of the car, pushing the door closed with her hip. She followed the sidewalk to the front of the house and let herself inside. "Hello," Lorri called out.

Mister let out one loud woof, then scrambled on the slippery wooden floor to greet her, his sniffer doing double duty on the bag.

"Hey there." Tinsley bounced up from the sofa. "We were just watching a movie. You're back way earlier than I thought you'd be. When I get together with my girlfriends time flies." Tinsley paused the movie and met Lorri halfway.

"It was such a nice visit. I'm glad to be home though." Mister gave her a slobbery kiss then whimpered like a pup.

"He missed you," Tinsley said. "He kept going to the front door and pacing, until I took him out back and brushed him. Sorry to tell you, but after that he kind of forgot about you. He's been so good."

"At least now I know I can leave him with you if I have somewhere I need to go."

"Anytime," Tinsley said.

After being in the city this afternoon, it confirmed what she loved about living in Dalton Mill. The slower pace, peaceful neighborhood, and beautiful homes with wide open spaces and neighbors like Tinsley.

"When I lived in Raleigh, I never realized how much traffic there was," Lorri said. "I used to love that town, but I couldn't wait to get back here."

Lorri took some money from her purse and handed it to Tinsley.

"No." Tinsley stepped back. "You weren't even gone that long. I'm not taking your money. It'd be one thing if I stayed all day, or overnight, but this was my pleasure."

"Take it. Really. You helped me out. I appreciate it."

"Well, ask me again some time. I'd love to spend time with Mister. Maybe some day you'll help me out with a logo for my new company or something."

"I'll hold you to that." Lorri knew Tinsley was destined for great things.

"Works for me." Tinsley gathered her things. "You know, I was thinking while you were gone. I don't know if you know about the Leafland County Fair, but it's a big to-do around here."

"I've been to the state fair once. I was in fourth grade, I think."

"Well, the county fair isn't as big or fancy as the state fair, but we have a really good one. I'll be working the aquaculture booth. You should come. It spans five days. Different things each day. The schedule is online."

"That sounds like fun," Lorri said. "I'll check it out."

"Fair food. Crafts. Local artists. The 4-H livestock shows, if you like that kind of stuff. Businesses from the county have booths too. Might be a good way to meet some of the trades-people. I mean, you never know when you're going to need a plumber or HVAC guy."

"Hopefully not anytime soon on a new house, but you're right." Wouldn't hurt to put her name out in the marketplace for potential clients too. "I'll look for you there."

Tinsley headed for the door. "Might not be too late to enter Mister in the dog show."

"I don't think he's the show type."

Mister sprawled out on the floor and dropped his head to the ground.

"It's not a breed show. There are fun categories like 'snoring' and 'couch potato.' He's Olympic-level at both of those."

Lorri gave him a soft pat. "We'll practice for next year."

"Hope to see you at the fair. Everything gets started this Tuesday night." Tinsley stepped outside.

Lorri followed her out onto the porch. "Hey, I meant to ask you about The Wedding Ranch. Do you know anything about it?"

"Yeah. I know the people who own it. It's the coolest wedding venue on the whole East Coast. Every event is unique. They transform the old tobacco barns into the most magical settings with lights and flowing fabric in different colors. Honestly, I don't know how they do it. You should look at the pictures online. They're booked three years out already. You better hurry if you want to secure a date."

"No. Not me. I just heard . . . well, it sounds very exclusive."

"Very expensive, too," Tinsley added. "Thank goodness they give a significant locals' discount. I'm not sure even with the discount if I could ever afford to have my wedding there."

"Country venue weddings are very in right now." Lorri pictured the glossy wooden signs with shiny gold lettering that read THE WEDDING RANCH in script with arrows to the venue, but she'd never driven down that way. "Aren't we lucky to be out here so close to it," Lorri said. "We live in the best location in town."

"I wouldn't say that so loud," Tinsley half whispered. "That's kind of a sore subject around here. Well, not right here in the neighborhood, but in town."

"Really? The Wedding Ranch? Why would that be a sore subject?"

"Not The Wedding Ranch. The location of this neighborhood."

"I'd heard it was an old cattle farm. The corporate farms are making it so hard for small farmers to thrive these days. I've seen that on television before. It's really sad."

"No, it wasn't like that. Part of the family who owned the land sold off their acreage without letting the others know until it was a done deal. When the rest of the family found out it had been sold to a developer, there was a lot of drama. I heard they put the stipulation of lot size in the deed at the last minute to ease the tension."

"I wonder what the developer's original plans looked like." She thought about how the spaciousness was such an important factor in her own decision to move into this neighborhood. "It wouldn't be the same with even twice as many houses, but they could have really packed them in."

"They could have."

"It's a gorgeous place to live," Lorri said. "I fell in love with it as soon as I saw the pamphlet, and I love all of the green features. I'd think they would've been pleased."

"Well, who ever said family fights made sense?"

Lorri thought of the long-running conflict within her own family. After Jeff's death so many things spun out of control. "They can live on way longer than the original issue."

Even now, years after his death, it was hard to talk about Jeff without someone getting bent out of shape.

"Yep," Tinsley agreed. "Best to just stay out of those. Good night."

"Thanks again for watching Mister today." Lorri went back inside and sprawled out on the couch.

Mister followed along.

"Hey, buddy. Did you know your dad is marrying the lady from puppy school?"

It was bad enough Craig had left her for the other woman, but to marry her? And so soon? No, she'd never seen that coming.

It took him five years to pop the question to me. Maybe Tiffany's pregnant. She has a two-year-old already. It's possible, and it would explain the rush to get married.

"He never wanted children. I'm glad he gave me you. You're the next best thing. Tiffany has a two-year-old." She looked the dog square in the eye. "Did you ever meet her toddler?"

Mister pulled his head back and turned away.

"Sorry. I shouldn't put you in the middle. It's okay."

Can't live your best life on yesterdays.

Her laptop lay on the end table. She reached over and grabbed it to search online for information about the county fair. The website was well done with bright graphics and lots of smiling faces.

It was an occupational hazard that she could never just look at a website without a critical eye. Years of experience in marketing had ruined that for her. A checklist of missed opportunities always took over, but the county fair did look fun. Well, not the rides—she wasn't the ride type—but there were lots of shows. Even pot-bellied pig races. That could be fun to watch.

She found the schedule of free craft classes. Pottery, mosaics, even a birdhouse-building session. She'd quickly grown to love all the different birds in her backyard. She had some flexibility in her schedule, maybe she could catch the birdhouse class. Anything to keep her mind occupied and off of Craig and Tiffany's upcoming wedding.

The next thing she knew, her fingers were flying across the keyboard, typing in "Craig Walker," searching for engagement announcements. At least they hadn't been so tacky to have posted anything so soon after the divorce.

But it was just timing. It didn't change the fact that they had to have been planning their wedding for a good long while. It takes time to book and plan a wedding in a venue like The Wedding Ranch, and from the sound of it this was going to be a big one.

A picture of Tiffany at the Golf Club Fund Raiser with that Yorkie in her purse popped up on her screen. She zoomed in on the picture. *She isn't that pretty.*

Craig's comment about Lorri not being a purse-sized-dog type of woman irked her. At the time she'd thought it was a compliment. *Who wants to be a purse-dog woman anyway?*

She reached for Mister, giving him a pat on the back.

Not me. Let all this go about Craig and Tiffany, she told herself. *I'm living the life I dreamed of in a beautiful home, with this sweet dog, in a town of nice people. Working from home in pajamas is pretty awesome, and I'm in the best shape of my life.*

"You know what I'm going to do, Mister? I'm going to make a forget-about-it jar and put it on my desk." She got up and went into the kitchen. Scouring the cabinets for something that would work, she tiptoed to reach a mason jar on the top shelf. With a grunt she stretched just enough to tip the jar and grab it before it fell. "This'll work."

Mister stayed right at her hip. Ever curious, he pressed his nose to the glass jar. "There's nothing in it. Not yet." She walked back into the living room and sat down at her desk.

Pulling broad-stroke permanent markers out of the caddy in her drawer she started decorating the front. She hadn't hand-lettered anything in a while. She used to love doing that.

Finally, happy with it, she turned the jar toward Mister. "What do you think?" He stuck his nose inside the top of the jar and sniffed, then backed out and sneezed. "Every time I waste a minute thinking about my old life, I'm going to put five dollars in this jar. The goal is to keep it empty." She set it in the right front corner of her desk. "Can I get a high five on that?"

Mister lifted his huge paw and tapped her hand.

"I probably owe it twenty dollars just for today, but we'll start now." The jar wasn't a painting, but at least it was a little crafty. She got up and walked upstairs to the loft. She flipped through the paintings she'd stored there, along with the old projects in different stages of completion.

She pulled out a canvas. One beautiful tree on a rolling hill. It had never seemed quite finished. It needed some balance. She placed it on the easel. Pressing her finger to her lip, she stared at the image before her.

What the painting needed became clear. It was darn near a recipe for her own life. She knew now what was missing. *Life.*

Balancing a palette in her hand she squeezed a dab of three different colors and then stood back for a moment before dipping her brush into the paint and pulling the brush across the canvas. That first stroke filled her with inspiration. *Maybe I do still have this gift.*

Chapter Six

The next week on Tuesday morning, Ryder sat in his truck in the Ruritan barn parking lot while the 4-H-ers loaded their goats into his livestock trailer for the short ride to the county fairgrounds. It was a much better-looking group of meat goats this year. Couldn't have made a good soup out of some of the entries last year. They'd been mostly dairy goat culls. Sure, any goat can be a meat goat, but people were finally learning that the conformation of meat and dairy goats was very different.

Joe slapped the side of the trailer. "All in. All clear."

Ryder raised his hand and inched forward, the trailer lurching as a few wild bleats rose from the back as the truck bounced over the unlevel terrain.

By the time Ryder got to the main road, there were two pickup trucks full of kids—the two-legged kind—following behind him. He waved them around, then followed them into town.

The children's voices filled the air as they belted out "Old

MacDonald Had a Farm" at the top of their lungs as they cruised by.

Ryder sang *cluck-cluck here and a cluck-cluck there* along with them, tapping the rhythm out on his steering wheel.

When they finally reached the fairgrounds, there was a line at the gate. Getting the animals loaded into the tents took time, a lot longer now it seemed than it had when he was showing at the fair. Then again, there were more entries these days.

The fairgrounds brimmed with excitement. Huge tents had been erected for the livestock activities, and the old concrete buildings were surrounded by cars and people unloading their wares into booths inside. Those buildings weren't fancy, but at least they had ceiling fans and air conditioning in them now. A real must when the North Carolina summer humidity was as high as the temperature. He remembered how hot and miserable it was in those buildings in the summers when he was a kid.

Later this afternoon, when the fair officially opened, this place would be a flurry of activity. Carnival rides were set up on the far side of the property. Though he'd never known anyone to get hurt on one, he'd never trusted those rides. To think they could haul them in on a trailer and bolt them together in a few hours made him nervous.

He backed up to the gate at the sheep and goat tent, then went to unload the trailer. A series of corral gates kept the trailers of animals separate until the fair veterinarian could check them in and validate that they were correctly tagged and held the proper immunization paperwork.

Once all of the goats were unloaded, Ryder closed the gate and moved his truck and trailer out of the way so the next group could unload. With six towns in the county they pulled in lots of entries.

Across the way he saw Ross and Reece unloading a display for their booth in the main exhibit hall. Ross waved. Ryder waved back, then heard someone yell, "Hey, you going to stand there and watch or are you going to help us?"

He'd recognize his sister's voice anywhere. "Hey, Diane. I just saw the twins unloading stuff."

"Come help. They are so excited about their booth this year. It's a big step up from last year. I bet they'll book a few more weddings." She tugged at his arm, and he fell into step with her.

"Did they tell you they kicked me out of my own house?"

"That's not exactly the way I heard it."

He laughed. "No, they did let me think I had a choice, but you know I can't say no to them. I'm not sure a high-profile wedding is as profitable as they think. It could lead to more problems than it's worth."

"It'll be fine," Diane assured him.

"I hope so. I keep reminding myself my house is insured. We'll get through it no matter what."

"They will make sure of that. You know they don't want to disappoint you."

"I know, but those famous types. Some of them don't know manners from mayonnaise."

"Well, let's hope this couple is different."

"At least Cody Tuggle was brought up by good country folks."

"Have some faith, brother."

He walked with her into the main exhibit hall and offered kudos to the twins on their booth. He was proud of them for not being completely absorbed by the big new contract, and still taking the county fair seriously.

"Are you hanging out all week, Uncle Ryder?"

"No. I hauled the market goats over for Joe's 4-H club. I'll be back for the livestock auction though."

Reece reached over and picked up a stack of glossy business cards. "Here. Hand these out when you're chatting with people. Tell them to stop by and see us. The booth number is on the back. We have an awesome giveaway in our booth."

"Good thinking. Sure." He tucked the cards in his pocket. He wasn't a big talker, but he could strategically leave cards in different places for people to find them.

"Ryder Bolt? Is that you?" The southern lilt swung like a lasso around him, turning him around.

He caught the passing glance between Reece and Ross as he turned.

Dressed in a white sleeveless blouse and blue jeans tucked into bright turquoise western boots, that woman always could make an entrance. "Penny Driscoll?"

"Mayor Blevins to you, Ryder."

"I know you're the mayor. I voted for you, but I still can't believe you married Marty Blevins. You'll always be Penny Driscoll to me."

"Believe it. Poor Marty may not have been worthy to even pick up your sweaty football towels in high school, but that nerdy math wizard has been working financial magic ever since." The light caught her silver and turquoise necklace, and then the hefty diamonds on her ring finger. "Turning money into more money. It's what he does best."

Ryder shrugged. "Poor dirt farmer can't compete with that."

"Mm-hmm. I know better than that, darlin'. How've you been?"

"Good. I really did vote for you."

"Of course you did. We always did think alike."

She'd been Valerie's best friend. He'd barely spoken to her since the accident. It was just too painful to relive happy memories Penny had of Valerie. That's when Penny and her first husband, Buster, split up and she went on to marry Marty Blevins. "Yeah. Those were the good old days."

"That they were. We should catch up some time."

He pulled a few of the cards from his chest pocket. "Here. Reece and Ross have transformed the old barns on the bottom acreage into an event venue. It's called The Wedding Ranch, but they host all kinds of parties. Fit for a mayor, or the governor even. You should throw some business their way. You'll be impressed."

She swept the card against the palm of her hand. "I'll get on their calendar."

Ryder heard a tiny squeal out of Reece from across the way. He loved earning hero status with her. It never got old.

Penny lifted her hand in a finger wave. "I'll see you around, Ryder." She strode off with the air of success. She'd always been audacious.

He watched as she left, wondering how on earth someone like Marty Blevins managed to get even a first glance from someone like Penny Driscoll.

Joe walked up behind Ryder. "Now that's a fine—"

"That's Penny Driscoll."

"Oh. The mayor. I didn't recognize her from behind! And to think I was going to set you up with the lady who opened the new bakery on Main Street. I may not know anyone flashy enough to appeal to your taste."

"Real funny. She's married. I'm not interested. Not in her or anyone else."

"You haven't been to the bakery yet, have you?"

"No. Why?" Ryder wondered what Joe was hiding. "Are her cookies that good?"

"Definitely. I've just about eaten my way down the first whole row of treats in that glass case already. That gal can bake, and she's nice."

"I'll pass on a date, but you can set me up with a cupcake and I won't turn it down."

"Never say never, my friend. One of these days you're going to finally wake up again."

Maybe when I see Valerie holding Ronnie Dwayne's hand in heaven.

Chapter Seven

Lorri checked her watch. Ever since Tinsley told her about the Leafland County Fair she hadn't been able to get it off her mind.

Each day was packed with things to do, and she already had a spot all picked out for one of those birdhouses. She had every intention of being the first in line for that Make Your Own Birdhouse class today.

She grabbed the copy of the schedule from the printer and looked it over. If she left now she'd catch the 4-H opening ceremonies. She'd never been to a livestock show. She'd seen dog shows before, but she couldn't imagine how children could run around a ring with farm animals. Her curiosity was piqued, and for certain the younger age classes would be adorable no matter what.

She updated her project records so she could shut down early for the day. There were two new projects in her inbox. One was a simple logo for a land developer, the other for a California vineyard. She'd done a whole campaign for them five years ago and ever since they hired her to do all the labels for their high-end wines and marketing materials to support them. It always earned her a few cases of the good stuff too, and her wine rack was impressive for it.

She set her out-of-office message and changed into a pair of jeans and a soft green shirt that was almost the color of her house. She grabbed her purse, but decided to tuck a credit card and cash in her pocket instead. One less thing to keep track of while she browsed and shopped.

"Come on, Mister." He got up from where he'd been lying in the sun on the patio and trotted inside. He'd probably have been fine outside, but there was a chance for rain and if there was one weird thing about this dog it was that he loved play-ing in mud puddles. Even though she'd made sure there was a walk-in shower big enough to bathe him in, it was no easy task. Thank goodness he never seemed to mind lazing inside in the air conditioning.

Mister sprawled out on the cool terrazzo tile near the patio doors. *What a life.* "Can I trust you to be a good boy for a couple hours today?" He laid on his back and raised his paws in the air, twisting his torso like a candy cane. "That's a little dramatic, even for you. I'm not even sure what that means." She scratched his belly, then sat down with him for a minute to give him a belly rub.

Birds darted through the yard. A couple of bird feeders along with the birdhouse she intended to build today would be such a nice addition. "Here's the situation," she said to Mister. "I've got to go somewhere. Tinsley is busy, so I need you to behave for me. Deal?"

He rolled over and sneezed.

"Well, don't be put out. You've made quite the mess in the past. I'm going to close off the back bedrooms. If you're good, I'll bring you a treat. If you're bad, next time you get stuck outside for the whole day."

His eyes got wide, the whites accenting the dark brown centers.

"I know that's harsh, but you're in control. Do we have a deal?"

He put his chin down on his paws.

"Excellent." She pressed a kiss to his nose. "I'll see you in a little while. You be good now."

She wondered if she and Craig had had at least that much conversation over the past few years if their marriage may have stood a chance. *Why do I even care? I'm happier without him, and what's wrong with talking to my dog? He's a better communicator than Craig was anyway.*

Lorri walked outside. The sun was hot on her skin, but there was a breeze that offered a brief relief. She put on her sunglasses and pulled out of her driveway. Big, puffy clouds broke up an otherwise blue sky, making it an unusually comfortable day for August.

On her agenda, besides the birdhouses, was stopping in to show her support for Tinsley at the aquaculture booth, and since that was in the same location as the crafts, she was saving it for last, because she knew herself—she could spend a whole day looking at handmade things. She'd probably come home with a list of fourteen new projects. She'd start with the livestock tents, then attend the class before heading over to the craft building. If she could make the timing work, she hoped to see those racing pigs.

She drove across town toward the fairgrounds. In the distance, a red-and-white-striped tent top rose between two tall poles and a Ferris wheel peeked above the trees. Traffic slowed the closer she got, and then it came to a stop, inching forward at an incredibly aggravating speed.

Just as she was ready to try turning out of line and giving up altogether, traffic started moving. Colored pennant flags lined the entrance. Flagmen wearing bright orange safety vests waved people into the parking area, which was a dirt field. Thank goodness it had been a dry week.

She parked next to the truck that had been in front of her. Families walked hand in hand toward the gate. She fell in step behind them, awkwardly alone in the crowd of grouped families. She stepped to the counter, bought her ticket, and then went inside.

Music and ringing bells from the midway mixed with the smell of sugary treats and sausage dogs. Her stomach growled. She'd been so eager to get here she hadn't taken time for lunch. Not that most of this food was going to supply much good nutrition.

Across the way a trailer selling cotton candy caught her eye. She'd never had cotton candy. It was time to correct that.

Lorri walked over to the counter. "One cotton candy please."

"That'll be five bucks. Pink or blue?" the concession clerk asked.

"Are they different flavors?"

"No. Just different colors."

"Well, let's go with blue then." She handed the woman a five-dollar bill, who then plucked a paper cone from the top of a tall stack. She swirled it above her head as if it were a tiny baton, then spun it into one of the huge silver bowls twisting it in a circular motion in the sugary web until it was nearly as big as a bowling ball.

"Here you go." She handed the sticky puff to Lorri.

"Wow. I should've asked for a small!"

"One size fits all. Enjoy."

"Thank you." She pinched off a piece of the fluff between her fingers and thumb and brought it to her lips. It melted away into a sweet nothing. *Not bad.*

The airy concoction flattened in her touch, and it didn't take but a few bites before she realized she should've opted for the pink because her fingers were now blue.

She absently nibbled as she worked her way through the fairgrounds looking for the building where the birdhouse class was scheduled. She pulled out her map and got her bearings.

The livestock show was being held in the giant red and white tent. As big as a circus tent, it must've cost the county a fortune to put that up. She followed behind a group of people who seemed familiar with things. Strands of lights rose in a crisscross pattern across the entire tent. Duke-blue gates and panels filled the left side of the tent, and the ones on the right side were red. Banners hung above most of the pens. Pigs over here, goats and sheep in the blue pens, and cows at the end.

The pigs really didn't need a sign. She'd already guessed their location by the smell. The group in front of her moved forward and she caught her first good look at the animals. A double-wide pen hosted a big old momma pig that had to be the size of a Volkswagen Beetle. From the sign zip-tied to the fence, she learned the sow's name was Petunia. She appeared to be worn out, but then she had a bunch of hungry piglets vying for her attention even though Momma was trying to rest. They oinked and eeked, little tails wriggling in delight as they fought like brothers and sisters do for the best spot.

She stood there amused for a long time. A teenager stepped into the pen and refreshed the water and tidied things up.

"Is it unusual for them to have this many babies?" Lorri asked.

"Yorkshire sows usually have eleven pigs in a litter. This year she surprised us with fourteen, but she's handling them all just fine." He looked so proud.

"She's a good mom." Lorri was fascinated by this young man.

"I won a blue ribbon with her the first time I showed her. She was a lot littler back then. Her name is Petunia. She's retired except for this breeding swine project now. I use a younger gilt from one of her other litters for the showmanship class."

"Guilt?" Lorri had never heard the term.

"G-i-l-t." He smiled. "That's a young female who has never had a litter of her own." His cheeks reddened slightly.

"You must be very proud of Petunia." Lorri was impressed by his knowledge of the animals and how polite he was. "What happened to her ear? Did her piglets chew on it?"

The kid laughed, slapping his hand on his leg. "No, ma'am. Don't think she'd stand for that kind of behavior. We notch all of our pigs' ears. It's how we identify them. You know, for breeding, immunizations, and all that."

"I had no idea. Doesn't that hurt?"

"Only for a minute. Some of them don't make a peep. Can't be too bad."

"That is so interesting. Maybe I'll see you out there showing later."

"Maybe. My pens are the four at the end of this aisle." He pointed to where orange and blue banners hung. "I'll be in the senior showmanship class."

"I'll check it out. Thanks for chatting with me."

"Yes, ma'am. Have a good day at the fair."

The smell didn't seem as bad now that she was in here. Fans blew throughout and she wasn't really sure if it was to keep the animals cool or the stink down, but either way it seemed to be working.

She stopped to read one of the project boards hanging in the next pig pen. These kids worked hard on this stuff. There hadn't been a 4-H program in her school that she'd known of, but these posters would've been right up her alley. She enjoyed looking at all the different styles. Some of the girls had bedazzled their posters and even had what looked like a onesie on their pig, probably to keep them clean for the show, would be her guess.

Something tugged at her hand and she squealed and jumped back, laughing when she realized that a black and pink pig with a big notch in one of his floppy ears had reached over through the fence to snag a lick of her cotton candy. He looked innocent, except for the blue tuft on his nose that was a dead giveaway.

"You don't even look sorry." She glanced down at the paper cone. It probably wasn't appropriate to feed the animals, but he did start it. She lowered the cone and let him steal one more nibble before tossing the rest into the trash can. "What's fair is fair at the fair, Mr. Piggy."

Chapter Eight

Cheers rose from outside the livestock tent. Lorri made her way through the maze of pens to see what all the excitement was about.

There in the greenway between the big tents, a man announced the next round in a herding dog trial over a scratchy PA system. A whistle blew and someone in the middle of the field opened a gate. Five fluffy sheep stepped cautiously out of the pen, then took off running.

Lorri watched the first dog, a small black and white border collie, begin his run. He moved to whistles and hand motions from his trainer on the other side of the field. Stopping, lowering himself close to the ground, and walking forward slowly in that crouched position, then waiting for the next command. It was captivating. Finally, the dog forced the sheep right back into the pen where they started. Applause filled the air. The dog ran back to his handler, dancing and spinning in circles.

Another contestant stepped next to the flag at the starting

line, with his dog sitting at his side ready for their turn. The sheep were let out of the cage again. The judge raised his hand in the air, then dropped it. The handler immediately blew his whistle and the dog raced out, changing direction and speed with each subsequent tweet.

Across the way a small boy wearing a white collared shirt and black pants led a full-size cow into the tent adjacent to the one she'd just been in. All by himself!

Everywhere she turned there was something going on. She meandered through the crowd toward the other tent and poked her head inside. The bleachers were filling fast. She pardoned her way to an empty spot near the top. At least from here she had a good view of everything.

The emcee announced the junior showmanship class, explaining that the judges would be scoring the exhibitor on how he handled the animal and knowledge on the breed. They were also being scored on project books. There was a lot to this animal-showing stuff.

Twelve kids stood smiling at a judge with one hand on their lead line connected to a halter on the steer. Those steers had to outweigh the showmen by at least ten times. They used their foot or a stick to help align the large animals' feet, making sure they were positioned to show off their best features.

She lifted her phone and took a picture. It was hard not to pick a favorite among the class. A little girl with her hair in braids tied with green ribbons never quit smiling. Even when her steer moved his foot, she simply lunged against his leg to realign him. She made it look as easy as a dance move.

Across the way she spotted Tinsley talking to a man. Lorri

climbed down from the bleachers to grab a spot closer to the show ring for the next class.

A moment later, Tinsley slid into the spot next to her. "I'm so glad you made it. Are you having fun?"

"Yes, I am. I was going to come visit you in your booth after this. Did I miss it?" Lorri lifted her map and schedule. "See. I had it marked and everything."

"I'll be at the expo building all evening. You haven't missed a thing. I was taking a little break to watch the 4-H classes. I loved 4-H when I was a kid. There's so much work that gets put into these projects."

"I've been really impressed."

Tinsley leaned over and pointed at Lorri's schedule. "Oh, I see you have the birdhouse class marked. You'll love that. I made one last year. I gave it to my mom on Mother's Day. They do a different design each year, but they are always really cute."

"I've been thinking about that class all weekend. I know exactly where I'm going to hang it in my yard."

"Great. Well, I just wanted to say hello really quick before I had to go back. I guess I'll see you in the expo building later."

"Definitely." Lorri turned her attention back to the ring. For not knowing a thing about 4-H, calves, or showing animals, Lorri apparently had a knack for picking winners, because her favorites were winning. She was four for four.

She might not be as lucky now that they were moving to the market class, and she didn't know anything about good or bad traits in cows or steers. She found it all quite interesting though. She had every intention of contacting someone at the county to see how she could sponsor some of this next year.

She glanced at her watch. The time had gotten away from her. There were only fifteen minutes until the birdhouse class. She hated to leave her primo spot, but while the steers were cleared from the ring she hustled toward the exit. She took the map from her pocket to be sure she knew which direction Building L was in from where she'd exited. She spun in a circle, getting her bearings against the vendors surrounding her.

Something struck her at the shoulder and hip so hard it flung her forward. She caught a lungful of red dust gasping for air. Then everything seemed to go in slow-motion. An arm pulling her to the side, in a stronghold she couldn't escape, and then hitting the ground with a thud that made pretty colors dance in front of her eyes.

Struggling for a breath, she closed her eyes and tried to swallow.

"Are you okay?" The masculine voice was calm, but serious. "Can you see me?"

She blinked. Dirt scratched at her eyes. She wiped her hand across her mouth as she coughed again.

"Here." Someone shoved a water bottle in her hand. "Take a slow sip."

She sipped, but cold water dribbled down the front of her shirt. She got the bottle back to her mouth and took another drink.

"You okay, Miss? Can you talk?"

She tried to answer but talking made her choke up.

"Breathe in. Slowly. That's good."

Through half-open eyes, she saw a blurry crowd of people gathered around her.

"That's okay. Get you another good breath. Take your time.

Slowly." The man placed something cool and wet across her eyes.

"I'm sorry. I don't know—"

"Quit talking. We're right here. Catch your breath."

She inhaled. Her eyes were still gritty, but the cool rag had taken some of the sting away.

"Are you okay?" His voice was steady.

As her eyes focused, she noticed his tan skin and the five-o'clock shadow shading his cheek. "I think so. Yes. What happened?"

"You sure you're breathing okay? Take in a good deep breath."

She did, but her chest burned. "I think I got the wind knocked out of me."

"The EMT team is coming now. They'll check you out. I grabbed you and pulled you out of the way."

"Of what?"

His chocolate-brown eyes danced when he smiled. "One of the steers got loose and came running and kicking down this alley. I was walking by when it happened."

"Thank you."

He brushed dirt from her arm. "Sorry. I didn't mean to take you to the ground."

Heat rose to her chest and cheeks. She swept at her clothes, hoping he wouldn't notice. "No, it's fine. I'm fine. I'm sorry. I should've been paying attention." She touched her forehead.

"Did you bump your head too? Follow my finger with your eyes."

She did as he said, but it was hard not to notice how handsome he was.

He moved his finger in the other direction. "Now again."

She pulled away from him. She'd never been good at being fussed over. "I'm fine. I'm sure. I'll just get up and . . ."

"Not so fast," he said. "My name is Ryder. What's yours?"

"Lorri."

"Lorri what?"

"Is this a quiz or do you just want to know?"

"That was a pretty good answer." A smile curved at his lips. "Does it matter?"

She paused, sorry to have been short with this guy who was clearly just trying to help. "I suppose not. Walker. My name is Lorri Walker."

"Excellent."

She was more humiliated than anything. "Is Ryder your first name or your last name?"

His playful grunt was followed by, "Is this a quiz or do you just want to know?"

"I just want to know." Her eyes were finally clear enough to see that the man who'd rescued her from being trampled by a steer was very good-looking, which made her wish she hadn't been so brazen just now. It had been a protective reflex. She got snarky when she was embarrassed. It was a skill she'd learned as a younger sister who was picked on by her older brother.

"First name. Ryder."

The whir of a motor and tires skidding to a stop startled her. An EMT rushed over to them from a John Deere Gator with a medical kit. "She okay?"

"I think she'll be fine." Ryder wiped his hand across his face, still smiling.

He had a nice smile. She was horrified that she'd caused this scene. All she'd wanted to do was build a birdhouse. Next time she'd stay home, watch a video, and figure it out on her own.

The EMT insisted on cleaning up the scrapes, but he wasn't nearly as gentle as Ryder had been. "You're friends with Ryder?"

"Um. No. I mean, never met him until just now. I suppose a rescue earns at least one point toward friendship though."

"He's a good guy." The EMT pressed a bandage into place on her arm.

"I really think I'm okay here. I'm going to go home."

"We'll get you a ride to your car, ma'am. Actually, you might not want to drive after a fall like that. We'll get you a ride home."

There was a crowd of people around her.

"Nothing to see here." She climbed to her feet, happy that her legs seemed okay and she felt stable. "Thank you for your help. I'm really fine."

"Lorri?" Tinsley ran over to her. "Ryder told me what happened. Are you okay?"

"I'm fine." She leaned in and quietly said, "Embarrassed, but fine."

"Oh my gosh. Don't be. You could have really gotten hurt. I'm so sorry this happened, especially since I was the one who told you to come. Can I give you a ride home?" Tinsley asked.

"No. You're working the booth tonight," Lorri said.

"Hi, I'm Diane."

Lorri hadn't noticed the other woman standing there. Maybe she did need to take a minute to get her senses back.

"Ryder is my brother," Diane said. "I can give you a ride

home. We're friends of Tinsley's. She said you live down from her folks' place. It's right on my way home."

Lorri shook her head. "That's not necessary, I really do feel fine. Wait. Do I know you?"

"I'm the veterinarian. You look familiar too."

"That's it," Lorri said. "Yes. It's so nice to see you again. You took care of my mastiff. Mister."

"I remember him. What a great dog. I hope y'all are getting settled in."

"We are. Thanks."

"Glad you're up," Ryder interrupted. "You scared me."

Lorri realized now that he was the guy Tinsley had been talking to earlier. "I'm so sorry. I should have been watching where I was going."

"Well, yeah, that, but your lips." He pointed to her face. "They're blue. I thought you couldn't breathe."

She touched her lips. "Cotton candy." She began laughing. "It was the cotton candy. I'm a first-timer. Nobody warned me that I'd end up with blue lips. Next time I'll get the pink."

"You almost got unnecessary CPR."

Maybe she did have a concussion because something about that comment, stone-cold serious, absolutely hit her funny bone and if she was going to receive unnecessary CPR she couldn't have picked a better-looking guy to offer it. "That wouldn't have been the worst thing that happened to me this year."

"Yeah, well I'm sorry I tackled you to the ground. I'd just meant to pull you out of the way." He looked as flustered as she felt. "I was trying to help."

Diane piped in. "He was the best offensive lineman we had back in high school. Even got a scholarship."

"Haven't had to tackle anyone in a good long while. You weigh a lot less than those guys I use to play with too."

"Good to know," Lorri said. "Sorry I broke your tackle-free streak."

"It's okay. Here." He tossed something her way.

She raised her arms to catch it. "A T-shirt?" She unfurled it. "Oh, and it's from . . . The Wedding Ranch?" Her gut rolled like she was going to hurl. "Oh, gosh. I couldn't." She threw it back to him.

"Your shirt's a mess. At least it's clean." He realized the shirt was much bigger than the woman. "It's too big. Sorry. I just grabbed one. Didn't think to check the size." He thrust it in her direction again.

A stolen shirt from The Wedding Ranch? That did seem more appealing. "Thank you." *It's the thought that counts.* "I'm going home."

"You really shouldn't drive or go to sleep after a fall like that. I'll buy you something better to eat than blue cotton candy. I've got years of experience with fair food. Besides, we should keep you moving around and make sure you're okay."

"I don't know." Lorri looked to Tinsley, hoping she'd offer a lifeline.

"And you missed your birdhouse class," Tinsley said. "You were so looking forward to that."

"It's fine," Lorri said.

Diane piped up. "I offered her a ride home."

Ryder said, "I know the guy who teaches that class. I think I can pull a few strings."

"Really?" Lorri responded to Ryder a little more enthusiastically than she'd intended.

"Being a local has its privileges," he said. "I'd feel better keeping a watch on you in case that bump on the head is anything serious."

She eyed him surreptitiously. He didn't seem dangerous, and everyone seemed to know him. That had to mean something. She could think of worse ways to spend the evening, and if Mister made a mess of the house, she wasn't ready to deal with that yet anyway. "Okay, then. Yeah. Let me change my shirt. Thanks for the offer of the ride, Diane."

"No problem. You're in good hands with Ryder. I'd be more help to the steer," she teased.

"She's the veterinarian," Ryder explained.

She looked around to see where she could go and change into the clean shirt. "I knew that, but I didn't put it together until she told me. I took my dog to her when we first got to town."

He pointed out the tent toward the building next door. "The ladies' room is over there. I'll wait here for you."

Chapter Nine

Ryder waited while Lorri changed her shirt, and stood there second-guessing why he'd insisted she stay at the fair for a while. It wasn't his job to care for her in the first place. *I should've let Diane give her a ride home. What the heck has gotten into me?*

The internal banter had only just begun though.

I tackled her pretty good trying to get her out of the way. Watching over her for a couple of hours is the right thing to do.

Has nothing to do with the fact she's beautiful? No. Just to be on the safe side. A good neighbor.

She's lovely. Even covered in dirt with wood shavings in her hair. But I'm not interested. I only have room for one woman in this heart.

"Great. I'm talking to myself and answering myself too. That's it. I'm officially crazy," he mumbled.

Maybe it's appropriate we're going to go build birdhouses. I'm cuckoo.

He kicked his boot in the dirt.

"Good as new," Lorri said, interrupting his self-assessment. "This shirt is the softest material I've ever worn."

"Looks good." He cleared his throat and lifted his eyes from the logo on her chest, leveling his gaze with her deep green eyes. "That shirt is made from recycled milk jugs or something eco-friendly." *Milk jugs? Really? I'm a blundering fool.* "The Wedding Ranch is very aware of cause and effect on the environment. Recycling. Reduced carbon footprint. All that."

"I'd read about that. Here's a fun fact for you. I actually created the logo that's on this shirt."

"You know Reece and Ross?" She was a little shorter than he realized now that she was on her feet.

"No. Not exactly." Lorri shrugged. "They must be the owners. They wouldn't know me either. I work for the graphic arts firm out of Raleigh that was contracted to do the work. I was living there—in Raleigh—when the project came in," she explained.

"Small world."

"It is sometimes," she agreed with a smile that was beautiful even though her lips were still bluish.

"Yes." He cleared his throat. No need to tell her he was related to them. He probably wouldn't see her again after tonight. "The shirt works. Good."

She nodded.

"So, new in town?" He started walking toward the big block building.

"Is that your best line?" The toying edge to her comment came across as playful.

"Yeah. Guess so. I mean, I know everyone in this town, and I haven't seen you before."

"So, it was a statement?" Lorri commented. "Not a question?"

"Right. That and Tinsley told me that you lived down from her mom which means you moved into Mill Creek Highlands."

"Yes, I did," she said. "From Raleigh."

"Right. You said that. I could've guessed you were from Raleigh though. You have that city attitude to you."

"Really?" Her eyes narrowed. "Why not Charlotte?"

"No." He was sure of himself. "You don't have that banker look. Not a computer geek either. More of a Raleigh look."

"And how does a Raleigh person look?"

He was in over his head. The banter was quick. He and Valerie had always gone at it like that. He'd been able to think fast on his feet back then, but that had been seven years ago now. Out of practice, and a little uncomfortable, he bailed out. "No comment."

"Probably a good idea." She winked, a perky smile lifting her cheeks.

He laughed. "Come on. This way." He jogged ahead to open the door. "After you, ma'am." Air conditioning flowed from inside, a relief from the afternoon heat.

She made a beeline for the rows of baked goods. Valerie had always insisted on looking at all of them too. What was it about ogling food you can't even try that intrigued women? All the entries looked pretty much the same to him. He moved along at her pace since she seemed to be enjoying it.

"Do you bake?" he asked.

"No. That's why I admire the people who can. I can barely get the pop-can biscuits to come out like the picture."

His laugh came so quick, it almost choked him. "There's an art to homemade biscuits, but those canned ones, they don't require much skill. I think I can give you some tips on those myself."

"Thanks." She mused, glancing around. "I'd starve if I had to rely on my cooking. Thank goodness there are a few good restaurants in town."

"Speaking of food, I promised you some. I'm going to grab us a couple barbecue sandwiches. These are the best. Keep looking. I'll catch back up in a minute."

He kept an eye on her as he waited in line at the BBQ booth. She wasn't making an obligatory pass. She was really into it, checking each of the entries out and truly enjoying herself. He got the sandwiches and two bottles of water. He caught up with Lorri, who was looking at batches of homemade cookies.

"This might not be what you're craving after staring at all those baked goods, but I think you'll like it better than that blue cotton candy."

"Thanks." They ate while walking down the last row of baked goods—the tiered cake category. There were lots of traditional wedding cakes, but also contemporary and theme cakes.

"I like this one." Ryder stood in front of a four-tiered cake.

"I'm drawn to the trendy semi-naked cake. The sugar flowers are so realistic and the bluish-green eucalyptus is such a nice contrast to the pinks."

"Are you kidding?" Ryder laughed. "Looks like someone just swept their finger around the edges to steal the frosting. I turn every cake that sits on my counter too long into something that looks like that. Doesn't take much talent, just an appetite for sweets."

"Well, it's a good thing we just ate, or some of these cakes might be in danger."

"Truly," he said with a nod.

"Thanks for the sandwich. That was the best barbecue I've ever had, and I've had my share," she said.

"Glad you liked it."

She took a sip of water from her bottle then lifted on her toes. Delighted, her eyes flashed. "Quilts!"

"You quilt?"

"Oh no." She flipped a hand in the air as if he'd made the craziest assumption possible. "I don't quilt either. In fact I don't do much in the domestic area at all." She double-stepped over to the display of quilts. She wandered through the ones hanging from the ceiling, her chin to the sky moving as if she were navigating a maze. "These are gorgeous."

"Takes a lot of work." He shoved his hands into his pockets. "Mom used to spend hours in front of her quilting frame, hand-stitching the final patterns. She always said that was the most precious part of the quilt, although you didn't even notice it unless you really looked."

The black and red quilt on his bed now was one his mom had made for him. In the hand-stitching in one of the corners she'd sewn the words, "Sleep soundly every night knowing I love you, son," something that no one knew but the two of them. That memory made him miss her. Some days it was like she'd been gone forever rather than on a road trip with his dad, especially when weeks went by with no phone call. He wasn't even sure which state they were in now. "Mom loved quilting."

Memories of her holding the ribbons she'd won in this fair went back as far as he could remember. She used to have an old Christmas tree in the corner of her project room that was filled with mostly first place ones.

"Oh, I'm sorry. When did she—"

"She's very much alive. Sorry. I just haven't seen her in a while."

"Where does she live?"

"She and Dad took off to see the country. Sold the house and bought themselves a fancy RV. Thing is as big as a cotton baler. I get postcards. Sometimes they stay in one place for a few weeks. Mostly I think they are letting life lead them to the next adventure."

"That sounds amazing." She tossed her hair back. "There are so many beautiful places I've never visited. I bet it's wonderful."

He liked the way her dark hair waved this way and that. "For them maybe. I couldn't do it."

"Honestly, as awesome as it sounds it's probably not for me either. I'd never be brave enough to do that." Her brows pulled together. "I'm kind of a creature of habit. I like to know where I am and what I'm going to be doing."

"I'm with you on that," he said. "And tradition. I like to do things that I know make me happy. Those are what should become tradition. Right?"

"Yes. And don't repeat the things that don't bring joy." She seemed pleased on their meeting of the minds.

She admired the quilts, reading the information about each one. She ran her fingers across fabric in muted greens and blues. "I love this one. It would go perfectly in my house."

"I like the green. It's a different shade."

She snickered. "Not like John Deere green, huh?"

"Nothing wrong with John Deere green."

"Not if you're a tractor," she teased. "This is more of a sage. My house is about this shade. It attracted me instantly."

"You know, most of these quilts will be for sale this Sunday. I mean, if you think you might be interested."

"Really?" She stepped closer to the quilt. Each stitch was so precise that if she hadn't read the card she'd never have guessed it was hand-stitched. She liked the way the top stitching left the fabric in puffy tufts along the pattern. She traced the stitches with her fingertip. "Look how intricate the continuous swooping flourish is on this one. It's like they tried to copy the path of a bumblebee's flight on a spring day."

"That was rather poetic. You sure you don't know something about quilting?" He stared at her. One moment she was trading snippy banter with him, the next she spoke as delicate as a feather.

She dipped her head as if she hadn't realized she'd uttered those words out loud. "No, but I know a lot about patterns and color. I was an art major. I work in marketing in the design area."

"Which explains how you created the logo on that shirt." He twisted the tag on the quilt to see who had crafted that one. "Patsy Faber. I'm sure you can negotiate a deal on this one. She's been sewing quilts for years. She's one of Mom's close friends. She'll definitely be here on Sunday after church."

"That would be wonderful." She pointed to the quilt. "I'm coming back for that quilt."

"I'll introduce you two."

"Thanks. Oh, gosh. I'm sorry, I'm sure this isn't your idea of a good time. I can come back and stroll through this stuff another day. Let's make those birdhouses."

He pointed toward the far side of the building and they walked together.

There was no one in the booth, but the tools and supplies were still sitting out. "Come on." He pulled a metal chair out for her. He picked up two stacks of precut wood, handing her one as he took the seat at the head of the table to her right.

"Are you sure we're not going to get into trouble for making ourselves at home like this?" She leaned in. "Those people over there are looking at us."

"They're just enjoying the show."

"If we get arrested, you are posting my bail." She wagged a finger in his direction. "Got it?"

"Welcome to Leafland County, where anyone can build a birdhouse without getting arrested." He lifted two pieces of wood and positioned them. "Like this."

She followed his lead, lining up the edges, gluing and clamping them before nailing them together.

They worked quietly. He liked that she wasn't the type to fill every quiet moment with words—talking just to talk. He valued comfortable silence. Each step of the way there were nods and smiles as they built the birdhouses. She followed direction well.

"Now for the roof. We have old license plates that can be bent to create the pitch or there's live-edge wood. What's your pleasure?"

"What's live-edge wood?"

"They still have bark on one side."

"That's a hard decision."

"Let's do one of each. I'm giving you mine anyway. I don't need a birdhouse."

"Great. I'd love to have both. Thank you."

He bent a license plate across the roof of his birdhouse, while she nailed the live-edge slices of wood into place on the other.

"Not bad." She looked very pleased with herself. "These are great. Who do we pay for them?"

"On the house," he said.

She looked like she was going to argue, but then she simply said, "Thank you, sir."

"Least I could do for bumping your noggin." He swept her hair from her forehead. "Let me see that." He winced. "You've got quite the goose egg there."

"Lovely." She brushed her hair back into place. "Could've been worse. So quit apologizing."

As if on cue the Cody Tuggle song "If I Say I'm Sorry" played. She laughed, pointing toward one of the speakers. "See!"

They both noticed the coincidence at the same time. "Alright already," Ryder said.

"I love this song," she admitted. "He's one of my favorite singers."

"Really?"

"Mm-hmm. He's a good guy."

"How do you know?"

"I can tell," she said. "If you listen to the words of his songs, he's a genuine guy. He writes most of his own lyrics."

"I'll let you know what I think when I meet him." Ryder leaned in to whisper in her ear. "Don't tell anyone, it's top secret, but he's getting married at The Wedding Ranch next month."

She shook her head. "No way. But if it is true, and it's a secret, you shouldn't be telling me." She waved a finger at him. "Or anyone else for that matter."

He looked stumped. "You're right. I don't even know why I did that." He stood there looking at her. "I guess . . . I was trying to impress you." *Have I gone completely mad?*

Her cheeks reddened. "Well, don't tell secrets. That'll impress me."

"Yes, ma'am." He placed both birdhouses into a box and slid them under the table. "We'll pick these up later. We should get you something to eat. Are you hungry?"

"Not after that barbecue, but I kind of had my heart set on trying a fried Twinkie."

"Dessert then."

"Deal."

"We have to cut through the midway to get to where they park all the really good food trucks. I happen to be pretty skilled at those games."

"Are you bragging?" The playful tilt of her shoulders made him regret the comment.

"Isn't bragging if it's true."

"It's still bragging."

He steered her by the elbow to a tent with one of those

games where you have to throw the ball and hit bottles off of a platform.

She shook her head. "Doesn't matter how good you are. You know this game is rigged to keep you from winning."

The booth operator feigned offense at her accusation. "This joint is not rigged. I promise you that." He handed Ryder three balls. "I run a fair game. Get it. Fair. Go for it. Wait a second. Miss, pick out what you want to win."

Lorri pressed her finger to her lips as she scanned the stuffed animals, laser-lit hats, and feather boas. "That teddy bear."

Ryder gave the guy a nod, then winked at Lorri. "Here goes."

He threw all three balls and nailed all three. He took a bow, and the operator presented her with the giant stuffed bear.

"That thing is huge." Ryder lifted it over his head, balancing it on his shoulder and back.

"You haven't seen huge until you've met Mister."

"You mean to tell me there's a Mister Lorri? You're not wearing a ring." Yes, he'd noticed.

"Not that kind." She took her phone from her pocket and scrolled to a picture. "Here. No. There's no Mister Lorri Walker, but there is a Mister in my life."

"Holy cow. That's your dog? I've got feeder calves that size."

"That's why I named him Mister."

"I would too. How much does he weigh?" Ryder had steer-wrestled calves smaller than that.

"One hundred and eighty pounds last time we were at the vet."

"He's a cool dog. If you're not already, you might want to

start buying your large-breed dog food from the mill in bulk. It'll save you a bundle."

"That *would* help."

"I've known those guys forever. I'll hook you up down there."

"Thank you. That's really nice of you. You do know everyone around here."

"Nothing of it," he said. "It's the neighborly thing to do." He walked forward and realized she had suddenly dropped back. She had an odd look on her face.

"Yeah, sure, neighborly is good. As long as that's all it is. I mean, I'm not married. No ring as you said, but I'm not looking either." That sounded harsh. "I didn't mean to insinuate that you'd even be interested, but—"

"Don't dig yourself in any deeper. I'm not looking either."

Her smile came back. "Oh good, because my ex was a real jerk. Bought me that giant dog, then left for a lady with a Yorkie from puppy class."

"I never did like those little barking breeds."

"Tell me about it." She looked like she might have regretted giving him too much information.

"No worries. We're just neighbors. No time for more than that. I've got a very busy schedule," he said.

"Me too. I've been accused of working too much, but what does that even mean? We're supposed to work hard, aren't we?"

"Being a hard worker is a very important life skill. I completely agree."

"See! Thank you." She stopped and looked for a moment, then turned back to him. "I need to get home to my big dog before he gets hungry and eats the couch or something. Today's been fun."

"It has. I'm glad you're okay." He lifted his phone and moved the flashlight in front of her eyes, then raised his finger in front of her face. He didn't even have to tell her to follow it as he gave her the remedial field test for a concussion again. "No nausea or dizziness?"

"Nope."

"I think you're fine. Do you think you can drive? I'd be happy to give you a lift."

"No." She answered quickly. "Thank you. I'm fine to drive. I'm going to go get those birdhouses and head home."

"I'm a little worried about you driving. I could follow you to be sure you make it home okay."

"I'll tell you what. If I feel like I can't drive, I promise I will stop. Believe me, the last thing I want to do is drive recklessly, or have people think I'm driving drunk. You don't want to get me started about drunk drivers."

"You're not the only one with strong opinions on that. But tonight, I just want to know that you're safe, and that I didn't give you a concussion trying to rescue you. Can I at least carry the birdhouses to your car for you?"

"No. You've done enough, babysitting me all afternoon. I can handle it. Thank you." She turned to leave, then lifted her hand in a wave. "Bye," she called out over her shoulder as she walked away.

"See you around town." He didn't want to sound interested. He wasn't. "It's a small town. I'm sure we will. Cross paths, I mean." He wasn't so sure that was any more convincing.

Shut up.

He watched her walk into the building, resisting the temptation to help her with the birdhouses to her car after she'd already said no.

Ryder turned and walked over to the arena where the horse show was in full swing, but then jogged out to his truck to follow her so he could be sure she wasn't on the side of the road somewhere.

Chapter Ten

Lorri was thankful she didn't experience any blurred vision on her way home. The EMTs were probably being overcautious, but they'd kind of scared her.

Aside from the fall and the knot on her head, the evening had been a lot of fun. She was still replaying the day's events when she turned into the neighborhood.

She wrangled the two birdhouses out of her car and carried them to the house, setting them on the porch to unlock the front door.

The county fair had far surpassed her expectations. With the lingering smell of cotton candy and barbecue still on her, she turned the key in the lock, glad she hadn't missed out.

"Mister? Where's my boy?" He was like a toddler. When it was quiet, she worried what he was up to.

His heavy paws plodded against the hardwood floors with all the heft of a man's weight.

Just as she laid her things on the table in the foyer, Mister spotted her and raced over.

"There you are." She patted him on the head and received the expected warm welcome. "I didn't mean to be gone so long. You wouldn't believe the day I had. Let's check the place out together. You didn't destroy anything while I was away, did you?"

He looked up with wide-eyed innocence. She'd been fooled by those puppy eyes before.

She slapped her hip for him to follow along. The living room looked undisturbed. Every throw pillow was how she'd left them.

"Good boy." She pressed her hands to the sides of his face and bent to kiss him on the forehead. "You are getting to be such a big boy."

She took a quick look through the rest of the house and to her delight he hadn't gotten into any trouble. Not even a stray paper towel, which he loved to snag from the kitchen counter and shred when she wasn't looking.

"I guess my puppy is finally growing up." She placed her hand under his chin. "I'm so proud of you. I bet you're hungry for some dinner."

Mister barked.

"I'll take that as a yes. Let's go out first. It's been a long afternoon for you."

She let him outside while she put her things away. She hadn't asked Ryder what his last name was, and that had been intentional. She wasn't looking for anyone in her life. Things were much easier and predictable without a man in the picture, and she was beginning to really treasure this new lifestyle.

But as much as she commended herself on being strong and

independent and keeping the handsome man at arm's distance, she couldn't help but think about how much fun they'd had tonight.

When she let Mister in, he ran straight to his food dish and scarfed down his food.

She stood there watching him but thinking of Ryder. It was an interesting name. It fit him though. Unique. Strong. Serious, but fun in a way she'd never experienced before. He seemed fine with his plans for the day changing after he rescued her, just shifting gears on a whim. Something she never did. Planning was in her DNA. She excelled at it, and having plans also meant that there were routines in place. *Or traditions, like Ryder had said.*

Mister trotted out of the kitchen and stood by the back door again.

"Creatures of habit. Not the worst thing in the world to be." She got up and let him out. "At least we know what to expect."

From her desk, she hit a key on her keyboard and the computer screen brightened. Emails began loading like a waterfall in her inbox. She scanned the long list then clicked on a new assignment from her boss, Franklin. She'd once thought she wanted his job. As creative director he got first look at every project and was on point to handle the ideation process and pitches to the clients. She'd filled in for him when he and his wife had their first child last year, and that had been a blessing. Not because it was a test drive of her dream job and a chance to prove she was ready for the additional responsibility, but for the realization that the very things she loved about her work were elements she'd lose if she moved up to that next level. She'd never been happier than the day he came back from paternity leave.

Technically it was after working hours, but she had taken almost the entire afternoon instead of just a couple of hours away as she'd planned. She opened the files and printed them. Her best ideas were usually from tiny golden nuggets that came to her during the initial review, and she'd found she worked better with paper in hand and reading out loud, rather than on the computer screen.

On the couch with the stack of papers she began reviewing the details. Budget and timeline would drive a lot of the decisions, and the attached ideas from the client with pictures and links to other companies doing similar things always helped her get a feel for what might delight them. If experience had taught her anything it was that clients knew what they liked, but they didn't know what they wanted . . . even when they thought they did.

In fact, most often the solutions that got approved were not the client's idea at all. That's why they paid her the big bucks to come up with something fabulous that would stick with the consumer and garner sales or impressions depending on the goal.

This project came with a hefty budget, which was good, because it was a tight timeline. Not impossible, but definitely tight. This looked like a project that her coworker John Pitts would usually run with, but as she continued her initial review, she could see why Franklin had given her the assignment this time. The client was the real estate developer who had built the rural sustainable community where she now lived.

True, John Pitts had done lots of similar projects, even the first two for this company, but Lorri knew she was the right person for this job, having bought her home based on the quality and craftsmanship of this company's work. Franklin probably thought her recent experience moving out of the city might give her an interesting perspective on it.

She was known for mostly food and beverage accounts of late, so it was a nice switch-up. Her mind was already conjuring up color wheels and themes to capture the best things about this style of living.

Mister let out a single woof at the back door, his way of letting her know he was ready to come inside.

She placed the project printout on her desk. There was such great light here, and on these long summer days that was extra nice.

Mister pranced inside and over to his favorite spot next to her chair.

Sitting behind her desk, she pulled out a box of markers to start brainstorming. She jotted down a few ideas, changing colors for different types of promotions since the client was interested in both print ads and trade show materials including banners and signage.

The name of the company leant itself to some fun ideas too. Bloom. The logo was simple lettering right now, and although it was clean and legible—which often they were not—it didn't have much first-impression power. She'd work on that first thing in the morning.

Meanwhile she let her thoughts flow, filling pages with ideas. Good ones. She was excited about the direction. The client would either adore them or hate them. She worked up a simpler version. Sometimes clients liked vanilla, so that was a good thing to have in the package. She found, however, that by showing the vanilla version after the preferred one, it only highlighted how good the other was.

It was getting late and she needed to shower off the county fair smells and get into bed. As she showered the music and playful sounds from the children at the fair filled her head. Even being talked into staying by a complete stranger after almost being run over by a fleeing steer had turned into a good chain of events. It'd definitely be a fun story to tell her kids someday. Or Pam's kids, if Lorri never remarried.

Lorri had always been more of a traditional thinker in the parenting area, and raising a child alone wasn't something she wanted to do. She'd given up on marriage; maybe it was time to give up on the dreams of being a mother too.

She stepped out of the shower and wrapped herself in a big bath towel. Her fingers grazed the huge bump on her head, causing her to wince. She brushed her teeth and changed into pajamas.

It was probably too late for ice to help now, but she went into the kitchen and grabbed a bag of veggies from her freezer. She lounged back against the pillows on the couch and pressed the cold pack to her forehead.

Her phone played the special ring tone that she only used for one person. She didn't even open her eyes, clicking the answer button with her thumb. "Hi, Pam. I was going to call you. Everything okay?"

"Yes. I just got off the phone with Cody. Oh my gosh, you won't believe his news!"

Lorri almost blurted out that Cody was getting married at The Wedding Ranch next month, but then she'd be telling the secret too. Ryder's face when he admitted he'd been trying to impress her looked as surprised for saying it as she'd been hearing it.

Pam and Lorri had gone to high school with Cody, a fact Lorri hadn't disclosed to Ryder earlier. After high school, Pam and Lorri had gone on to college together, but Cody went to Nashville to chase his dream. No matter how much stardom he achieved, he always stayed in touch. Even though Cody Tuggle was now one of the most popular country-western singers, he was still the same down-to-earth guy they knew in school. He'd been Cody Allan Hill back then. Cody Tuggle was his stage name. The one the rest of the world knew him by. He'd always be Cody Hill to her.

"How is he?" Lorri asked. "I haven't heard from him since Christmas. He was at his mom's ranch in Tennessee."

"Well, it's a small world, my friend." The tone in Pam's voice piqued Lorri's curiosity. "Just the other day we were talking about The Wedding Ranch, and now guess where Cody is getting married."

"The Wedding Ranch." She lowered the frozen bag from her head, the smile on her face causing the swelling to pull. "You are kidding me. Please tell me he's marrying that nice photographer he was so crazy about. The one with the little boy. She sounded like the best thing that had ever happened to him."

"Kasey Phillips. Yep. Isn't it great? She lives in Virginia, you know. So it's really not that crazy that they'd get married at a venue here in North Carolina. Driving distance and all."

"I'm so happy for him." Lorri feigned surprise. Ryder had been telling the truth. Score for him. After her ex she had no tolerance for liars.

"Sweetest part of the deal is he plans to carve out a little time for us. I told him we could get together at your house. That's okay, right?"

"Of course. He can even stay here. I've got plenty of room for you, and them."

"They've got accommodations all worked out, but the wedding is a big secret. We can't let anyone know he'll be in town," Pam said. "We'll have to be really careful about that."

"No problem. I don't want to share the little bit of time we can get to catch up with him with anyone else anyway." Although she might have to give Ryder a real keep-it-quiet speech now. That is if they even crossed paths between now and then.

"I know! I feel the same way," Pam said. "There's more good news."

"As good as Cody finally tying the knot?"

"Better. We're invited to the wedding." Pam's voice rose with excitement.

"Of course we are," Lorri chimed in. "He couldn't leave us out of his wedding. We'd never let him live that down."

"I made that abundantly clear." Her laugh held mischief and Lorri could imagine the verbal assault Pam would've laid on him. "Actually, I told him we'd show up in hideous gowns to embarrass him if he didn't invite us."

"Sad thing is we would do that." Lorri laughed so hard she snorted. "I know exactly which bridesmaid dress I'd wear too."

"Me too. Carmen's. Am I right?" Pam said. "Her dress was drop-dead gorgeous. Why she put us in those frilly mountains of fluffy fabric I'll never understand."

"Me either, but Cody would never have been able to miss us in those big SweeTart-colored things."

"We'd have taken up a whole row ourselves," Pam said.

The laughter made the goose egg on her noggin throb. She pressed the veggies against her head again.

"This is going to be so much fun. We can't bring dates, and for that I'm grateful," Pam said. "You know how Bobby hates weddings."

"Fine by me too. I hate being the third wheel. When's the wedding?"

"End of August, but they'll be in Dalton Mill the better part of the week."

"I'm putting it on my calendar and marking off the days before and after so we can be flexible to his schedule," Lorri said.

"I did the same thing."

"You should spend a few days here. I'd really love it if you would," Lorri said.

"I might do that."

"I'll even take time off from work."

"Sure you will," Pam said.

"No. Really. In fact, I took the whole afternoon off today. I went to the county fair."

"You did not."

"I did. I have a big old knot on my head to prove it."

Pam stopped laughing. "What happened?"

"Apparently, one of the 4-H market steers went a little wild and I almost got run over by him."

"What? Are you okay?"

"I'm fine. Someone pushed me out of the way, and the paramedics showed up and everything. I was so embarrassed, but honestly it was the best day I've had in a long time. We made birdhouses, ate barbecue, and I picked out a quilt I'm dying to buy at the end of the fair."

"This someone? Would it happen to be a handsome man who rescued you?" Pam's question was filled with hope.

"As a matter of fact, he was very handsome. His name is Ryder. Local guy. Knows everyone. It was fun."

"I can't believe it. You sound like you really did have a big day."

"He won me a giant teddy bear and gave me the birdhouse he made too."

"Better watch it. That's probably a marriage proposal in a small town like that," Pam joked. "But seriously, I've been telling you to get better work-life balance for half our lives. I'm glad you're finally working on it."

"I am. I also set up my painting stuff up in the loft."

"Is this Lorri Walker?" Pam teased. "Did you hijack my workaholic best friend?"

"No. It's me. I'm learning how to enjoy this new life I've got and feeling pretty darn thankful about it."

"I promise I'm coming to see this for myself. I can't wait."

"Me either." Something about this day had changed her priorities.

She hung up, feeling excited about the reunion with Cody. At least the knot on her head would be long gone by the wedding.

What am I going to wear to a celebrity wedding?

Chapter Eleven

Ryder walked into his sister's veterinary practice on Main Street at noon. Ruby, the receptionist, was on her break as he knew she would be.

He'd gone to the county fair every day last week but hadn't crossed paths with Lorri again. She hadn't shown up to buy the quilt on Sunday either. He'd even asked the guys down at the mill if she'd come in looking for big bags of large-breed dog food, but so far, she hadn't.

Soft instrumental music played in the background. Diane swore it kept the animals calmer. He was uncertain of it. He played a lot of George Strait in his barn and his animals seemed fine with or without it.

He walked around the counter to the reception desk where the file cabinet with the patient charts was. He knew this place as well as the back of his hand. He'd built this animal hospital for Diane a few years back when she'd outgrown the small building where she'd started her practice. Here they'd expanded the kennel for long-term stays and added stalls for larger animals so folks could bring their horses to her. It saved her customers money, and cut down on driving time to make farm calls for a quick Coggins test—a win for everyone.

He slid open the metal drawer and began flipping through the files. He'd only gotten through the first few when a woman with a cat in a light blue carrier walked in through the left entrance.

"Hi," he greeted her politely, as if he were the one who was supposed to be behind this desk.

"Hey, Ryder. How've you been?"

He didn't recognize her. "Good. How's your mom and them?" That worked on just about anyone around here.

"Everyone's doing great." She nodded to the pet carrier. "Well, except for Tux. He's here to get fixed. Poor little guy has no idea what's getting ready to happen to him, but I know it's the right thing to do."

"It is," he agreed. "Don't need more feral cats running around."

"No. That's not good for anyone, although I'm grateful to have found him. He didn't take a week to tame down, and he's an excellent mouser."

Diane walked out with a lady leading an old swaybacked Basset Hound toward the front.

Ryder leaned back against the file cabinet closing it without suspicion. Perfect timing. He didn't want to have to make small talk with the cat lady any longer than necessary.

Diane glanced over at him. "Everything okay, Ryder?"

"Yeah, fine. I was in the neighborhood and thought I'd take my favorite sister to lunch."

"Really? I'd love that. I'll be free right after this next appointment."

The cat lady smiled.

Ruby came in carrying a takeout box. "Hey, Ryder." The smell of good North Carolina barbecue filled the air. The Basset's nose wiggled as he inched toward the scent.

Ruby edged by Ryder and sat in her chair. "I can finish going over the follow-up with Barkley's mom," she said to Diane.

"Thanks, Ruby." Diane turned to the cat lady. "Ginny, you can bring Tux right on back."

Ginny Matthews. The librarian. That's her. No wonder I couldn't place her. Haven't read much more than the farm auction brochure in a long while.

He stood there, kind of stuck while Ruby went over Barkley's follow-up instructions and settled their bill.

Barkley and his mom left, and Ruby spun around in her chair. "Ryder Bolt. What are you doing here behind my desk? Are you trying to steal my job?"

"Not in a hundred years," he said.

"Good," Ruby said. "So, then what are you doing back here?"

He fumbled for an excuse. "Thought I'd take Diane out to lunch. You weren't here so I came around to leave her a note, but then she came out and the cat lady came in and you showed up. It turned into a party."

"I see. Well, from what I hear you could use a good party now and then."

"Excuse me?" Since when was his business anybody's business? "I'm fine, thank you very much."

"If you say so."

Ginny walked back out to the front empty-handed. "I guess I'll be picking up Tux in the morning."

"Don't you worry," Ruby chimed in. "I'll call you as soon as he comes out of sedation. He'll be a little loopy, but they bounce back super fast. By the time you pick him up he'll be his old self."

The woman held her hand to her heart. "I feel kind of bad about it."

"Oh, don't. It's the responsible thing to do. We'll take great care of him."

"I know that. Y'all always do." Ginny twisted the handle on the door and walked out with her head low.

"Poor thing," Ruby said. "Sometimes those procedures are harder on the owners than they are on the animals."

"Guilt's a crippling thing." He knew that better than anyone.

"So, do you want to wait here, or should I send Diane over to meet you for lunch when she's done?"

"Oh, yeah. I guess she could just meet me across the street."

"Sure thing."

"Okay." He slowly turned, taking only one step before he stopped. "Did a lady with a mastiff come in here? Lives in the new neighborhood up near my place?"

Ruby cocked her head. "A lady?"

"Anyone, really. A big mastiff. Like a hundred and eighty pounds."

She leaned back in her chair and folded her arms across her generous chest. "Oh yeah. You must be talking about Mister."

"Yes!"

"Mh-hmm. Ryder Bolt, were you back here looking through my files?"

He glanced back to the operating room. "Stop that. I'm just asking a question."

"Oh, I know what you were doing." Her lips curled up like she was in the know. Ruby was enjoying this way too much.

"I'm not up to anything. I met her at the fair. I was supposed to give her a number for something, but I lost hers."

"Really?"

"Why are you giving me such a hard time about this, Ruby?"

"Because I know you. We all worry about you. You're acting all goofy as heck, but own it, man. This is a good sign."

"There's nothing to own." He shrugged. "I figured she'd have had to come here, and I'd get her number. Since I lost it. I . . . never mind."

Ruby pulled out a lateral file to her left. With a quick finger walk across the top of the charts she pulled one out. "Get your pencil out."

"Thanks, Ruby."

She pursed her lips. "You owe me." She called out the numbers, watching him the whole time. "Now would you do me a favor and use that number for something besides a good deed?"

"Nothing wrong with good deeds," he said.

"No. Not at all, but just relax. You might have fun. She's real nice."

I know.

"You're really not going to tell me anything?" Ruby fluttered her lashes. "Come on."

"Nothing to tell."

"Well, then get out of here. I'll send your sister over when she's done."

"Thanks, Ruby."

"Oh, don't thank me. I'll call in that favor one day." She flipped her hair back and spun around in her chair.

He waved as he walked out.

The Dalton Mill Diner was busy, but he spotted an empty table near the window. Not really his favorite place to sit. It was weird to eat on display like that. Made him feel like one of those Siamese fighting fish in a teensy bowl, but the sooner he got lunch with Diane over with the sooner he could call Lorri. His heart pounded. He clutched the brochure he'd written her number on, then tried to commit it to memory.

"What are you having today, Ryder?" Maggie Mae slid a cup of ice water onto the table.

"Diane's meeting me between patients. How about two specials. You know she'll be in a hurry."

"You got it. And two sweet teas?"

"That'll do."

He took out his phone and keyed Lorri's name and number into his contact list, still unsure of what he was going to say when he called.

Diane slid out the chair across from him and sat down. "To what do I owe this nice surprise? Is this so you can get out of the family party tomorrow?"

Tomorrow was her birthday. "No. Of course not. Can't a guy take his big sister to lunch?"

"Yeah. You just never do."

"Well, I'm going to do better on that. Now that Mom and Dad are wandering the nation, we need to fill in some gaps."

"I know. I really miss them. Sunday dinners too. One of us needs to learn some of Mom's recipes."

"It should probably be me," he said with a smirk.

"You're right. You *are* the better cook."

"Don't much like to follow a recipe, but this is a serious situation," he said. "We have traditions that need to be continued."

"How about we plan on Sunday supper after church this week? I'll tell the kids to carve out an hour or two for us."

He couldn't hold back the snicker. "You know all those two are going to talk about is that celebrity wedding?"

"You better lower your voice." Her eyes darted side to side.

"Whatever. I didn't mention a date or a name." He looked around. No one was paying them any mind.

"They are really busting their buns to make that happen," she said. "I've never seen them work so hard."

"They have time for family. If one or two hours will derail that project, then they are already in trouble." He wasn't about to let them skip out on this.

"I know, you're right. You leave them to me," Diane said. "I'll handle that, and I'll tell them all business is off the table."

"Might be a quiet dinner," he teased.

She shrugged. "At least we'll all be together."

Maggie Mae brought out two lunch specials and placed them in front of Ryder and Diane.

"This looks so good." Diane placed a paper napkin in her lap. "I'm so far behind at work from being at the fair last week. This was really nice timing, Ryder."

She grabbed his hand and they said a quick prayer before

digging into the smoked barbecue plate, tomato pie, slaw, and skillet cornbread.

Ryder took a bite, but his stomach was busy doing somersaults. He hated to keep a secret from Diane. It was just a phone number, but those digits would spiral her into giving endless advice that he wasn't ready to hear. He didn't want to get Diane's hopes up since all he knew was that he'd enjoyed spending time with Lorri and wouldn't mind doing it again. But they'd also both said it was just as friends. People never think a man and woman can be friends. Other people anyway, not him.

"I have something to tell you," Ryder finally blurted out. He'd never lied to her and he wasn't about to start now. Lying by omission was still a lie after all.

"Oh no." She put her fork down. "I knew it. There's more to this than lunch. What's wrong?"

"No. It's not bad. Well, kind of. No, it's not that kind of bad."

"What?"

"Remember the woman who got about rolled over by that steer on the first day of the fair?"

"I was there, remember? I told Mrs. Helms that Billy Ray was not ready to show that steer. He barely worked with him. Little brat. He thinks his parents can buy him into first place with a good steer and not put in the work." Diane had strong opinions. They ran hot like that in the Bolt family.

"Diane, I'm sure you're right, but sometimes that stuff just happens. They are animals after all."

"I saw that one coming. Is she okay?"

"She was when she left," he said. "Haven't heard anything else about it."

"Thank goodness."

"I spent the better part of the afternoon with her. I mean, you know, just to be sure she was okay to drive after that knot on her head. She might've fared better if I hadn't tackled her out of the way."

"I doubt it. That steer outweighs you by several hundred pounds." She took another bite and lasered a look at him. "She brings her dog in. She's really nice."

He sucked in a breath. "Yeah. Very nice. We built birdhouses. Had some laughs. She's friends with Tinsley's family, that has to say something. I mean, she's from the city, but she seems . . ."

Diane put her fork down. Swallowing dramatically, her teeth showed as she grinned. "You came to get her phone number, didn't you?" She pounded her fists on the table. "I love it."

"Did Ruby tell you?"

Her mouth dropped open. "Ruby gave it to you?"

Ruby hadn't told her. He stepped right into that one. "Not without some arm-twisting. All I know is she lives in Mill Creek Highlands, and has a dog named Mister."

"And now you have her phone number. Well, good for you, little brother." Diane raised her hand up in a high five.

"Put your hand down. People are looking. It's not like that."

She lowered her hand to pat his cheek. "Well, maybe it could be. Lighten up. Ryder, you're too young to live your life alone."

"I know the speech."

"Well then quit making me repeat it. Trust me, I don't like giving it over and over and over and over—"

"Okay, okay. I got it. I'm just going to call and check in on her."

"That's a good start." Diane took another bite of her lunch. "You know, I'm surprised you're willing to talk to her at all since she lives in the neighborhood. You still harbor such anger about it."

"Not her fault she's benefitting from our family stupidity."

"Be nice. We were born into that family."

"I'm just telling it like it is." Over seven years had passed since the day Valerie and Ronnie Dwayne died in that car accident. Just the thought of calling Lorri was twisting in his gut, and re-igniting guilt he thought he'd put to rest. But why? You'd think by now he'd have forgiven himself for not being with them, but that wasn't as easy as it sounded. He couldn't picture himself with another woman, but he had enjoyed Lorri's company. It had felt good to laugh, and he could do with more of that.

No strings. No expectations, just two neighbors checking in once in a while. And as for that neighborhood, Joe was right—it wasn't going anywhere, and even if Ryder and Diane hadn't benefited directly, this town had.

If Diane wasn't on him about dating, then she was on him about letting go of grudges. She was the second person this week to comment about his moods. Maybe he *had* become more bitter over the past few years.

"Well, you not holding it against her that she lives in the neigh-borhood has to be a step in the right direction." She took a long slug of her tea and set the glass down. "I've got to run. I have a packed schedule. Thank you for lunch. This was a treat, but you know what was even better? You. Almost living again. I love you, brother." She made a beeline for the door, not giving him the chance for a rebuttal. Not that it would have done any good.

Family. They know all your soft spots. No hiding from them.

Chapter Twelve

Lorri had been up and down all night. The ideas kept coming for the new Bloom campaign. She'd given in to the creativity, letting it drive her out of bed again and again. Bleary-eyed, she could still see that what she'd put together overnight may have been one of the best campaigns she'd done in her whole career.

She shot off an email to her boss with the project package, citing her love for her new home as inspiration and letting him know she planned to take the rest of the day off. She hoped he loved the graphics as much as she did.

Lorri texted Tinsley to see if she could stop in and check on Mister a couple of times throughout the day. Tinsley responded quickly that she could.

With that taken care of she dialed Pam. "What are you doing today?"

"Working. Why?"

"I thought we could shop for dresses for the celebrity wedding."

Lorri knew she wouldn't find what she needed here. "Can you take a few hours off?"

"Definitely."

"I'll meet you at the boutique at ten." She knew Pam knew where she meant. It was the place to go for designer dresses, and they'd bought many there over the years.

By 10:15 Pam and Lorri were holding champagne flutes in one hand and flipping through racks of gorgeous dresses with the other.

"I'm not even sure what I'm looking for," Lorri admitted.

"He said dressy, but not overly so." Pam pulled a simple black dress off the rack and held it up.

"You have fourteen dresses just like that," Lorri said.

"I'm always drawn to them. It's a country-themed wedding, but there's likely to be a little bit of everything from denim and fringe to sequins and pearls."

Lorri shrugged. "Should we wear boots and a bandit's bandanna with our sequined gowns?" She laughed. "I'm not doing that even if everyone else is. It would be hilarious though."

"He'd kill us, but honestly I have no idea what we should wear." Pam shrugged and slid aside the next dress, a sequined number with a halter top. "No sequins."

Lorri said, "I'm sticking to a black dress and pearls."

"Wait a minute. If I can't buy another black dress, neither can you."

"Fine. You're right. I didn't need to drive an hour and a half from home to buy another black dress. Here's the deal. We'll both buy something with some color."

A blond woman who had that Miss Texas look approached.

Beautiful, very put together, and tall. She towered over both of them.

"Did I hear someone say color? You know color is the new black," the saleswoman said.

"No it's not," Lorri said matter-of-factly. "It's actually the absence of color."

Pam elbowed her.

"Well, it's not," Lorri reiterated. "There is no replacing black."

"We all have our safe colors." The woman air-quoted the word "safe."

"Is Ms. Travis here? She always helps us." Lorri would give anything for that sweet old woman to help them today. She used to work with Gloria Vanderbilt back in the day. She was old, but she had the best taste, and she never let Lorri walk out of this place looking like less than a ten. This Miss Texas? She wasn't sure about her.

"Ms. Travis retired."

"Retired? She wasn't *that* old."

"No? I never met her, but I happen to know that she found herself a very fine man who wanted to spend lots of time with her, so she left. I promise you're in good hands with me. Trust me."

Lorri gave Pam a look.

"We're struggling with what look we're even going for," Pam said. "It's a high-profile wedding. Not too flashy. Not too casual."

"Excellent." Miss Texas took note of their sizes and the style of dresses they'd already picked out, then darted off to pull other dresses for them.

They sipped champagne until the woman came back and led them each to their own dressing rooms. She'd already placed several options in each room. "And don't worry. I didn't pick the same dress for either of you."

Lorri went into her dressing room and picked her least favorite dress to try on first. *Might as well get this one out of the way.* She wriggled into it and twisted to zip up in the back. "You ready for dress number one?"

"Zipping," Pam called out.

Lorri stepped out of her dressing room and looked in the mirror. The hideous pattern wasn't nearly as bad on, but as she'd suspected that ruffle down the front was not doing anything for her.

Pam opened her door and started laughing. "You look like there's a snake crawling up the front of that dress. Why would someone put a ruffle there? That's a definite no."

"I agree. That one looks good on you though."

Pam smoothed the skirt. "You don't think it's too short?" She hunched down a little. "I'd like it better if it was about two inches longer."

"You've got the legs for it."

"Maybe so, but I don't have the confidence for it. I'd be self-conscious all night long." She tugged at it dramatically.

"Then it's a no." Lorri twirled her finger, sending them both back to their dressing rooms. "Next."

A couple of minutes later they both stepped out of their rooms again. There were more bad dresses than good ones, and Miss Texas seemed to be getting a kick out of the two of them.

"Okay, ladies. You've had your fun, but if you want to find

the right outfit for your big event, we need to get to work. I've been watching, and I think I've found the perfect dress for you." She was looking right at Lorri. "Now, stick with me on this. I can see you're a fan of the little black dress, but you have the perfect figure and complexion for this dress." She pulled a dress in a black zippered bag off of a rack. "No peeking. Take it into the room and put it on. Then come model for us." She handed the dress to Lorri, then clapped her fingertips together.

Lorri tried to hide her concern, stepping into the dressing room before she rolled her eyes. She unzipped the bag. The dress was almost emerald green. Sure, she'd warmed up to the color green since she bought her house, but that was a soft Zen-like sage green. Not top-o'-the-mornin'-to-ya emerald green. She stepped into the dress and fastened it behind her neck. The lines were clean and simple, and honestly the color did perk her complexion up a bit. There was intricate stitching along the shoulder line, and it fit perfectly. She opened the door and took a giant step out, not even chancing a look into the mirror.

"Oh wow." Pam stood there staring at her.

"Was I right?" Miss Texas nodded. "Seriously beautiful. Stunning."

"She's right, Lorri. You look beautiful. Your eyes absolutely sparkle, and it fits like it was made for you."

Lorri cast a sidelong glance toward Pam, not sure if she was teasing. She stepped out past the two ladies and looked in the mirror.

"All you need is the right jewelry now." Miss Texas was already fumbling through wooden felt-lined drawers.

"I'd planned to wear pearls. I don't like big and flashy. This dress is doing plenty of that."

Miss Texas spun toward her. "Good pearls are always okay. They never go out of style." She dove back into the giant jewel case. "I have a great strand here you can try on with it to get the look. Oh, and here." She stepped out of her black pumps. "They'll be big, but they are the right height. Go on, step into them."

Lorri stepped into the shoes and lifted her hair for Miss Texas to hook the pearls around her neck.

"Am I right?" She nodded with her bright blue eyes twinkling and too-white teeth flashing a stage-worthy smile.

"You're so right," Pam said. "Find me a dress as great as that one," she begged.

Miss Texas strode off in her stocking feet since Lorri was still standing in front of the mirror in her shoes.

"I love this dress," Lorri whispered. She'd never have picked out something with such straight lines, afraid it would grab at all the wrong places, but it didn't. "I can't believe it, but I really do."

"You look great." Pam craned her neck trying to see which racks Miss Texas was perusing in search of the perfect dress for her. "I hope she finds something special for me too."

"I'm going to get out of this before I wrinkle it." Lorri kicked off Miss Texas's pumps next to the mirror. "Here, I don't know if these are magic slippers, but you're going to want to try your dress on with them too."

From her dressing room Lorri heard Pam talking to Miss Texas.

"I don't know if this is really my style," Pam said.

"Just try it for me. I think you'll be pleasantly surprised. If not, I'll find the right one. Give it a try-on. Yes?"

"Okay," Pam said, but she sounded a little disappointed.

Lorri hung her dress in the zippered bag. She couldn't wait to wear that dress to Cody's wedding. She walked out of the dressing room and hung the bag on the garment rack next to the love seat in the fitting area.

"I'm so glad you like the dress. I knew it would be perfect on you." Miss Texas clearly loved her job. "Wait until you see what I picked out for your friend."

Pam walked out with a smirk on her face. "I've never been one for lacy stuff," she said, but when she looked into the mirror the smirk fell away.

"Pam, you look beautiful in that dress." Lorri stood there shaking her head. In a million years she'd never have suggested that style, but it was perfect.

Pam turned, the skirt floating across the lower half of her well-toned legs.

"A strappy sandal would be great with that. No jewelry. That dress doesn't need a thing. Don't you agree?" Miss Texas stood there nodding.

Pam shook her head.

"You don't like it?" Lorri was stunned.

"No. I love it," Pam said. "I just can't believe it. When she brought this to me I thought she was crazy, but I feel so . . ." She didn't even finish the sentence. Instead she twirled in front of the mirror. "I could dance all night."

"We might," Lorri said. "Although with Co—"

"Our friend," Pam interjected with a stare.

"Yeah, we'll probably be line dancing or two-stepping."

"Well, ladies, you can do whatever you like in those dresses. You two will own that place."

"We may overshadow the bride," Pam said. "But she'll have to forgive us, because we look amazing."

"I think we're done here." Lorri turned to Miss Texas. "You have been amazing. I don't think I even caught your name."

"Jody. I'm so glad you're happy. Ms. Travis is a hard act to follow."

"Well, it's nice to meet you and I think you're going to be as great as Ms. Travis has been to us all these years. Thank you for your help."

"You are so welcome. Let me get your dress."

Pam opened her dressing-room door and held her dress out in one hand. "You can ring this one up too."

"Excellent," Jody said. "I'll take these up front."

"We hit the jackpot," Pam said as she came out of the dressing room, with her shoes in her hand. "I can't believe we both found something so beautiful, and I'd never ever, not in a million years, have even tried on that cocktail dress."

"I know, but it's perfect, and it's lacy but not over-the-top girly at the same time."

Pam sat on the loveseat and put on her shoes. "We are going to have the best time."

"He'll be here in just two weeks. I've been thinking about what to get them for a wedding present. It's not easy to buy something for someone who has everything they've ever wanted."

"Should we do something together for them?" Pam asked. "Please tell me you've thought of something wonderful."

"I've been racking my brain over it," Lorri said. "I wish I'd met Kasey before. It's so hard to think of something I know they'll both love when I haven't met her."

"She's so down to earth. You'll love her. Honestly, if Cody will like it, she will. I say we just think of him. If he's happy, we're happy. Right?"

"What if I created a picture for them out of his album covers or tour pictures and some of her photographs, pulling out parts to make up the letters that spell 'Tuggle'? I've seen some of those that were really cool, and made out of things personal to them. It would be one of a kind, and it would be something that we put ourselves into."

"We both know how special that kind of stuff is to Cody. You could make that, couldn't you? I think it's an awesome idea."

"Do you think she'd be offended if I used her pictures? I mean, I'd technically be infringing on copyright, but since I'm not selling it and it's for her . . . that's a gray area with not having her permission."

"It's a wedding gift, and we're friends with Cody, like family. She'll love it. She has an artistic eye too. You two are going to be fast friends. I just know it, and wait until you meet her son. He's such an angel, and I know how you love kids."

Lorri's heart ached at the thought. She'd wanted children of her own for so long and Craig kept making them put it off. It was never "the right time." It would be a shame if she never had children because she listened to him, rather than her own needs. Seeing those children at the fair had brought that desire back. A child was part of what had been missing in her life, and now if she ever met someone she'd be sure they saw eye to eye on that subject from the word "go."

"Maybe we can find a photograph of her son to incorporate into the picture. I remember one of the pictures of him with Cody. I'll do some research," Lorri said. "Can you get Bobby to start working on the frame?" Pam's husband could make anything out of wood. His workshop was the envy of many.

"Absolutely. Just text me the size. I'm sure he'll be calling to ask you what kind of wood and tone of stain to complement the images."

"I'll think about that as I'm putting it together. I need to see the colors first. Oh, and could you ask Pete to get some of Cody and Kasey's photographs for us? He's probably the only one who could get his hands on them in such a short time." Pete was not only the lead guitarist in Cody's band, but also Cody's best friend.

"I'll text him right now."

They went up to the front counter and settled their bills, then walked over to the tearoom. Ms. Travis might not be at the boutique anymore, but at least this part of their shopping tradition remained the same.

Buchanan greeted them at the door. "You two have been away for way too long. I've been wondering what happened to you." He leaned forward and kissed Pam on the cheek, then Lorri.

"It's so good to see you," Lorri said.

"Just the two of you today?"

"Yes."

"I'll get you set up with a service for two and Paris tea, right?"

"You always remember."

"Because I'm the best." Buchanan drifted off into the back.

"And our favorite," Pam said to Lorri. "He's the best part of this place."

They hung their dress bags and purses on the coat tree at their table. Lorri loved this tearoom. The beautiful china place settings and fine linens made her feel the urge to raise her pinky. Here all those social graces that Granny had pounded into her tomboyish mind as a little girl were put to good use.

Over tea, scrumptious tiny sandwiches, and petit fours desserts, Lorri and Pam relaxed, both feeling better for having the wardrobe and gift decision resolved.

Pam brought Lorri up to date on everything that had been going on in her and Bobby's lives. Things were good, except Bobby had hurt his knee playing softball. "He isn't in his twenties anymore," Pam said. "I swear, this weekend warrior stuff is going to be a killer on his joints when we get older."

"That ought to be delightful. Especially the part where you're not supposed to say 'I told you so,'" said Lorri.

"Oh, I'll be saying 'I told you so.' And enjoying it. Hey, I've talked about Bobby and I all day. What is going on with you? Is Mister good? Run into the hero from the county fair again yet?"

"Things are good. I love Dalton Mill."

"Wait a minute. I thought the plan was to just live in that new house for a year and then move back. I miss you."

"I know. I miss you too, but the serenity of that small town is hard to beat. I'm telling you, you'd love it there too. Bobby could put a huge workshop on the acreage. He'd love every minute of it."

Pam held a finger up. "Don't you dare give him any ideas. He'd sell the house and the Prius, buy a pickup truck, and move us himself."

"Wouldn't be the worst thing to happen." Lorri would love it if Pam were closer. "You work from home. What's the difference?"

"I've lived in Raleigh my whole life. I can't imagine living anywhere else."

"But it's inspiring. I thought there wasn't an ounce of original creativity left in me until I moved here."

"It's your gift. That doesn't go away. You have such talent, and it's good news you're finding it again, but I'm afraid Dalton Mill is not on my wish list. I'm glad you're settling in there though."

"Yeah, I get out and walk the dog between meetings. I know every neighbor on my street. It's so different."

"And Ryder?"

"I don't know. He's nice. Very good-looking too." Lorri smiled, thinking of the way they met. "Did I tell you the part where he almost gave me CPR because my lips were blue?"

"No. Your airway must have been blocked."

"Nope. I . . ." Lorri started laughing, then completely tickled with herself, she laughed harder until she could barely breathe, which made Pam laugh too.

Pam was laughing and she didn't even know why. "What? Tell me."

"I'd been eating . . ."

"Stop laughing, I can't understand you."

"I'd been eating blue cotton candy and my lips were blue. He thought I couldn't breathe."

"Oh my gosh. That's hilarious."

"He said I almost got accidental CPR. I must have hit my head pretty hard because I told him that wouldn't have been the worst thing that could've happened." She nearly choked on her laugh.

"You did not. You were flirting!"

"I did. I don't know what got in to me. I was quite the smarty pants. I guess because I knew I wouldn't see him again."

"Did you exchange numbers?"

"No! Not even last names. Well, wait. He did ask me mine, when he was making sure I didn't have a head injury. Look." She swept her hair back from her forehead. "Can you still see the bruise?"

"I can. Lorri, don't let Craig ruin love for you. Y'all's marriage had fizzled a long time ago. Craig was your way out of your parents' house after all that mess with your brother. Who could blame you?"

"I still find it so hard to understand how Jeff and I could've grown up with the same parents, very same privileges and discipline, but turn out so different." Lorri would never understand it. "Even now, I can't forgive him for what he put my parents through. All he put other people through."

"The accident?"

Lorri nodded. "I know it's a high percentage of drunk drivers who hurt someone else and get by unscathed, but that is so unfair. He didn't even seem sorry, and I hated him for it."

"Craig was a rock for you through all of that."

"He was." She still remembered the night Mom called to tell her about the accident. Solely focused on her son, Jeff, she never mentioned that there'd been serious casualties in the other car. It was almost a week later before Lorri got that part of the story. Her parents were so angry when she later refused to testify on his behalf in the manslaughter case.

"Craig was there for that season of your life and maybe that's all that he was supposed to be. One of these days you're going to find your true love. There's someone out there for everyone. Yours is waiting."

"I don't know. I'm not overly anxious to test those waters again."

"You'll find real love. You'll know it when you experience it and Lorri, I don't think you have yet."

Lorri couldn't argue with her, because for all the romance books she'd read it all sounded like fairy tales, and surely there had to be more to love than what she and Craig had shared. Because there was no happily-ever-after there.

"Can we change the subject?" Lorri could only handle so much of that kind of talk.

"I talked to Cody. He will be coming after his concert in Oklahoma, so it'll be really late. He said Thursday early would work best for him," Pam said.

"I can't wait to see him. The three of us together is like a family reunion." She dreaded time with her real family. They could never get through a visit without a fight. Cody and Pam were her chosen family, and she couldn't wait for them to be back together again.

Chapter Thirteen

Ryder couldn't believe he'd tried to sneak Lorri's number from Diane's office. It wasn't like him to do something like that. He'd been so worried about what she'd think if he asked Diane for the number that he'd gone and made it worse.

He cursed himself all the way up the block.

Should've just waited. Bound to run into her eventually. Town isn't that big. What was the hurry anyway?

Diane would never let this go. Her imagination was already running wild.

Spending the afternoon with Lorri had been more fun than he'd had in a long while, and he'd liked that she seemed like a strong woman.

There'd been a familiar comfort, like they'd known each other forever. She didn't look anything like Valerie—it wasn't anything like that. She wasn't like Valerie at all. Or maybe she was in the ways you want friends to be. Pleasant. Kind. Unassuming.

He snickered. *She's definitely quick-witted, even with a bump to the head. I used to be known for my quick wit, but she'd got me a couple times. Yeah, I'd like to talk to her again. Nothing wrong with that.*

He went inside and sat in his chair in the living room.

Everything seemed so complicated. Even his own home wouldn't be his in a matter of days. The lock had already been installed so Reece could begin decluttering for their guests, as she'd so kindly put it.

Imagining anyone else in the home he'd once shared with Valerie and Ronnie Dwayne was difficult. He'd finally packed up his son's room last year when it became hard to see all those little kid toys knowing he would've outgrown them by now. He would never have agreed to letting someone else stay here for anyone but Reece and Ross.

Reece was always saying, "You're the best uncle in the world."

It was the best job in the world if you couldn't be a father, and ever since that wreck he'd made being the best uncle one of his priorities. They were teenagers when it happened, and it had been hard on them. They'd clung to him, and he'd needed that so much. They were his reason to go on.

He lifted the wooden frame holding the picture of Valerie and Ronnie Dwayne from the side table.

I miss you both so much.

He held the photograph to his heart and sat there for a good long while.

You were my one true love. Nothing will ever replace that. This isn't that. I would never even try.

He pulled the pamphlet with the phone number from his pocket. He'd wasted half of his morning on this. He picked up his phone and looked at the screen where he'd keyed the number in. His thumb hovered over the call button.

I can't call her. There is no reason for me to interrupt her life. I don't know what I was thinking.

He turned off his phone and crumpled the paper with her number on it into a tight ball, tossing it into the leather wastebasket across the room.

"My life is full enough."

She'd been clear she wasn't looking for a relationship. They had that in common. Maybe that's why it seemed okay to contact her.

Then again, if you have to explain what you're up to, it's not worth doing.

Now that Diane knew he'd gotten her phone number it would be like pulling a dog off a freshly smoked brisket to get her to drop it.

He walked back outside, agitated with himself, every muscle fiber twitching. It wasn't a good day for sitting a tractor, with nothing but time for thinking.

Ryder went out to the barn, grabbed a pitchfork, and started clearing stalls. The rigorous routine released some of the pent-up energy, but by the time his mind cleared, he'd completely cleaned out two of the stalls down to the mats, something he hadn't planned to do until next month when the weather was more tolerable.

It was dark and he was tired and thirsty when he got back up to the house. He didn't even have the energy to make something to eat. Instead, he grabbed a bag of peanuts and sat in front of the television shelling them into the basket Reece had made for him for his birthday a few years ago. She'd taken some kind of grass-weaving class in college. There were two compartments in the basket, one for peanuts and one for shells. She'd even burned the farm brand on the wide band around the top.

He munched on peanuts until after the weather report. It would be another hot one tomorrow but clear for the next few days, thankfully.

Ryder slept in until seven Saturday morning, then saddled up Thunder and rode the fence line. The color of a storm cloud, the gray horse moved at an even pace up and down the hilly terrain. The sun rose above the trees, promising another steamy day. Thunder blew out a breath as he took their usual path up the hill that led to the old tobacco barns. The piece of the property that used to adjoin Dad's.

Pop-Pop, why can't I let this go? I know I can't change that Dad sold that parcel, but I feel like he gave away a part of our history with it.

Ryder closed his eyes; Pop-Pop's gentle blue eyes were so clear in his mind. He'd ride with his weathered hand resting on his Wranglers, much like Ryder rode now.

Ryder patted his hand on the saddle horn, wishing he could turn back time to the days Pop-Pop was around and they talked about everything from the crops and soil preparation to family and fellowship. There was nothing he couldn't talk about with Pop-Pop. Momma had always said Ryder was more like her than he was like Dad. Maybe that's why he'd always been closer to Pop-Pop.

Ryder regretted not having more time to make good on his

promise to be a good father to his son. Four years was barely a start.

The morning of the accident had started out so good. He'd helped Pop-Pop into his saddle, and they rode the fence line together. He didn't get around good much anymore, but once Ryder got him in the saddle he'd ride for hours. They'd ride side by side and Pop-Pop never rushed a day.

They'd been almost right where Ryder was now when that call came. *Thank God you were here. I'm a better man because of you, Pop-Pop.*

Valerie and Ronnie Dwayne had planned to be home that Sunday morning in time for them to go to church together. With the weather forecast forcing him to bring in the hay, he'd been unable to drive them as he'd planned. That was one thing about crop farming, sometimes you had to shift your schedule due to Mother Nature, else risk losing the opportunity. Those hay bales meant payday, and it couldn't be avoided.

Valerie didn't want to reschedule their monthly visit, so she and Ronnie Dwayne headed off to visit sweet Miss Agnes, who used to be their neighbor in Dalton Mill, that Saturday while he was working in the field. He'd worked all day and under the light of the moon and the tractor lights until he got every-thing in that night. He'd missed their call, but they'd left him a message of "I love you"s and evening prayers. He still had that message on his phone.

Sunday morning he'd been saying to Pop-Pop that his boy should be here in the saddle with him this morning when the phone rang.

He'd never forget the cadence of the state trooper's voice that day.

Who would be calling this time of the morning? He didn't recognize the phone number. "Sorry, Pop-Pop. I better take this." He answered the call. "Ryder here."

"This is North Carolina state trooper Ellis. I have you as the emergency number for Valerie Bolt."

"Yes. That's right." *His heart raced—every nerve ending itching in wonder.*

"I'm sorry, sir. There's been an accident."

Pop-Pop sensed something was wrong. His hand came across the horn on his saddle to reach for his arm. "What's wrong, Ryder?"

Ryder shook his head. "Are they okay?" *Ryder prayed for help.* "Where are they?"

"I'm sorry. It's not good. We've airlifted your son to Duke."

"I'm on my way." *He'd hung up, unwilling to waste one more second. He had to get to his family. He'd spun Thunder in a tight circle and galloped all the way to the barn. Pop-Pop followed and was right there beside him when he stopped to dismount.*

Blind with concern, he turned to see Pop-Pop sliding off of his own horse. He rushed to steady his landing. "I'm sorry, I shouldn't have taken off like that. It's Valerie and Ronnie Dwayne. There's been an accident."

"No. You go. I'm fine." *His grandfather pressed his palms together.* "You've got to believe it will be okay, Ryder. Have faith. Pray, and drive careful."

"I will."

"I'll take care of everything here. Call me and let me know what's going on."

"You'll be the first to know as soon as I do."

He'd driven with his flashers on as fast as that diesel truck would run, daring anyone to try to blue-light him on the way. Prayers and promises rose with every passing mile. The thought of either of them hurting tore at him.

He didn't even park his truck. Just left it sitting with the keys in it under the emergency entrance.

"My son was airlifted. My wife? The last name is Bolt. Valerie. Ronnie Dwayne is my son."

"Let me check, sir." The attendant had reacted with little surprise. "I'll have the doctor come out and talk to you. Please take a seat."

He'd stood there for a long time. The hospital sounds muffled by his heartbeat.

"Mr. Bolt?"

Ryder spun around. The doctor, dressed in blue scrubs, wasn't any older than he was. "Where are they? I need to see them."

"You can follow me."

Ryder breathed a sigh. Thank goodness. He'd see them. They'd get through this. He was here for them now.

The doctor led him through a set of shiny automated doors, then turned into a waiting area. Ryder noticed how tired and worried the people looked. The doctor walked to the far end of the waiting area.

"We can have some privacy here," the doctor said as he opened a door.

"Privacy?" Ryder dropped into the chair.

"Your wife sustained life-threatening injuries in the crash. We did everything we could do, but the internal . . ."

Ryder sat there not hearing any of the words. It was as if this man were talking in another language.

"Valerie? My wife?"

"She's gone, but your son is in the ICU. He's in critical condition, but I can take you to sit with him. He should be your focus right now. If you have other family that you want to bring in, it's a good time to make those calls."

Valerie was gone and his son was clinging to his life.

"Please take me to my son."

The doctor took him to the intensive care unit and introduced him to the nurse there. "She can help you contact family. We're here to answer questions. The next few hours are critical for your son."

Ryder remembered staring through the glass at his son, so swollen and bandaged that he wouldn't have recognized him. He'd almost tripped racing to his bedside.

When he stood there looking over that tiny body he sobbed when he saw the tiny freckle on his earlobe. There was no mistaking this child was his. He touched his own ear, where he had the same freckle.

"Mr. Bolt, I brought you some water. Who can I call for you?" She'd pushed a pen into his right hand and a piece of paper onto the table next to him. "Write down the numbers and I'll call them."

He looked through tear-filled eyes.

The older woman held her soft blue eyes on his. "Let me help you."

He scratched down the numbers and she slipped out, closing the glass door behind her with a whoosh of air.

"Ronnie Dwayne. Son. Can you hear me? It's me. Dad." He smoothed the covers across his body.

"You are the best thing I ever made in this lifetime. You are my heart, young man. We have so many more things to do together. Fishing. Riding. Learning to ride a bicycle. Kiddo, that's a lot harder than riding a horse. I still have a scar on my forehead from when I learned. Fight, little man. You have a cowboy heart. We'll get through this."

He sniffed back a sob. Ronnie Dwayne's tiny hand was so cold.

Ryder held his son's hand between his trying to warm it. "I love you, *son. Mommy and I both love you more than our own lives." He sat there wondering how he'd tell his son his mother was gone. That was something he'd have to figure out later. "Come on, buddy. Stay with me." He took in a stuttered breath. "I need you."*

Ronnie Dwayne never moved. There wasn't a hand squeeze or a blink. Just a fragile life accented by the noise of machines in the room.

Hours went by. Ryder hadn't moved from the chair. A strong grip on his shoulder grabbed his attention. Pop-Pop stood there, tears in his eyes too.

"You will get through this, boy. Pray to Him. It's His plan. You must journey forward," Pop-Pop said.

Mom and Dad took up on the other side of the bed.

"Come with me." Diane took his hand. They stepped into the hall and she hugged him, and they both cried. Pop-Pop stepped up and wrapped his wide arms all the way around them both.

"They will be in our hearts forever. They live on like that," he'd promised.

Ryder didn't know how that could be possible. It wasn't until the next morning, when Ronnie Dwayne was pronounced dead, that Ryder mustered the courage to see Valerie. He'd wanted so badly to be able to tell her their son was okay. But then, she knew well before Ryder how things were playing out. She had a front row seat.

"Lord, you got yourself two fine angels to do your work. Don't you need me too?"

But those prayers went unanswered and he had to find his way. Often he thought if he'd only lost one that it would have been easier, but the truth was they were all one working unit. It would have been heartbreaking no matter what.

And putting his life together without those two cornerstones—Valerie and Ronnie Dwayne—was darn near impossible.

Anger replaced some of the grief when the police reported the driver of the other vehicle had been intoxicated. With a blood alcohol level of over .32, he shouldn't have been conscious, much less driving.

Ryder lost it, smashing things in the barn, putting his hand through a cabinet door. Even Pop-Pop couldn't console him the morning they got that news.

Pop-Pop passed away three weeks later. Just didn't wake up one morning. HSB. That's what Pop-Pop had always called it when one of the cows died for no apparent reason. HSB. Heart stopped beating.

In one short month, Ryder had buried his wife, son, and grandfather, and his life unraveled like a rope in the wind.

It had been a slow go rebuilding his life. *Survival is a sorry way to live a life.*

Ryder's heart hung heavy in his chest, burning with each breath. He hated days like these. He never knew when they would happen. And he still couldn't control his emotions. Raw and painful tears slipped down his cheek. He ran the back of his hand across his face, then rested both of his hands upon Thunder's strong neck.

Lord, you've got to make sense of my life. I was a good husband. A good father. A good grandson. You took all of them away in one sweep. I'm tired. So tired. I'm humbled every day by the land and crops you've put me in charge of. I'm so grateful for the life you've given me, and thankful for Diane and Reece and Ross. If it weren't for them, I couldn't wake up every day. Help me, Lord, help me. All I ever wanted in this life was to be a good father, and my heart feels empty.

He lifted his chin to heaven, tears trailing down his face to his neck. Dropping the reins, he let Thunder keep moving. The horse knew the way.

In the small family cemetery, Ryder guided Thunder around the headstones. His great grandparents, whom he'd never known, only heard stories of. Grandma and Pop-Pop. Valerie and the tiny plot where he'd laid his son to rest. Only four years old, he hadn't even had the chance to skin up his knees.

Ryder threw his leg over Thunder and stepped to the ground, then took a knee in the soft grass. Thunder snorted and lowered his head, letting out a gentle vibrating puff, as if he too could still feel the gaping hole.

Ryder knelt there for a long moment, then stood and pressed a kiss to his hand and touched first Ronnie Dwayne's, then Valerie's, and then Pop-Pop's stones. The marble was as cold as the hard truth. He clenched his fist and tapped it to his chest.

He drew in a breath. The sweet smell of alfalfa hung in the air. Tomorrow he'd cut it and begin the process of bailing.

Thunder walked over to him, pressing his face closer to Ryder. "Thanks, Thunder."

He took the reins and walked Thunder down the path a good ways before stepping back into his saddle. They completed the lap around the perimeter, then loped back to the barn. Ryder took comfort in the routine of unsaddling and brushing the big gray horse down. Sweat made him look almost bluish gray in this light.

"I've got to finish Diane's present. You chill here for a bit, huh?" He gave Thunder a pat on the shoulder then went to his workshop. He'd been working on Diane's gift for weeks. Building, sanding, staining, and finishing the cabinet. He'd made it from reclaimed wood from Dad's barn. When he'd learned they sold the property, Ryder had spent every last hour salvaging everything he could. *Our whole life had been there.*

Ryder had to put up another storage building to hold everything he'd salvaged. He ran his hand over the breakfront. It had turned out even prettier than he'd hoped. Using the wood from the stall where Diane had kept her mare, he'd left the childish scrawl of her horse's name, Brandy, intact on the back of the piece. No one else would appreciate it, but he knew Diane would. The two of them had used nails to scratch the names of their horses on those boards. It had taken weeks to do it. A labor of love.

Ryder's phone rang. "Hello?"

"Hey, son, it's Dad."

The man had impeccable timing. "Hi, Dad. I was just thinking about you. I'm finishing up Diane's birthday present. I made her a breakfront from the wood I reclaimed from the old barn at your place."

"She'll love that."

Ryder's heart squeezed. *No thanks to you, old man.*

"I'm glad you were able to salvage that stuff."

"Could have been a lot easier if you'd told me what you were thinking about doing." Ryder regretted saying it as soon as the words left his mouth.

"We're not going to start this again, are we?" his dad said.

"No. I'm sorry, but this is something I can't seem to let go of, Dad." He let out a long breath. "Believe me, I've tried, and I know it's not good to hold a grudge."

"Son, that land was mine to do as I saw fit. I hope you won't find yourself one day having to answer for the way you decide to handle your own things."

"I hope so too."

"In retrospect, yes, now I wish we'd had a conversation, but you and your sister couldn't have matched the offer that developer presented me without going broke, and I wasn't going to have that either. Please forgive me and be happy for us."

"Thank you for saying you wish you had talked to us. I appreciate that. You're right, Dad. I'd have gone for broke to hang on to that land."

"I know. I couldn't let you do that."

Maybe some of his letting-go problem had to do with being forced to let go of Ronnie Dwayne. After all, he was the reason Ryder had always wanted the land in the first place—to have a legacy to leave to him. "I'm trying, Dad. I am. What's done is done."

"Yes." He cleared his throat. "I was calling because we shipped something to your house for Diane's birthday. It should be there today."

"I'll keep an eye out for it."

"You'll call us during the party? There's a two-hour time difference here," Dad said.

"Of course we will. How are y'all doing?"

"We're both doing really good. We're in Utah. Prettiest place I've seen in a long time. We found a great place to camp and we've made some friends. Your mom wants to stay here for a while. She even went horseback riding yesterday. It was really good to see her riding again."

"I bet. Should've taken a picture," Ryder said. "I'd love to see that."

"I'll send one to you."

"Thanks. I'll be sure the present makes it over to Diane's for the party. Tell Mom I love her."

"I will. Thanks."

They hung up without an "I love you" between them. Dad had never been one to dole them out. You had to go on blind faith that there was love in his heart.

Ryder put down the phone and ran the steel wool one last time over the piece, making sure there wasn't a single blemish. He was proud of how the breakfront had come out. He'd built it to fit the spot in Diane's dining room perfectly.

The finish shone with a rich hue that had taken a custom mix of colors to get. Satisfied that it was complete he ran a soft cloth across it one more time, then took a permanent marker to the back and wrote,

> *Sis,*
>
> *They say when you've gained the trust of a horse, you've won a friend for life. I love you more than all of my horses, and I will our whole lives.*
>
> *With love, Ryder*

He pulled his phone from his pocket and called Reece. "Hey, Reece, it's your favorite uncle."

"You'd be my favorite if I had twenty."

The conversation always started the same way, but he never tired of it.

"Did you talk your mom into going to Pastrami Joe's?"

"Yep. Ross and I have the cake being delivered at eleven. Joe is expecting it. We're taking her to the vineyard at noon to pick out some wine, and then over to Joe's. That'll give you enough time to get everything in place and meet us there, right?"

"Yes. Text me as soon as you leave the house. I'll have the breakfront loaded and ready when you call."

"Ten-four," Reece said.

"See you at Joe's."

He hooked up to the small trailer and backed it up to his workshop. Good thing Mark was going to help him move the thing. It weighed a ton. He grabbed a rag and wiped at a smudge on the seeded glass. That old wavy-looking glass in the cabinet doors gave the piece a timeless look.

He put Thunder out in the pasture and returned his saddle to the tack room before going up to the house to shower and change.

As he stepped out of the shower, he heard loud banging at the front door. "Mark, that you?"

"Yeah. You said noon, right?"

"Hang on," Ryder called out as he swept the water off with a towel and jumped into a pair of jeans to run to the door. It was only eleven thirty. Mark was always early. "Hey, man. Thanks."

Ryder and Mark walked down to the workshop.

Mark nodded with appreciation. "I've told people you could build anything, but you outdid yourself on this one. It's really nice, Ryder. She's going to love it."

"I think she will," he said. "Reece will text as soon as they leave the house."

"Let's get this thing loaded then." Mark took his end and they loaded it on the trailer. The text came just as Mark tied it down.

"Perfect timing. You riding with me or following me?" Ryder asked Mark.

"I'll follow you."

They made the short drive over to Diane's house. Ryder went inside first to be sure Diane was gone, then moved the old drop-leaf table out of the way so they could move the new piece in its place.

Ryder and Mark wrangled the hefty piece off the trailer and up the steps through the French doors into the dining room.

"That thing weighs a ton," Mark huffed.

"No. We're just getting older and out of shape," Ryder said.

"Speak for yourself."

Ryder slid the piece into place and centered it on the wall. A perfect fit.

"She's going to go nuts when she sees that. You did a great job." Mark opened the cabinet, admiring the inset hinges and dovetailed drawers. "Beautiful craftsmanship."

"Thanks. Pop-Pop taught me well."

"He was a good man."

"The best." Ryder took one last look at his work, satisfied that she'd be happy. One day, when she pulled it away from the wall, she'd find that note on the back, and it would make her cry big, happy tears. He couldn't wait for the day she called to tell him she'd discovered that. "Let's get on over to Joe's. Everyone should already be there."

Mark followed Ryder to Pastrami Joe's.

When they walked inside, Joe gave him the "hurry" signal. They hustled over to where Joe prepared to take the cake to Diane's table. Ryder and Mark followed behind Joe and everyone in the restaurant started singing.

Diane blushed. "Y'all! You are too much."

Mark looked as smitten now as he had when they were fifteen.

Diane blew out the candles. Joe sliced the cake and served it while Diane opened presents.

Just as Ryder took a bite of cake, he noticed Mark slip a small box to his sister. *Some guys never give up. Be gentle with his feelings, Diane.* He ate his cake, happy to sit back and watch family and friends celebrate his sister. The restaurant wasn't closed to the public, but everyone in the place was here for the party. He liked that about this town.

"This is the best birthday ever," Diane said. "This cake is amazing."

"It's not over. Dad sent something. It's getting delivered to my house. I'll have to meet you over there with it. I have a little something for you too."

"You didn't have to do anything, Ryder. You're so thoughtful." Diane blew him a kiss.

Out of the corner of his eye, Ryder caught a glimpse of a black Range Rover rolling down Main Street. He watched as they parked in front of the attorney's office. It was usually closed on Saturday.

Ryder stood, easing closer to the window with his cake plate still in his hand.

His fork hit the ground when he saw Archer K. Bloom step out onto the sidewalk.

Thought I'd seen the last of that guy. He'd better not be after more land in this town.

Chapter Fourteen

Lorri was at the farmers market Saturday afternoon picking out fresh produce for the week when her phone started ringing. She fumbled her basket and purse trying to answer. Finally, she hit the green button and before she could say "hello", she heard her boss's voice.

"Brilliant! Absolutely brilliant! How did you get all that done so quickly?"

The Bloom campaign. A call this quick, and on a Saturday, was totally unexpected. She hadn't expected him to see it until Monday. "It came to me so clearly. I couldn't stop once I got started."

"I simply had to let you know how impressed I am. I forwarded it straight over to him, and he's already called me. He's so impressed he can't wait to talk to you."

Lorri felt unsure about that. "What do you mean?"

"It turns out he has business in Dalton Mill today. He wants to meet with you and go over the packet with you in person."

In person? She wasn't thrilled about interrupting her personal life with business. She liked the clean separation of the two. "I'm not comfortable with clients coming to my home," she said.

"No. Of course not. I told him you'd meet him at Take the Cake & Coffee Shop. He said it's down the street from his attorney's office on Main Street. Do you know of it?"

"I do. Sure."

"He can meet you in an hour. Can you be there?"

It was a question, but Lorri knew she didn't have much choice. "The account manager usually handles these meetings. Why does he want to meet with me?"

"He wants to talk directly to the talent. That's you. He's promising another big project. I didn't think you'd mind."

"Give me an hour and a half. I need to get back home, change clothes, and print everything out."

"Done. Thank you, Lorri. Great work."

She ended the call still in a state of wonder. *Wouldn't it be funny if this account yielded the biggest profit and took the least amount of her time?*

She hopped in her car and sped home to change. Thank goodness she lived just around the corner.

Mister seemed disappointed when she ran past him without a hello.

Since it was the weekend, she stuck with her jeans but changed into a blouse and pulled her hair up. A gold chain, and she looked as pulled together as if it had been on purpose.

"Sorry, Mister."

She printed out some samples, then tucked her portfolio and her laptop under her arm and ran out the door.

Lorri stepped into the bakery on Main Street right on time. Inside, the sweet mingling of sugar and coffee made her hungry. A man sat at the table in the corner. He lifted his hand in a wave, and she walked over to join him. He was younger than she'd expected, but silver at the temples.

Lorri extended her hand. "Hi, I'm Lorri Walker."

"Archer Bloom." His voice was even. Void of emotion. "I wasn't happy about someone new working on my account."

"Oh?" This wasn't what she expected.

"But when I saw your presentation it blew me away. I didn't wait one minute before pulling the trigger on the whole deal. It's perfect, and when he told me you lived in Dalton Mill, well, I wanted to thank you myself. You really get what I'm going for."

"I used my home for inspiration. I purchased the model home and I love it. Originally I'd planned to stay one year and then sell it and move back to Raleigh."

"Oh?"

"Yes, but I have no intention of moving now."

"That's great customer feedback."

"I can't say that it's only the neighborhood. The farmers market right there is a huge plus, and I appreciate the neighborhood's attention to sustainability, a healthy lifestyle, and its eco-friendly features. I haven't had a single issue with my home. I'm completely delighted."

"That's wonderful." He took a long sip of his coffee. "Can I order you something?"

"No. Thank you." She removed her portfolio from her brief-case. "I brought the full detail plan for Bloom Homes with me. If you liked the proposal I think you're going to really love this."

He leaned in as she walked through everything with him. She had a couple of different concepts, but he was more interested in her favorite. Just as expected, when she unfolded the more simple, low-cost version, he swept it away as if it were cold leftovers. "No. This one." He punched his finger atop the stack containing her recommended approach. The one that brought the biggest profit too.

"I couldn't agree more, Mr. Bloom." Satisfaction rippled inside her. Understanding the customer's needs was important to her, and this was face-to-face proof that she did. His body language spoke volumes. "Nowhere in the materials did it mention where your next properties would be located. I'd be happy to incorporate those particulars into the program."

"Not necessary. We have several sights under review across the country. Let's keep it as high-level as possible."

"Evergreen," she said nodding.

"Exactly."

Archer Bloom left the bakery. *He loved my pitch.* She resisted the urge to fist pump lest he turn around and see her. That design had come together so easily. She practically skipped to the counter to order an assortment of treats. Something to celebrate this, and a few extras to try before placing an order for when Cody came to town.

She put the box of goodies in her car, then drove over to

Publix to pick up the groceries Pam had requested since she'd be doing the cooking.

Lorri pushed the cart down every aisle, marking off the items as she went. With more groceries than she'd ever bought in a single trip, she almost felt motivated to try to cook something herself. *Almost.* She knew it wouldn't really happen. Her best dish was takeout, and it may have been a long-standing joke between her and Craig, and that hadn't changed since the divorce. If there was one thing everyone in this town probably already knew about her, besides the size of her dog, it was that she ordered salads and dinners for pickup every Monday and Thursday for the week.

As she loaded her groceries from the cart into her vehicle, she heard the rumble of a diesel truck roll by, then back up. She turned to look.

"How are you?" the deep voice carried across the parking lot.

"Ryder?" She walked over to his truck. "You said we'd bump into each other."

"Small town. Bound to happen."

"And here we are," she said, peering inside the open window. His truck was meticulously neat. "I had fun at the fair. Thanks again for the rescue, and the private tour."

"You're welcome. It was nice to enjoy it with someone who'd never been before. How's your head?"

She raised her fingers to her forehead. It was still a bit tender to the touch. "Almost good as new."

"Put out the 'No Vacancy' sign yet?"

It took her a moment to get what he was talking about. "The

birdhouses! I saw a few birds checking them out this morning. I may need to make more."

"I know a guy."

"Of course you do."

"Hey, I was wondering." He paused, leaning over the steering wheel. "Have you ever been down to the old mill on the creek?"

"Didn't know there was an old mill. Is there a new one too?"

"No, but that neighborhood you live in was named after it."

"Oh, I thought it was named after the town, Dalton Mill."

"No. Dalton Mill was the big feed mill on the other side of town. The old water mill on the creek is practically right behind the neighborhood. It's really nice down there."

Was he just telling her about it, or asking her out? She paused, but he didn't say anything else. "I bet it's a beautiful sight."

Finally, he said, "Want to see it?"

Although she'd been hoping he'd ask, him actually doing it made her breath hitch. "I would." She held back a nervous giggle.

"Can I get your phone number?"

"Sure." She took her phone from her purse. "Give me yours."

He recited his number and she typed it to text, then pressed send.

His phone pinged, and the way he smiled tickled her when he read the text which simply read, "Just friends."

"Thanks. Can I help you load those groceries?"

"No. Thank you, I've got it under control."

"I thought you might like to make lighter work of it with some help."

"Next time, then."

"Deal. I'll give you a call Wednesday or Thursday depending on the weather? Does either one work better for you?"

Cody was coming to town and Pam would be there Wednesday night. "I have someone coming into town this week. Wednesday would be best."

His hand rested lazily on the steering wheel. His eyes narrowed as he spoke. "You weren't being polite giving me your number, were you?" He exaggerated a pout. "Don't go hurting my feelings now."

"No. I'd never. Just setting expectations." She loved how playful he was. It made it so easy to let down her guard and relax.

"Fair enough. Then I'll let you get back to it. Nice seeing you."

He rumbled off and she realized she was still smiling as he turned out of the parking lot onto the main road.

Nice seeing you again too.

She put the last of the groceries in her car, then rolled the cart back up to the store, snagging an orphaned cart along the way. It was her pet peeve that people left them in the lot like that. It didn't take two minutes to return them to where they belonged.

Lorri looked over her shoulder as she backed out of the parking spot. Her phone pinged, and a wave of disappointment came over her when she realized it wasn't Ryder. It was Pam. Rather than text back, she called her.

"Hi, Pam. I picked up all the groceries on your list. I've never bought this much in one trip. I'm on my way home now."

"Thanks. I was just texting you to let you know I was thinking to drive down there Wednesday. Cody won't be in town until Thursday, but I'll come early and work from there if it won't bother you. It'll give us some extra time together."

"That would be great. I'd love it." The thought of Ryder caused her to pause. "Um, so remember Ryder? From the fair?"

"You mean your hero?"

"Yeah, that guy. I just ran into him here at the grocery store."

"Already. Well, isn't that convenient?"

"It's a small town. It's not like he was hunting me down. Anyway, he might be taking me to see an old mill near my house on Wednesday. I can reschedule it though."

"No. You most certainly will not. I'm thrilled to know you're doing something fun with someone of the opposite sex."

"Just friends, Pam."

"Whatever," Pam sputtered. "Look, I'm your best friend. I can hope for more for you even if you can't. You're still gun-shy. What happened with you and Craig will never happen to you again."

"Darn right it won't."

"Smart is one thing. Aware is good even, but isolation is bad for the soul. We need relationships and to be part of other people's lives. It's what we're meant to do."

"I'll see you Wednesday" Lorri said shutting down the line of conversation.

"Oh, you can shush me off the telephone all you want. You know I'm not done here," Pam said. "Just leave the key under the mat!"

And Lorri knew that was true.

Chapter Fifteen

By Tuesday afternoon it seemed like a lifetime since Saturday, when Ryder had run into Lorri at the market. So long that he was beginning to wonder if he'd imagined it. He should've nailed down specifics right there on the spot. Instead, it had been torture waiting to make the call. He'd been tempted to text her every day, but he'd said Wednesday.

Thank goodness the weather held out. If that line of storms hadn't made that easterly turn he'd have had to postpone until the weekend, and honestly, he didn't want to wait that long to talk to her again.

Ross and Reece gave him a tour of The Wedding Ranch that afternoon. They'd completed the transformation for the big contract.

"I'm not just saying this because I'm your uncle. This place looks like a million bucks."

"I know," Ross said. "Reece, you still amaze me."

"It wouldn't matter how pretty it looked if the rest of the

stuff didn't go to plan. It's your plans that make the magic happen," she said. "Which, by the way, Uncle Ryder, your old friend Mayor Blevins called us. She's coming to tour this afternoon."

"Well, you're putting your best foot forward. It looks great," Ryder said.

"But we're focused on this project right now." Ross opened his computer and reviewed the project plan with Ryder.

"I was worried," Ryder said. "I'll admit it, but I don't see how this event can be anything but a success. Traffic flow plans are genius the way you've scheduled arrivals in intervals with a three-hour pre-wedding jam session to entertain guests during the security screening. The town will be none the wiser."

"That's the plan," Ross said.

"Wonder if I'll be able to hear the music down at the creek?" Ryder didn't mind some good music on a sunshine day.

"You can always come up and listen."

"No. That's not appropriate. This is a private event, and that means no outsiders, not even uncles. Besides I'm all moved in down at the Rest Stop." He'd parked his living quarters—a horse trailer—next to the great room he'd built his first summer home from college. The roof line was angled so he could pull his trailer right up to it, making it bigger than some houses in this town when the slides were out, expanding the living room and sleeping quarters. "I don't know why I haven't done this before."

"I'm so glad. I hated asking you to let us rent the house, but we appreciate it so much."

"My pleasure, kiddo. In fact, I'm going to head there now.

You two know you can call me if you need me for anything. I'm available."

"Yes, sir." Ross shook his hand and Reece hugged his neck.

He drove down to the creek and rolled out the rug under the awning. Twenty feet long, tan with a brown running horse in the middle, it would keep him from tracking in dirt and the dew that settled on these muggy summer nights. He was looking forward to the week of peace and quiet and limited chores.

He set two chairs next to the firepit. Maybe that was a little optimistic, but he thought Lorri might enjoy sitting around a fire at night. If she didn't stay, he'd still enjoy it.

This was something he should've been doing all along. Every man needed a place to quiet thoughts and be grateful for all he had. He hadn't focused on being grateful enough lately. This was a good place to do that.

He'd gotten all his hay baled and up in the barn yesterday so there wouldn't be any farm equipment noise during this week's events. Thank goodness the weather had held out to allow that to happen, else he'd have had to disappoint the twins, because although he wanted their business to flourish, he still had a farm to run.

Stepping his toe against the back of his left boot, he slid his foot out and then took off the other, standing them next to the front door. He pulled off his socks and laid them across the top of his boots.

Cell reception was lousy down here, so he removed the phone from his pocket and set it on the bar in the trailer, which was the only place he did get service.

He walked down to the water enjoying the tickle of the tall

grass beneath his bare feet. This region hadn't had much rain, so the creek bed was low—a ripple over the smooth rocks that was noisier than normal.

Sun sparkled in dots of light in the shallow water as shiny minnows darted in and out from the bank looking for food before they became something else's meal. The food chain. Some folks grimaced at the thought. He liked the order of it all.

A bird called from a nearby tree, and a busy woodpecker tapped a rhythm in the distance. He stepped into the chilly water, then bent forward to grab a handful, rubbing it behind his neck, cooling himself from the intense heat.

Later he'd bring Thunder down to walk the creek. Ryder liked the sound of the horse's hooves slapping at the water with each step.

Trees on both banks arched from one side to the other, creating a canopy. It was cooler under the shade here. A good place for a break.

And there she was again. In his mind. *Lorri.* Invading his quiet time.

He wondered if she'd ever ridden a horse. They could trail ride most of the way down to the mill on the creek trail, then tie the horses at the fence and hike the rest. It would make for a longer day that way. But it was so much more peaceful on horseback than on the Ranger UTV.

Pump the brakes. Don't get ahead of yourself.

He'd promised to show her the mill, not spend a whole day with her. Maybe he longed for companionship more than he'd realized.

Tomorrow the first guests would arrive to the wedding venue.

If he was going to move horses down, he needed to go ahead and do it today. Unless something went wrong, or they needed an extra hand, he'd be staying out of the way down here. Better to have options. He climbed back in his truck and drove up to the barn to get the horses.

He rode Thunder down to the creek, ponying Dottie, a black-and-white paint that was more of a babysitter horse. Even if Lorri had never ridden she could ride Dottie.

He tied the horses to a picket line, then started the long walk back to get his truck. He'd made it as far as the tobacco barns when he saw the black town car pull in front of the barn. He stopped just out of sight and watched as Reece and Ross came into view to greet their guests. It seemed like yesterday the twins were six years old and getting ready for their first day of school in matching outfits. They didn't need any help these days. They knew what they wanted, and were smart enough to make it happen.

He took the dirt path over to the barn then called Lorri. She answered on the first ring. "Lorri? Hey, it's Ryder. You up for the old creek mill tour?"

"Sure, when were you thinking?"

"Tomorrow if that still works for you. I can pick you up at your house."

"You don't mind?"

"Not at all, besides, I'd kind of like to meet that big dog of yours."

She gave him the address. "It's the fourth house on the left. Sage green. Last name's on the mailbox too."

"Great. I'll see you tomorrow."

He disconnected the call, then dialed Joe. "Hey, man, can I get you to make a picnic lunch for two for pickup tomorrow at ten thirty?"

"Sure. What's the occasion?"

"No occasion. Just lunch."

There was a pause, but Ryder let it hang.

Finally, Joe asked, "How about a Tuscan Turkey and one Hammer, homemade pasta salad, a charcuterie tray, and a bottle of red?"

"A couple tall bottles of water too, please. And dessert."

"I'll have it ready."

"Thanks, Joe." He hung up before Joe had the chance to ask any questions. With any luck he'd be too busy to chat tomorrow with the early lunch crowd.

Wednesday morning, he put a small cooler in the back of his truck and drove into town to pick up his order from Pastrami Joe's. When he walked inside, Gladys was standing there grinning at him.

Great. And I was worried about twenty questions from Joe.

"Hey, Gladys. Picking up a to-go order."

"So I hear."

He pretended not to notice her accusatory tone.

She turned and put a large brown sack on the counter, then slipped a bottle of wine and two large bottles of water into a four-pack carrier, tucking cups, utensils, and napkins into the other slot. "Here you go. All set."

"Thanks, Gladys."

"You're very welcome. You have a *really* nice afternoon."

"Okay." He started to leave, but he couldn't without asking first, "So what makes you think this isn't something for the twins or one of their customers?"

She leaned her arms on the counter with a grin. "Because when Reece was in here an hour ago picking up a deli tray, I flat-out asked her if this order was for them. She said no."

"That would explain it." He hurried out the door. Why did he ask? Now she'd be speculating for sure.

He drove over to Lorri's house feeling incredibly ill-prepared. *Just friends,* he reminded himself. *Relax.*

He pulled into her driveway and shut down his truck. Something he rarely did, it being a diesel, but somehow leaving it running in the driveway seemed like he was rushing things and he didn't want to give her the wrong impression.

He'd stayed as far away as he could from this neighborhood until now. He had to admit, her house was very inviting. He liked the big stained timbers on the front. Kind of a farmhouse-meets-mountain-lodge look. The sage green was nice against the landscaping too. Every house on the road looked well maintained. The five-acre lots were deeper than they were wide, so it still had the feeling of a neighborhood to him.

He rapped his knuckles against the solid wood door. A deep woof gave him a start, followed by quick footsteps, probably hers.

The door swung open and Lorri stood there smiling in western boots, jeans, and a blue and white blouse. "Hi, Ryder. Come on in. Meet Mister."

"Thanks."

He stepped inside. The mastiff sat at attention about six feet back from the entry way. "So you're Mister?" He held out his hand for Mister to check him out. "I'd have called you Ranger, short for Lone Ranger, with that black mask you're wearing, but Mister suits you fine."

Mister stood, sniffed his jeans, then pushed his forehead under Ryder's hand.

"He likes you," she said.

"I like him pretty good too." He rubbed Mister under the chin. "Big as you are, folks better call you 'Mister.'"

"You ready to go?" she asked.

"Yeah. Sure."

She grabbed her purse, then dropped a kiss on the top of Mister's head and made him promise to behave before following Ryder outside.

She walked down the sidewalk to the passenger side of his Ford F-450 and reached for the door, but he was right there behind her and he grabbed the handle first to open it for her. Something he'd always done for Valerie.

Lorri smiled at the gesture, then stepped on the running board and hopped in.

It's not a date. His jaw tensed. *Feels like a date. Maybe I should've let her open her own door. This is harder than it should be.*

He went around to the driver's side and got in.

"I've been looking forward to this all morning," she said.

"Me too." Only honestly, he'd been looking forward to it since Saturday. He backed out of the driveway, then turned west, taking her to the far side of his property, opposite The Wedding Ranch to be sure they didn't stumble into any of the goings-on over there today.

He pulled in front of a bright blue pole gate.

"Are we allowed to be here?"

"Of course. I come here all the time." He got out and opened the gate, then drove the truck through it and then hopped out to close and latch it behind them. "The paved entry used to lead to the old mill. The state has long since taken it off their maintenance list, but it remains in good shape."

Lorri seemed to be enjoying the ride. "Look, there's cows."

"Just some young feeder calves," he corrected her. "They won't bother us."

She kept an eye on the small herd as he drove down the overgrown path to the creek. The fescue was dotted with soft purple aster and bellflowers, and an occasional shot of goldenrod. Queen Anne's lace peeked its head above the grasses too.

"I picked up some lunch. I've got my horse trailer up here at the Rest Stop."

"Rest Stop? Like on the side of the highway."

"Not exactly. Just a little place I built. I call it that because it's in the middle of a field along the creek. The perfect spot to rest. There's some chairs and an awning, or we can go inside where it's air-conditioned. I thought we'd eat and then hike or ride down to the mill."

She didn't ask for further details. "I like the sound of that." Her easy smile made it hard to take his eyes off of her.

Chapter Sixteen

Ryder found himself in strange territory. He pulled off the pavement onto the private gravel road that led to the Rest Stop.

She looked surprised when the tires crunched against the gravel, staring out the side window, presumably at the dust billowing around them.

"We can ride to the mill if you're up for it. It's about forty-minutes on horseback, but the views are breathtaking. Unless you'd rather me drive."

"I've never ridden a horse, but I've always wanted to. Can we do that?"

"Absolutely."

Lorri fidgeted, her eyes darting around as if she didn't want to miss a single thing.

"Here we are." He pulled into the campsite.

"Wow. That's one long horse trailer. Is it yours?"

"Yep." He hopped out of the truck and walked toward it. "Fits four horses, plus living quarters."

"Do you live here?"

He looked around and laughed. "This is more like camping, don't you think? It's beautiful out here though, isn't it?"

She took a step back. "It really is. Is that the water I hear?"

"It is."

She raised her palm as a bright yellow butterfly danced across the top of the tall seed heads ahead of her. Lorri held her palm up, and the little yellow-winged insect seemed to hover mere centimeters from her fingers.

She spun, inhaling deeply. "Did you see that?"

"The butterfly?"

"Yes. Dancing in my hand!" She practically danced as she stepped forward.

"That was a lisa," he said.

"You name the butterflies out here?" She looked at him like he was crazy.

"No. That would be a big job. Have you seen how many butterflies there are out here? Lisa is the type of butterfly. Very common. *Eurema lisa* means 'little lisa' or 'little sulphur.'"

"I like lisa better."

"Me too."

Her quiet laughter was as soft as morning fog. She walked over to where Thunder and Dottie were tied. "Can I pet the horses?"

"Sure. Like I tell the kids, they have teeth, so they *can* bite. But they are both very friendly."

She placed a flat hand above Dottie's nose. "You are so beautiful."

The horse raised her chin, her mane shifting in soft strands across her neck.

"I think she likes me," Lorri said.

"She likes everyone. I've had Dottie since she was a baby. My sister named her, because of the polka dots."

"That's cute. How old is she now?"

"Dottie is twenty-eight."

"I didn't know horses lived that long."

He laughed. It was fun watching her delight in the things he'd taken for granted for so long. "Yeah, they do. My horse is Thunder. He's a cutting horse."

"What's that mean?"

"He helps me work cattle. He's a good horse. They both are."

"Hmmph."

He wasn't sure what that little *hmmph* was for, but he figured it would become clear soon enough.

Ryder retrieved their lunch from the truck. "Think it's too hot to eat outside?"

"No. It's a perfect day. What can I do to help?"

"Not a thing. Follow me." He led her over to the chairs he'd set up under the awning. "Have a seat." He placed the cooler between them, then divvied up the food. "My buddy owns Pastrami Joe's. His sandwiches are the best. We've got a Tuscan Turkey or the Hammer." He took both sandwiches out of the bag. "Your choice. Figured since you ate barbecue at the fair I didn't have to worry you might be a vegetarian."

"Heck no. My favorite food is hamburgers."

"Oh, you haven't had a hamburger until I've cooked one for you on the grill. I'm kind of known for them."

"I can't wait," she said without hesitation. That made him happy.

He handed her a sandwich and put his to the side, then pulled out the container of pasta salad. Handing her a cold bottle of water, he smiled as his hand grazed hers, then pulled off his ball cap and bowed his head, blessing the food with a quick prayer.

When he lifted his eyes, she was smiling sweetly. "Amen," she said.

"Dig in."

"This is a great lunch. I've eaten there often. It's always good, but I think eating outside makes the food taste even better. I could get used to dining outdoors like this."

"Best view in town, and it's always changing."

"I bet it's beautiful in the spring too."

"Yes. It's great every season, even in the dead of winter when most of the leaves have dropped and the trees are bare. The white haze on frosty mornings when the fog hangs just above the pasture. Nothing like it."

"Sounds pretty."

"It is." He slugged back some water. "You ready to go down to the mill?"

"Definitely."

Both horses were already saddled in hopes she'd agree. "All right. You're going to mount from the left side. Come on over here."

She went over to the horse. "Now what?"

"Put your left foot in the stirrup." He steadied her as she got her foot into position, and placed her hands. "Okay, now you're going to take a little hop and lift that back leg up and over."

"Seriously? I don't think that's going to happen." Doubt arched in her brow as her head tilted to the back of the horse.

"I'll help you."

"Okay. Here we . . . go!" With a teensy extra nudge from him she was sitting tall in the saddle.

"How's that feel?"

"High." Her giggle wavered, exposing her nerves, but she leaned forward and stroked Dottie's neck. "You're going to take good care of me, right, Dottie?"

"Okay, let's see what we've got here." He spent the next few minutes getting her set in her stirrups and walking her forward, to the left and right and backing Dottie up. "She neck reins. Just slight movements of the reins will tell her where you want to go. Nothing to it."

"Seems easy enough."

"She knows what to do. All you have to do is sit and enjoy the ride."

She let out a breath. "I'm so excited."

He swung up onto Thunder with ease. "Here we go."

Lorri was a quick study. No one would ever believe it was her first time in the saddle.

"Those are some nice boots you've got on. I was going to take us down to the creek and ride that path most of the way, but I'd hate to ruin them."

"Don't worry about these boots. Let's take the horses in the water. Oh my gosh, this is like a dream. I can't believe we're riding." She stretched her arms above her head. "I love this."

He turned Thunder toward the creek's edge, and Dottie fell right in line behind him.

He heard Lorri gasp as the sound of the rushing water became louder. It always took his breath away too.

Dottie stepped down the bank and leaned forward to drink. Lorri squealed. "Am I going to slide off?"

"I hope not. She's not a giraffe. Lean back."

She straightened, noticeably relaxing.

"There you go," he said. "You're fine. She's just thirsty."

The horses drank and then they began clip-clopping through the creek side by side.

He reached up and bent back a low-hanging twig as the path narrowed and he moved in front of her. "You doing okay?"

"Perfect."

"We're going to have to go single file for a bit, then the horses will climb up the bank where it widens again."

"I'm following you."

It was an easy pace, and he enjoyed her quiet company. As they approached where they were going to climb the bank, he twisted around in his saddle. "Okay, let Dottie take care of the climb. Sit and balance, that's all you have to do. She'll take it slow."

Thunder bounded up the bank. Ryder spun his horse around to keep an eye on Lorri, but she didn't flinch, just let Dottie do the work. Lorri smiled with every step. He got down off of Thunder and helped her from her horse.

"We'll tie them up over here." He grabbed both lead lines and took care of it.

"That was wonderful," she said. "Thank you so much."

"You haven't even seen the mill yet."

"I can't believe it's going to get better."

"Better start believing." He gave her a quick wink. "Get your land legs."

She jogged in place. "Ready to go."

They walked along the bank. She stopped and picked a wide blade of grass. "When I was a little girl my grandfather taught me to whistle with grass." She licked her thumbs and put the grass between them, puffing between them. "That was not the way I remember it."

He snagged a piece and made a loud duck-like whistle. "Like that?"

"Yes! What am I doing wrong?"

"Try again." It only took her a couple of tries to get it right, and by then they were trying to name songs. He guessed "Jingle Bells" to her "Stairway to Heaven." Laughing so hard, she could barely blow.

"The mill is just behind the tall rhododendrons over there."

They marched through the thick brush near the water, and then there it was.

"That building looks so tired."

"It's old, but we've shored it up over the years."

"It's built so well. Look how thick the wood is. My house isn't even framed with wood that heavy."

"No, it's not." He reached for her hand. "It's safe. Come on. You can see the stone wheels in here. The water used to be much deeper and would run this mill. Unfortunately, years of land development, well drilling, and grading have affected the waterway through here. I played here as a kid."

"It's really neat. It should be a landmark."

"People don't appreciate this kind of stuff much anymore."

"They should." A hint of sadness hung in her words. "This has been such a great day."

"It's only half over. We still have to get back."

"I know, but I didn't want to forget to thank you. I thought you were going to drive me past a waterwheel off the side of the road. I had no idea I was in for an adventure like this. And lunch too."

"You're welcome, my friend Lorri." He liked the way she wrinkled her nose when he called her that. It was silly, but it was nice to have that special little something between them. Just their own. "You know, I should have done this sooner. I owe you an apology."

"For what?"

"The other day. The only thing I can come up with, and it's stupid, is that I was showing off a little. I never break a confidence. I don't know why I told you about that celebrity wedding. . . ." He let out a breath. At least he'd set the record straight. "Anyway, I hope you'll forgive me. I really am a man who is good to his word. I want you to believe that."

"I understand," she said. "It's fine. I'm kind of flattered in some weird way, but don't you turn out to be the town gossip." She shook her pointer finger at him. "I won't be impressed by that at all." She bent down to pick up something. "A feather. Just out here in the middle of nowhere."

She took a few steps then tossed the feather in the air, letting it spin to the ground.

"The Wedding Ranch, this event," he continued. "It's a big deal for them."

"I'm sure it is."

He bent over and picked up the feather she'd tossed. "No, I mean, really big. My niece and nephew run that place. They'd be so upset if anything went wrong. And if I had anything to do with even so much as a hiccup this week . . . well, I'd never want to let them down like that."

"Don't worry. I have no intention of telling a single person. I'm always good to my word." She cocked her head. "You're bragging on them a little. A proud uncle?"

"Definitely." He tucked the feather into his pocket. "I can't believe they've made such a big success out of hosting events. Who knew you could take a falling-apart barn and a couple of tobacco barns and breathe new life into them like that? People are coming from across the nation to have their events there. I don't really understand it, but I'm very happy for them, and hope it lasts."

"Country is very cool right now. Even if it's a passing fad, they will be learning valuable entrepreneurial skills," she said. "Venue weddings have been trending for a long while now, but the country stuff, it just keeps getting more and more popular. Country music. Country homes. Country cooking. Country weddings."

"Don't have to sell me on it," he said. "I grew up this way."

"I'm a city girl through and through, but I'm totally sold too." She lifted her arms out to the side. "I love all of this."

Well-toned and tan, she was as graceful as a ballerina. She closed her eyes, lifting her chin to the sun.

"I bet heaven is like this," she said, "but the deer will walk up and eat from my hands, and birds will rest on my shoulders." She twirled. "It's so peaceful."

"It is." He squatted, plucking a wildflower, twirling it be-tween his fingers as he watched her thoroughly enjoy nothing but nature. Her lips slightly parted, embracing the moment she seemed to be in no hurry at all. He couldn't take his eyes off of her.

He realized he'd kind of hoped today would be like this. But now that it was real . . . as much as he was enjoying the day, it scared him too.

What if he found that feeling again? Could he bear the possibility of losing it?

Chapter Seventeen

Riding the horses back through the creek was twice as fun as the slow trail ride down to the mill. Lorri had gotten brazen and taken off, but Ryder had way more experience, splashing her and leaving her soaking wet.

"Hey! No fair! I don't know how to do that yet." Not that she really minded. It was warm enough that the cool water was refreshing against her skin.

They unsaddled the horses back at the Rest Stop.

"If you're not in a hurry we can brush these guys down." He propped his saddle up against the trailer.

"I'd love that. I've got nowhere to be." Lorri was glad she had nothing else pressing to do today. Anything on her work calendar she could catch up on tonight.

He showed her how to hold the brush, and how much pressure to use starting at the top and working her way down the sweaty horse.

It was amazing how wet the horse was underneath where the saddle had been. She'd never thought of them building up a sweat as they ran. It wasn't easy work, although it had sure seemed like it. She enjoyed feeling close to the horse that had just served her so well.

"I wasn't scared for one moment." She brushed Dottie like he'd shown her, in long sweeping movements. "Dottie seems to really like this. Can I brush her mane?"

"Sure."

The thick, coarse hair was so shiny she was tempted to pull it into braids to keep it from getting all tangled again.

She glanced over at Ryder as he cared for Thunder, mimicking his movements. She could see how girls fell in love with horses. There was something so personal about being on horseback. She placed her hand flat against the warm smooth side of the paint horse where the black spot faded to gray against the lighter pigment. She saved that memory, hoping to translate it to canvas, imagining her brush fading and blending the colors almost too pretty to look realistic.

Lorri watched Ryder. He seemed like a good guy. Not just handsome, but genuinely kind. He'd even opened doors for her. That never went out of style. It was cute that he had to admit that he'd been showing off for her by telling her the secret about the wedding. Embarrassed by it too.

It had to have been a humbling moment. She was relieved he had though, because it had bothered her that he'd told her that secret. Maybe more than it would have since it was about Cody, but then Ryder didn't know that she and Cody were friends.

Not being good to your word was a character flaw. A serious one. Daddy had always said, if a man isn't good to his word, then he's good for nothing.

They finished tending to the horses, then Ryder took her home. The sun was beginning to set when they pulled into her driveway. She wished the day didn't have to end.

He walked her to the door, not hesitating a single moment as he dropped an innocent kiss to her cheek just in front of her ear, then stepped back. "I'd like to do this again."

The sweet gesture practically melted her. "Me too. Soon."
Please stay.

He didn't ask to come in, but his face brightened when she said "soon." Or maybe she'd just hoped it had. He turned and walked away, lifting his hand in a wave as he got into his truck.

She stood there as he backed out of her driveway, wishing she hadn't already told him she'd be busy the whole weekend. Waiting until next week to see him again seemed like such a long time.

Lorri had just fed Mister when the doorbell rang. With her mind still on the day with Ryder, for a half second she hoped it was him, but she knew it would be Pam. Lorri ran to the door to let her in.

Pam stood there with a rolling suitcase in one hand and a large picture frame hanging over her shoulder with a roll of wrapping paper and a huge spool of white satin ribbon in the other. "I was so hoping you'd still be out."

Lorri hugged Pam. "I haven't been home long."

"Good!"

"What all do you have there?"

Pam lifted her arms.

"Since you created their gift and Bobby crafted the frame, I thought I could at least wrap it really nicely." She tapped Mister on the head with the tip of the wrapping paper tube. "I love this dog. He's gotten even bigger."

"You think?"

"Definitely."

"Come on in." She snagged the rolling bag from Pam and led the way to the guest room. "You'll be in here."

"I love what you've done with this place. It's even prettier than when we toured it when it was the model home."

"New start." Lorri smiled appreciatively as she took the frame. "This is going to look great. The stain is perfect. Bobby does such great work."

"I'm glad you like it. He had fun messing with it." Pam walked over to the armoire in the corner. "I love the antique touches here and there."

"Thanks. I've got kind of an eclectic mix going on, but I think it works."

"It does. Now, enough of the small talk. Tell me about your date with Ryder."

Lorri pressed her lips together unable to hold back her smile. "We went on a picnic, and then rode horses down to an old mill. It was amazing."

"I can tell by the look on your face you had a really good time."

"I did. It was so easy. Oh my gosh, gorgeous. Nature. The creek. He was a complete gentleman."

"Well, don't hold that against him."

"Stop it. He earned points for that."

Pam opened her suitcase and took a small bag from the top and handed it to Lorri. "Here. This is for you. A little hostess gift."

"You didn't have to do that." Lorri held the shiny purple bag. "But thank you. What's in here?" She reached in and lifted out a long box tied with a ribbon. Her brows pulled together as she lifted it and shook it. Something clanged around inside. "I have no idea what this is."

"That's why it's in a box. So you'll be surprised. That's how it works."

Lorri tugged the ribbon and peeked inside. Three very nice paint brushes lay nestled inside. "Thank you. This is perfect timing, too." She took them out, enjoying the feel of the smooth wooden handles and the weight of the long brushes in her hand. "Nice balance. I love them."

"You're special. You deserve only the best, and I'm sorry I didn't get a chance to tell you about Craig before Stacy blurted it out over lunch. I really am. I hope you can forgive me. It's really been bothering me."

"Well, stop worrying about that." She waved her hand. "It doesn't matter. We're divorced. He can do what he pleases. I really don't care."

"You seem far better off without him."

"I am. I love my home. I've made friends—none as good as you, and I miss you, but I'm doing okay. And I'm trying new things. I rode a horse today."

"I've never ridden one." Pam snickered. "Unless you count

the kind you put a quarter in for a ride at the grocery store. I've done that."

"A real live breathing horse. With a name even." Lorri sat on the bed next to Pam and poured out every detail of being with Ryder today.

Pam shook her head. "You don't know how much I love seeing you like this. If I'd showed up a little earlier, would I have perhaps interrupted a kiss at the door?"

"No. He's a gentleman. And it's strictly friends. That's why it's so perfect." Okay, he had given her a little kiss, but just on the cheek, and that was unique enough for her not to want to share it.

"So, he's single? Divorced?"

"I don't know, but he doesn't wear a ring, and he was very clear he's not looking for a relationship. It was nice. We don't ask each other a million questions. I like that. It's different."

"Maybe that's because this guy is genuine, and Craig . . . well, we know what he was."

"I can't wait to paint what I saw today. I hope I can do it justice. I've never felt so close to nature in all my life."

"That's because the closest we get to nature is watching Discovery Channel and even then you're always curled up in a ball worried about who's going to eat who next."

"Those shows are sad. I don't watch those anymore."

They changed into their pajamas, chatting nonstop like a couple of schoolgirls, almost falling asleep, and then thinking of something else they had to talk about.

"Oh gosh. It's after two," Lorri said. "We've got to get some sleep. I'm going to my room so we can't keep talking."

"Party pooper."

"The party will continue in the morning. Love you. So glad you're here. If you wake up before me the coffee maker is ready to go. Just hit the start button."

"Good deal."

"Come on, Mister. Time for bed." He lifted his head and then put it back down. "Looks like you have another best friend."

Pam leaned over the side of the bed and petted him. "Fine by me."

Lorri walked down the hall to her room and climbed into bed. She closed her eyes. *This has been a perfect day.*

Lorri woke up to the smell of bacon. Something that never happened. She got out of bed and went into the kitchen.

Mister sat to the right of Pam, his nose wiggling.

"It smells so good," Lorri said. "Don't you feed my dog bacon. He'll expect me to start frying it up on weekends, and that is not going to happen."

"Just one little piece?" Pam tick-tocked the spatula in front of him. "That's what aunties are for." Mister cocked his head, putting on his best begging face. "Seriously. How do you say no to that?"

Lorri poured a cup of coffee. "When he outweighs you, you keep the boundaries clear."

"Fair enough. I'm almost done here." She put a bowl of scrambled eggs on the table, then took the last pieces of bacon out of the frypan. "All set."

"This is a treat." Lorri sat down and made her plate. "I just bought fresh tomatoes. The produce at the market has me completely spoiled." She went to the kitchen and brought one back, slicing it into wedges to split with Pam.

After breakfast they went upstairs to the loft to look at the wedding picture.

"Lorri, I know this is what you described, but this is amazing. Cody and Kasey are going to love it. I just got chills."

"I'm really pleased with how it turned out. Pete sent over some pictures from Cody's things, and I was able to find a ton of Kasey's stuff online."

"I love how you incorporated The Wedding Ranch into the 'E' of 'Tuggle' and then wrote 'everlasting' underneath it. Wow. You are so creative. You haven't lost a thing, girl. I can't wait to see what you end up painting from here."

"Thanks."

They matted and framed the picture, and then Pam wrapped it in the beautiful white-on-white damask-patterned paper. The satin ribbon was soft enough to be part of the bride's bouquet and formed a perfect bow on top.

They carried it downstairs and set it by the fireplace. Cody could take it with him when he left. No need to tote it to the wedding.

The driveway alert rang. Both of them ran to the door. "It has to be Cody!"

"It's a Mercedes," Pam said. "I thought he was supposed to be all incognito. Yep. It's him." She opened the front door.

Lorri squeezed Pam's arm. "It's been too long since the three of us got together like this."

Cody spread his arms open, a wide grin on his face. "How're my two favorite girls?"

"Feeling like we've become number two and number three on your list, but we're okay with it," Lorri said. She skipped out to meet him halfway on the sidewalk. "It's so good to see you."

He wrapped his big arms around her. "It's been too long. You both look great."

"You're bigger than I remember," Lorri said.

"That's blubber. My bride-to-be has learned to make all of my favorite meals, and I just can't say no to them. That, and being on the road is more than my metabolism can keep up with." He patted his belly which still looked completely flat.

"Well, you look great. We're so excited for you. Thank you for making time for us." Pam stepped up for her hug.

"I'd have made time for y'all if I had to do it in the middle of the night. Man, it's good to see you. I'm beat though. The last week has been nonstop. Scrunching the tour dates for the wedding was a real pain, but we managed it."

"Come on in," Lorri said.

"I like it a lot better than your other house. This is more my style."

"I never knew it was mine," Lorri admitted. "I'm loving it though. So tell us what to expect at the wedding. Is it going to be fancy? Traditional? Are you going to sing?"

"I am. I wrote a song just for it. I love that gal so much, and Jake, that child is a real gift from God. I couldn't love him more if he were my own." His eyes shimmered with the unmistakable sheen of joyful tears.

She had to ask. "Think you two might have one of your own?"

He grinned. "We've been talking about it."

"Oh my gosh. That's so great."

"Will you play the song for us?" Pam pleaded.

"Where's the guitar," he said with a groan. "I know you've got one around here somewhere."

"I do. Always just in case you show up."

"My kind of girl."

She got the guitar and handed it to him.

He strummed a few notes. "It's even in tune. Here we go." He sang a love song that was sure to make everyone at the wedding cry, then capture the hearts of his fans. As he played the last chord, they applauded with gusto.

"You know that's going to be the next big wedding song, don't you?"

"Well, that'd be nice, but all I want is to make Kasey happy."

"And that's why it'll be a hit. It's real."

"How about this one." He played their college favorite and Lorri and Pam sang along.

"Are you hungry?"

"You're not cooking, are you?" Cody teased.

"No, but I did do the shopping for Pam."

"I am hungry, but I have to see Kasey. We want you both to come to the cookout on Friday night."

"We'll be there."

"I'll text you the details. As for Saturday, just come and enjoy yourself. Wear whatever you want and prepare yourself for a good time. Mom will be there. She's dying to talk to you, so be ready."

"It'll be great." They walked him to the front door. "Wait, Cody. We have your wedding present. Take it with you so there'll be one less you have to deal with at the reception." She ran over and got it. "It's from the both of us."

"You didn't have to do this."

"We wanted to," Pam said.

He tucked the long frame under his arm like a surfboard. "Thank you."

"You're welcome. By the way, you know," Pam added, "that Mercedes isn't exactly low-key."

"Hey, I'm trying to keep up with this Walker girl." He gave Lorri a wink. "The Pinto was already rented. It's all they had."

"Right," Lorri laughed. Her first car had been an old Ford Pinto. It had been her grandmother's and she'd put less than thirty thousand miles on it before Lorri ever got it. It was like brand new, and she knew she should've appreciated it, but the other kids had teased her mercilessly about it. "Real funny."

As soon as Cody backed out of the driveway, Pam practically melted. "Please tell me you are okay with taking a nap. We did not get enough sleep last night!"

"I'll race you." Lorri scooted past her and didn't stop until she reached her bedroom door. She poked her head back out. "Pam. I'm glad you're here."

"Me too. I miss you, but I feel so much better seeing for my-self how happy you are here."

Lorri slid across the bed and hugged her pillow. *I am happy.*

Funny how her life had changed since the divorce from Craig. There'd been a time when she was dressed up more often than not. Now she chose blue jeans and pulled her hair back. No makeup. No jewelry.

I have better things to do with my time. She glanced over at Mister, who sat next to the bed with his head held high.

"You're the best thing Craig ever did for me, even if his intentions had been less than honorable." She brushed her left hand over the mask of dark hair surrounding his eyes and ears. "Good boy."

She'd be glad when the telltale notch on her ring finger finally went away. Pulling her hand into her lap, she twisted the skin at the seven-year indentation. It wasn't noticeable to anyone else, and hopefully soon she wouldn't notice the wedding ring missing or why. Like it had never happened.

She questioned now if it had ever been love, or rather the expected natural progression of steps since they'd been together from their school years. Time served. Companionship and being able to afford things—two paychecks were easier than one. Feeling like adults by moving out onto their own. She'd landed the graphic design position right out of college; he'd hopped from job to job. Playing more than planning.

With him off her back financially, and the extra cushion from the sale of their home, she was living more comfortably than ever.

Chapter Eighteen

Saturday morning, Lorri smoothed her party dress, twisting in the full-length mirror and relieved she still loved the emerald green. She stood in front of the mirror. It had been a splurge. She wasn't sure what kind of wood it was, but the slightly reddish hue made her think it was either cherry or pecan. It had been simply leaning against a wall in a furniture store marked "Not For Sale" the day she saw it. She'd tracked down the manager anyway. She told him that she'd fallen in love with the piece the moment she'd laid eyes on it, knowing it would cast beautiful light across her bedroom from the window across the way.

The manager seemed to enjoy her excitement, admitting he'd bought the mirror at a sample sale from a company that was no longer in business. He'd underestimated its size and it wouldn't fit where he'd planned to use it. "It's not for sale, young lady, but I have to say you'd give it a much better home than I'd intended. I'll part with it for you."

She'd almost fallen down. Those kinds of things never happened to her, but here it was, proof that life wasn't always predictable.

The whole time she'd lived here, she'd barely used it to check her image. Working at home meant jeans or jammies, but it was nice to dress up again. Heels, earrings, and the pearls Mom and Daddy had given her when she'd graduated from college. She was excited for Cody. Moments like this were exactly what this mirror was meant for.

"Are you almost ready?" Pam leaned inside the door. "Wow, you look beautiful."

Lorri turned to Pam, who looked elegant in her black lacy dress.

"That dress . . . wow. . . ." Pam shook her head. "Twirl. Let me see the back."

Blushing, Lorri did as Pam said, kind of enjoying the moment. "Think we'll fit in with all the famous folks?"

"Definitely. I can't wait to see who was on the guest list. Dressed like this they might think we're famous. We could make up something."

"Not like we haven't done that before," Lorri said. "It's been a long time since we've gotten this dressed up for anything."

"Bobby would much rather go to a sports bar and eat wings than go somewhere fancy."

"We should do it more often. Get the girls together and go somewhere fancy," Lorri said. "Quarterly maybe."

"We deserve it," Pam said, "and without grumbling husbands it would be so much more fun. Poor Bobby can barely swallow in a tie. He'd be happier if we went without him."

"Wasn't it sweet how Cody gushed on and on about Kasey, and when he talked about Jake . . . he truly loves that little boy."

Pam lowered herself to the edge of the bed. "He does. The bond he and Kasey formed when Jake was missing goes deep. What they've got is the real thing."

And Cody had written that song about her. A song that went triple platinum, and all he cared about was helping her find Jake.

They sat quietly, remembering the circumstances that Cody and Kasey had met under, and the subsequent events that became the foundation of their friendship and love. It was such a strange way for two people to find each other. The only explanation was that it was meant to be.

"You'll have that kind of love someday, Lorri. I know you will."

"I wasn't thinking about that. I'm happier than I've ever been the way things are," Lorri said. "And I'm glad you're here."

"Me too."

"We'd better get going." Lorri grabbed her handbag and checked herself one last time in the mirror. "No tags, right?"

"Wouldn't that be classy? Sounds like something I'd do." Pam double-checked Lorri, then herself. "Nope. We're both good."

Even though The Wedding Ranch was not far as the crow flies, detour signs had been placed on the stretch of road leading to it, forcing anyone who wasn't a guest of the wedding to take the long way around.

Lorri ignored the sign as she'd been instructed and drove past the bend in the road to where a portable guard shack was set up. Two official-looking guys in three-piece suits stood there wearing headsets.

The tall one stepped toward the car. "Can I help you?"

Lorri handed him her and Pam's driver licenses as detailed in the invitation. The guy checked them against his electronic list on a tablet, then gave the other a nod.

"Enjoy your day. Follow the road up to the white tent. Someone will valet your car there."

"Thank you." She raised her window.

"He looked like a young Clint Eastwood," Pam said. "He's already making *my* day."

"Stop." Lorri stifled the giggle. "We have to behave."

"Cody was kidding when he said that."

Lorri pressed the accelerator and followed the signs to the venue. The valet raised his hand to stop her. He took Lorri's car at the entrance and she and Pam walked into the giant party tent. It was as big as the one at the fair—except this one was open on two sides, with sails as big as a pirate ship in shiny navy blue. Lengths of white fabric with sparkling sequins softened the appearance. Fans lofted the fabric, which created a breeze, making it quite comfortable inside.

"This. Is. Gorgeous." Pam's eyes darted around the beautiful decor and well-dressed people already mingling with crystal champagne flutes in hand.

"I don't know how they did all of this just up the street. I never heard a thing. Crazy." Lorri snagged two glasses from a passing waiter. They tapped crystal flutes and sipped the fine bubbly champagne.

With every strum of the guitar and tinkle of the ivories from the shiny grand piano, excitement built. Big overstuffed couches around the edges and bar-height tables throughout

created inviting conversation nooks. She and Pam comman-
deered one of the tables so they could have a clear view of the
celebs as they arrived.

Staggered arrival times meant it would take much longer for
the attendees to gather, but there was already a good crowd. A
jam session by Cody's friends kept folks entertained with music
and the vibe was elegant yet casual.

"I can't believe we're here." Goose bumps chased up Lorri's
arms as she scanned the room, recognizing several musicians
and a very well-known actor. *This may be the best week of my life.*

Chapter Nineteen

Ryder sat in his lawn chair under the horse trailer awning enjoying a cup of coffee while checking messages. He wasn't normally one to spend a lot of time on his phone. The way he saw it, phones were for phone calls. The only reason he had a fancy one was because his old flip phone finally stopped working and he'd been forced to get something new.

He had hoped he might hear from Lorri though.

A little lisa butterfly skittered across his shoulder. Maybe it was the same little lisa that Lorri had been delighting over the other day. Her spontaneous delight of the simplest things resonated with him.

He pictured Lorri riding the creek trail on Dottie. The way her hair moved in the light breeze, her skin kissed by the sun. No one would have believed she'd never ridden before. He remembered her squeal when he'd splashed her, and the reckless laughter that followed. It made him laugh now.

She'd talked to a ladybug, and when she walked through the

tall grass back toward the old mill house, her fingertips sweeping the green growth as high as her waist, he'd caught his breath.

"One last look," she'd said, taking off before he could answer. "One last goodbye."

"I'll bring you back," he'd promised. "It's not really good-bye."

"I'm going to hold you to that, Ryder."

And he'd found comfort in that. *Don't threaten me with a good time.*

It had been a good day. Seeing these all-so-familiar things through her eyes, fresh and new, brought new respect to the good fortune under which he lived his life.

It had been a long time since he'd spent time in the company of a woman. There'd been a few dates over the years since Valerie died, but they'd been awkward. And not of his doings. Friends invited him over for dinner only to find they had also invited *the perfect girl*. They meant well. He tried to remember that, but he didn't appreciate it much.

He'd had the same thought every time that happened.

I already met the perfect girl. Married her and vowed my life to her.

What made his friends think he needed a second best?

Grief was a funny thing. Just when he thought he was making progress, someone would push him and he'd clamp onto the past again even tighter than before. Giving up that empty spot where his heart used to feel happiness felt too much like letting go of all the good memories.

He missed Valerie and Ronnie Dwayne every day. It was fine by him if he relived those good memories every last day of his life.

If he died an old man only clinging to the memories he had with them—his wedding day. The birth of his son. Sunday dinners. All of Ronnie Dwayne's firsts. Every goodnight kiss—if that's all he died with, he'd have so much more than many people would ever experience in their lives. He was thankful for that.

Lorri was different. She wasn't a divorcée looking for a replacement, or a single mother hoping for a new dad for her kids. She was just another person, like him, hardworking, honest, and playful. Beautiful in a girl-next-door kind of way, her confidence intrigued him. The way Lorri enthused over the small things that made this town special delighted him as much as the first vine-ripe tomato of summer. He couldn't wait to show her more of Dalton Mill, and there was nothing more to it than that. No pressure. No expectations.

He hadn't asked many questions. Hadn't even wanted to, but today he found himself wondering about her. Where she grew up. Her favorite foods. She'd mentioned she didn't cook. Did she eat takeout or those little frozen cardboard-box dinners? What was her career like? He knew she'd created the logo for The Wedding Ranch, but how does someone fall into that kind of job?

Ryder's phone rang—disappointment fell over him as he saw that it was only Ross.

"What's up, Ross? Is everything okay at the venue?"

"We have a slight hiccup. I could use your help if you have time." Ross blew out a breath. "Sorry for the last-minute ask, but Cody loaned out his rental car to one of his friends, and that's how he and Kasey were going to move from the ceremony to the reception. Do you think you could bring the horse and carriage down to take them back to the tent after the vows? I can come up with something else if you can't. I get it, but—"

"Not doing anything but staying out of the way today as promised. I'm happy to help, Ross."

"Great. You're the best. They'll be surprised, and I think they'll really like it."

"What do I need to wear? I didn't bring much down here with me."

"Doesn't matter. Jeans and a black T-shirt would do. As long as you're wearing your cowboy hat, it'll be fine. I know you've got that."

"Got my pants on, don't I?"

"Yes, sir. Yeah, nothing fancy. The horse and carriage are fancy enough. All eyes will be on the bride and groom anyways."

"I'm on it." His mind was already thinking about what he'd need to do to pull it together in a hurry.

He always stored the carriage in tip-top shape after every use, but that barn got dusty, especially in the summer, and this summer had been drier than normal. He grabbed a decent pair of jeans and a clean shirt and tied them to the back of his saddle, then climbed up on Thunder and loped over to the barn to get things ready.

The wedding wasn't until one, so he took his time shining up the carriage and readying the horses. A quick change of clothes in the barn, and he'd be over there in plenty of time to take the bride and groom from where they were tying the knot in front of the tall tobacco barn back over to the big tent for the reception. A whole hog, apple in the mouth and all, had been on coals since last night. When the wind shifted, he could catch the smoky smell of it. At least now that he was working the ceremony, he could grab a nice hot meal that he didn't have to cook before going back down to the Rest Stop for the night.

He sprayed off the carriage and wiped away the last droplets with a chamois made of goat leather, then hitched Thunder and another horse, Buckshot, giving everything a quick polish as he went. It looked good as show day. No one would ever know it was a last-minute decision.

Ryder had just changed clothes when Ross texted a message they were ready for him to head that way.

Ryder walked back into the barn and pulled the champagne bucket from the storage room, filled it with ice pellets, then slipped a bottle of good champagne down into the sterling silver pail. He'd done this routine of driving the happy couple to the reception a few times by now, so he was prepared. By the time the "I dos" were done it would be perfectly chilled. He placed the silver bucket and two long-stemmed glasses in the wooden rig he'd built into the wagon solely for that purpose.

He climbed onto the raised seat and lifted the leather reins into his hands. One flick of his wrist and they rolled forward at an amble. He loved driving these horses. He looked out over his property as they moved across the field.

A good life we have here.

He propped his boot up on the wooden rail as the carriage rattled over the pasture. Noticing the dust on his boots, he slid the toe of one behind his pant leg giving it a quick shine. *Better.* Not that anyone would be looking at his footware, but it made him feel better. He had to admit he was kind of glad he was going to get to see Cody Tuggle up close and personal. He enjoyed his old country style of music.

He rode over humming one of Cody's older songs.

Ryder stopped the horses on the back side of the second building out of sight. From here, the carriage was out of view, but Ryder could see the huge wooden cross he and Ross had spent weeks building, sanding, and staining. It was gorgeous and rugged, and rose nearly ten feet into the air.

Together they'd also built wooden planters that were now filled with fresh flowers.

Today Reece had piled gorgeous arrangements with fluffy white hydrangeas that looked almost like clouds. White flowers spilled over the sides, some big and some small, the greenery adding a soft touch.

Using the carriage to move the wedding party wasn't something new. Ryder had been happy to oblige whenever the kids needed him for these events, and the horse and carriage had turned out to be one of those special options that had become a popular choice.

They'd done this carriage exchange so many times, Ryder had the timing down to a science. As soon as the bride and groom took the first step of their walk back down the aisle as Mr. and Mrs. he'd pull the horses up. The guests were so focused on the couple, clapping and cheering, they wouldn't hear the noisy carriage. It was as if the horse and carriage magically appeared as the crowd parted. The bride and groom would step right up and onto the carriage and he'd drive his horses over to the reception area.

The pathway was made from old cobblestones, adding to the

rugged sound of the iron and wooden wheels. Ross and Reece had somehow found a deal on a container of cobblestones that had been brought over to the US on sailing ships in the 1800s and used to pave the streets along the coast. The shipping container had been long forgotten. The town had purchased them at some point, but no one knew by who or for what, so they'd put them in the auction along with some old furniture and outdated, rode-hard utility vehicles. There were no other bids on the container.

Ross had bought the whole lot for two hundred dollars. Of course, it cost way more than that to get them delivered and laid, but they'd turned it into a family project. The worn edges of the cobblestones made for interesting work, like a puzzle, but it made for good old-fashioned curb appeal and the horseshoes sounded so good, almost a hollow clip-clop, against the hard stones.

Ryder pushed his cowboy hat back on his head to cool down; at least in the shade there was a bit of relief. He rested his arm on his knee.

Across the way, music from the party tent seemed like background music in a movie, with him, the star in an old western movie, waiting for his big entrance. Skulking back here behind the barn, his imagination drifted. In his mind's eye, four bad guys wearing black hats and bandannas pulled across their faces raced over the hill in his direction, guns blazing, horses snorting. He imagined what it would be like to slap the reins and roll the wagon out full speed toward them, pulling his Winchester from below the wooden seat. Slipping the leather reins under his boot not to lose control of the carriage, he'd stand, cock that rifle low, and take them out one by one.

Okay, so maybe I've seen one too many westerns.

Voices nearby stole his attention. Guests made their way over from the big tent, chasing his John Wayne moment away. The first few rows in front of the cross where the bride and groom would take their vows filled quickly.

People of all ages in a wide range of attire, from blue jeans and trendy short dresses to long gowns and suits, drifted in taking up every seat and flanking the surrounding areas. Ross and Reece had once told him that standing room only was the preferred amount of seating in a fancy wedding.

Didn't make sense to him. If he were having a highfalutin wedding he'd want to see to it that everyone had a chair. Showed what he knew about this stuff.

Conversation got louder until the pastor took his place. The crowd quieted in anticipation.

Cody Tuggle entered from between the buildings wearing Old West–style tails and a silver belly cowboy hat with a cattleman crown and that low tug on the front of the brim he was known for. Four other men in matching suits joined him. Ryder only recognized one of them and that was the lead guitarist in Cody's band.

There was a quiet moment and then suddenly music flowed from the speakers. Not the wedding march, but rather an instrumental piece with a country-western flair to it.

A little girl who couldn't have been more than four or five years old wearing a long white dress over cowgirl boots and a ring of flowers in her hair started down the aisle. Ryder remembered when Reece and Ross were that little.

The little girl took a step, sprinkled a few petals, and then looked around and waved, giggling the whole time she was weaving in and out, trying to avoid trampling the delicate petals she'd just tossed in front of her.

As she zig-zagged her way down the aisle, Cody's chin lifted, his smile so wide all you could see was teeth beneath the brim of his hat. The little girl walked toward him, sprinkling more white rose petals.

A young boy in a silver belly cowboy hat that matched Cody's carried a pillow down the aisle. He didn't dawdle or look around. His boots and spurs jangled as he marched straight up to Cody and stood next to him. Cody gave him an appreciative nod.

The pastor said something to the children, and both nodded, then the little boy took the little girl's hand in the sweetest moment. Ryder wasn't the only one to think so, because audible approval swept across the crowd.

Both children stepped in front of Cody. He placed a gentle hand on each of them as four women began walking down the aisle one at a time. Everyone twisted in their seats waiting for the big moment when the bride would make her appearance.

A vision in white, Kasey stepped out of the tall tobacco barn. The white-washed boards and the tobacco stick star on the front of the building was a nice contrast to the image of femininity seeming to float her way toward him in the white gown.

She paused and squeezed the hand of an older woman as she walked by, and then stopped next to Cody. They exchanged a heartwarming moment. Kasey handed her bouquet to her maid of honor and faced Cody, placing her hands in his.

It was a simple, but lovely ceremony.

Ryder thought about his wedding day. It was in a stuffy church. His rented suit was so tight he could barely breathe and the patent leather shoes pinched his sweating feet until his toes were numb. That preacher had gone on and on longer than any Sunday service. He'd have killed for a bottle of water, but he toughed it out, because the most beautiful girl he'd ever known—not just on the outside, but the inside too—had agreed to marry him. He could still feel Valerie's tender shaking hand in his as they said their vows.

'Til death do us part.

This ceremony wasn't long and drawn out like that though. Not scripture after scripture. It was short and sweet. Musical interludes paced it nicely, but it was still done in record time. *My kind of wedding.*

The pastor announced the couple as husband and wife, and then introduced Mr. and Mrs. Tuggle for the very first time.

The boy ran into the bride's arms and then Cody grabbed him and lifted him into the air, taking his bride's hand and leading her down the aisle.

Everyone cheered.

Ryder clucked his teeth and flicked the reins. The carriage rolled forward on cue, stopping right on the mark for his guests.

Ross gave him the okay sign and mouthed "thank you."

Ryder sat face forward with his hat tipped low, so as not to take any attention from the bride and groom. Across the way though, he spotted two beautifully dressed women talking. One of them almost looked like Lorri.

Girl is in all my thoughts.

Chapter Twenty

❧

With the Tuggle family safely in the carriage, the crowd moved back from the path and Ryder moved his team of horses forward, slowly transporting the couple to the reception while offering picture-worthy moments.

Reece hopped up onto the step at the rear of the carriage and motioned the rest of the bridal party to set the pace. Guests followed on their own. It wasn't far to the reception. This was all for show really.

Ross waved the bridal party and guests into the tent, and Ryder drove one more lap around the perimeter, letting the newlyweds exit on the far side in preparation for their big entrance. Huge bubble machines were at the ready. An explosion of colorful bubbles would fill the air as soon as the couple walked inside.

Ryder waited until everyone was off the carriage, then he dismounted and tied the horses to the hitch, offering them some water from the trough on the other side while the bride and groom went inside.

Excitement rose. Bubbles cascaded in a swirling frenzy, even drifting outside the tent. Ryder popped one. Thunder lifted his nose from the water, watching a flurry of bubbles float by.

Across the way there was a step and repeat banner with PT FOUNDATION in the silhouette of a family, and a clear plexiglass donation box. In lieu of gifts, the couple were accepting donations for the cause that was so dear to their hearts, finding missing children and reuniting them with their families. Ryder crossed the room and pulled every last dollar from his wallet. He dropped all of it through the slot—happy to be a part of the solution. It was a good thing they were doing.

His work was done here for the day. He'd drive the carriage back over to the barn and put Buckshot up for the night, then ride Thunder back down to the Rest Stop.

He scanned the room looking for Reece or Ross to make sure they didn't need anything before he left.

Reece ran up behind him. "Uncle Ryder. We've had a security breach. There are pictures all over the internet of the wedding. I need your help."

Across the way, the woman in the emerald-green dress stood there with another woman, and she was looking right at him. She smiled. He recognized the confident lift of her chin.

His heart dropped. Lorri had promised she wouldn't tell anyone about this, but there she was. *She crashed the wedding? It's my fault.*

"Can you help us try to weed the crasher out?" Reece paled. "Whoever it is is live posting all over social media. I've already alerted the sheriff and security so we can keep it contained, but we need to stop it."

"Don't worry. I'm on it." If it got back to them that he was to blame for the security breach, they'd never forgive him. Heck, he'd never forgive himself. *I can't believe I couldn't keep my big mouth shut.*

He stared at Lorri in disbelief. How had he become such a poor judge of character? He wouldn't have thought this could happen in a million years.

She lifted a hand and waved, her fingers dancing as if playing an invisible trumpet. The playful gesture hit him wrong. He hoped the twins hadn't noticed the uninvited guest. He stayed close to the outside edge of the tent, working his way over toward her. If he could get her out of here before Reece and Ross got word the unwanted party crasher was his doing, maybe everything would be fine.

His body tensed. *How could she do this?* She didn't look the type to break a promise. When she'd said she had plans all weekend, it never dawned on him it was to crash this party.

"What's wrong with you?" Diane put her hand on Ryder's shoulder sending him two steps back. "You look like you're about to explode."

"You scared me."

"That's not what has you riled up. I saw that from ten feet away. What's wrong?"

"That woman." He pointed toward Lorri.

"Is she famous?"

"No." Although she looked that gorgeous today. "That's Lorri. She's the lady I rescued at the fair."

"Wow. I wouldn't have recognized her. Of course, she was laying in the dirt with a knot on her head the last time I saw her. She looks beautiful all dressed up." Diane's face lit up in approval, which only made him snarl.

He pushed through the crowd. People were having a good time. Milling about, talking about the ceremony. "Pardon me. Excuse me." He made his way across the room, finally standing right behind Lorri.

In a voice low enough only she could hear he asked, "Lorri? What are you doing here?"

She spun around. "Hey there! Ryder. You're here." Lorri flashed him a million-dollar smile, then reached for her friend's arm. "This is my best friend, Pam." She gestured between the two. "Pam, this is Ryder."

Pam extended her hand. "The guy with the horses. I heard. Nice to meet you."

Wish I could say the same is what he wanted to say but being on his best behavior for his niece and nephew were top of mind. "Thank you." He gave her a polite nod, then lowered his voice. "May I have a word with you, Lorri?"

She looked utterly confused. "Um. Yeah. Sure." She shrugged to Pam who gave her an exaggerated wink.

He led Lorri by the elbow outside of the tent and out of earshot. He turned to face her. "So this is what you were busy doing all weekend?" *I've been such a fool.* He clenched his fist. "I told you how important this was."

"I know, I—"

"Let me finish, please." He didn't have the patience right now. "I can't believe you'd show up like this. This event is important to my niece and nephew. I realize it's my fault because I was the one who blabbed, but I really didn't expect this from you."

Her smile relaxed. "It's fine, Ryder. It's not what you think."

"Then what are you doing here? Why on earth would you crash a wedding? I get it. He's a celebrity, but it's his wedding day."

"I'm well aware of that."

"I'm asking you to leave. I'm not going to make a big deal out of this or tell Reece and Ross, they have enough on their plate today."

"You seriously think I crashed Cody's wedding?"

"You're here, aren't you?"

"Yes. I'm here, because I was invited." Her balled fist batted at the air as she leaned in. "I'll thank you not to go around making assumptions about me in the future."

"Then why didn't you say something the other day, when I told you about it, or when I apologized for breaking the confidence to begin with?" He rubbed the sweat from his neck. "I can't believe I did that."

"I didn't tell you that I knew Cody, or that I was invited to his wedding, because I was told not to tell anyone." She leveled her gaze. "I *can* keep a secret."

That comment hung in the back of Ryder's throat like cold peanut butter.

At that moment, Pam and Cody came toward them, catching them standing toe-to-toe. "I thought I saw you sneak off this way," Pam called out. "Cody wants us to do something to surprise Kasey."

Ryder looked at Pam and Cody and then back at Lorri who had one eyebrow arched and her arms folded across her chest.

"Oh man." He wanted to crawl off and disappear. He caught movement across the way. Reece and a deputy were escorting out a man wearing skinny pants and a black jacket. Lorri wasn't the crasher.

Lorri's nostrils flared slightly and he wondered what kind of scene she was about to make, but she didn't. She laughed and stepped closer to him. "Cody, you have got to meet my new friend, Ryder. He grew up in this town. He's part of the family business that's hosting your wedding."

Cody shook his hand. "Thanks for the excellent transportation. That was awesome. My mom went crazy. She's a horse lady, you know. You'll have to talk to her. She's over the moon about your gray horse."

"Thunder. He's a good horse. I'll look for her."

"She'll love that." Cody clapped his hands together. "I hope you don't mind, but I wanted to grab my two favorite dance partners for a quick twirl for old time's sake. We went to high school together. Kasey has heard me tell this story no less than one hundred and fifty times and still doesn't believe it. She's going to die!"

"He was like our big brother back then. We knew him before he was famous, when he still hit the wrong chords and la-la-la'd through the verses he hadn't written yet," Lorri teased.

"It's true. They knew me when I was the geeky guitar dude." He put his hands out to each of them. "Come on, Ryder, you can cut in when we're done. I know Lorri would love to dance all night."

"Y'all go on. I was leaving. I was just here to offer transportation." He felt about two inches tall. If there was ever a time that he could disappear, right about now would be nice timing.

Cody's deep voice boomed. "Don't be silly. Any friend of

Lorri's is a friend of mine. You get on in here with us. There's fun to be had."

It didn't look like Cody expected to not get his way, so Ryder followed them inside. Cody clapped him on the shoulder like an old buddy. "Really nice to meet you. Lorri is amazing. I'm glad she's meeting good people here in Dalton Mill."

Cody signaled to the guys on the band platform and they started playing his hit song "A Mother's Love."

Cody and Kasey danced their first dance. Everyone gathered around the dance floor, swaying to the music. Ryder could almost read the thought bubbles above the dreamy-eyed females in attendance wishing and hoping they'd have a wedding even half as beautiful as this one someday.

When the song ended, Pete announced from the stage, "Mr. and Mrs. Cody Tuggle. One more round of applause." As the cheers began to die, Pete said, "This next song we're going to play is a special little something for you, Kasey. I think you're in for a treat. I know I'm anxious to see it myself. Here's to seeing is believing."

Kasey turned and looked at Cody with a questioning look. "Do you know what this is about?"

Pete strummed the first few chords and the band switched into an up-tempo song. Cody walked out to the middle of the dance floor, leaving Kasey watching from the side. He hooked his finger toward Lorri and Pam who rushed out, giggling the whole way.

Ryder felt like a complete jerk as he watched Lorri walk out to join them. Of course she wouldn't crash a wedding. *What has gotten into me?*

"Here we go," Cody's voice boomed and then the three of

them eased into a well-choreographed two-step kind of dance including spins and dips and switches. He'd never seen anything like it. There was no disputing those three had been close friends for years, and this was not their first dance rodeo.

Idiot. He felt the red rush of heat climb his neck again.

The song ended and Lorri walked off the dance floor toward him.

"I'm *so* sorry," he said.

"I'm honestly not sure if I should be flattered that you'd think I might crash a wedding, or mad that you didn't think enough of me to just outright ask before jumping to conclusions."

"I'd love to roll back the clock, but then I might miss that dance and I'm so glad I didn't."

"I would have given you the courtesy to have at least asked you about something like that."

He blinked but didn't say a word.

"I appreciate how much you care about your niece and nephew and their business," she went on. "It's an admirable trait to care that much about your family. But friends are just as special, and I thought we were building a friendship. I've enjoyed my time with you, but I don't think you're the kind of friend I need." She turned to walk away.

"Wait. Lorri."

She stopped but didn't turn to face him.

"I really am sorry," he said. "I think you're great. It hurt my feelings to think you'd break that trust. I overreacted. I'm sorry. Please give me a chance to make it up to you."

Pam walked over still out of breath, laughing as she put her hand on Lorri's arm. "Oh my gosh. That was too fun." She must've noticed the tension between him and Lorri because Pam stopped laughing almost immediately. "Is everything okay?"

Lorri didn't answer, instead she turned and narrowed her gaze on Ryder.

He almost choked on that look.

"I made a mistake," he said to Pam. He glanced at Lorri; she wasn't going to bail him out this time though. "I thought your friend here crashed the wedding. I asked her to leave."

"Bwah!" Pam stepped back and laughed even louder. "Priceless. You really don't know my best friend at all yet. She's the rule follower in this group."

"Well, I hope she's also the forgiving one. I could use a get out of jail free card right now."

"You're handsome." Pam took a sip of her champagne. "I'm sure she'll give you another chance, but you better not mess up again, or you'll have me to deal with. I've been known to break rules." Pam nudged Lorri. "Let it go. Honest mistake. Right?"

Lorri shook her head, but then the line that had thinned her lips relaxed just a smidge.

He jumped at the opportunity. "Think I can talk you into that dance with you that Cody promised?"

Lorri let him lift her hand. "Really? You dance?"

"I'm rusty, but there was a time when I could really impress a gal out there." He took her soft hand in his and guided her out to the dance floor.

"I'm willing to give it a try, but you better watch your toes."

Pam let out a whoop, and Ryder lifted his arm, spinning Lorri, then moving her with purpose in a dance he hoped she wouldn't soon forget.

Chapter Twenty-one

Lorri melted into Ryder's lead, dancing in perfect time to the music. It was as if they'd been dancing together for years. When he twirled her, she hitched a breath as she got lost in his blue eyes for a fleeting second. She and Craig had danced in high school, but once they got married it was all she could do to shame him into even a slow dance. She'd missed dancing.

She and Ryder danced the whole song, barely realizing the band had moved on to a different one.

By the time the second song wound down she needed to catch her breath. She let go of his hand, ready to walk off the dance floor.

"No, ma'am." He closed his fingers around her hand. "Let's keep dancing."

"Longer?"

"Until you forgive me." He spun around with her in his arms, dipping her back just a few inches, his mouth a mere whisper from hers. "How long do you think that's going to take?"

You're forgiven. But she didn't say that. "I don't know. Guess you'll just have to keep trying."

He nodded. "Okay. I'm all right with that."

When they finally came off the dance floor three songs later, it was only because they started playing the bunny hop and Ryder quickly informed her that he was no bunny hopper.

Lorri heard a man say to Ryder, "I haven't seen you dance like that since you last danced with your wife. Good to see you, boy."

When she turned to see who had said it, she realized it was the pastor. The old white-haired man was beaming. Ryder hadn't mentioned being married. It would probably make a whole lot less sense if he'd never been married at his age, but it bothered her a little that she didn't know. She wondered why they split up. Had the same pastor performed the wedding ceremony for Ryder and his wife? There was so much she didn't know.

She followed him over to the food.

"Best barbecue in the state," he said, picking up a plate.

She wondered if he was going to explain the pastor's comment. "Sounds good. I haven't eaten all day." She started piling on a bit of this and a portion of that.

He used the silver tongs to pull a hefty serving of the fresh pork onto his plate, opting for the home-cooked local specialties on the spread.

They carried their plates to a small four-topper. A server came by with mason jars of sweet tea, which they both greedily slurped down before eating.

"I really am sorry I jumped to conclusions," he said. "But really, what are the odds you'd be friends with Cody Tuggle?"

"I get it. I'd have probably thought the same thing, but if we're going to be friends we need to trust each other. Let's just forget about it, and promise to be better friends than that in the future. Deal?"

"Count on it." Ryder ate a few more bites then placed his napkin in his lap. "You know, I went looking for you at the fair that Sunday. At the quilt sale."

She stopped chewing. "You did?"

"You said you really wanted that quilt. I thought you'd be there." He paused for a moment. "I wanted to see you again."

"I wish I'd made it back, but I got busy doing things at the house and the weather was so messy I got lazy. I wonder if she sold the quilt." She took a sip of water. "Maybe I could call her."

"I've got her number. Even if she did sell it, you'd make her day telling her how much you loved it. She is an exceptional quilter, and I really don't know how she keeps churning them out at her age. She's a little machine. She has no family."

"That's sad."

"Not really. She's everyone's family now. She's at all the church functions."

"I'd like to give her a call. You'll text me her number?"

"Sure." He pulled his phone out of his pocket and sent Patsy Faber's number to her.

Lorri's phone pinged in her fancy clutch. "Thanks."

Pam walked over carrying a plate of food. "Do y'all mind if I join you?"

"Not at all." Ryder stood and pulled out a chair for her. "I need more sweet tea. Can I get you some?"

"That would be great. Thank you." Pam sat down and slid her chair to the table. She watched him walk away then leaned in. "You two look like you're having a good time. Did you know he was going to be here?"

"No. I didn't. He's a lot of fun."

"This wedding makes me wish I could do mine all over again. Not that Bobby would ever agree to it."

"This venue is amazing. I'd be lying if I didn't admit I've been choking on the fact that Craig is marrying Tiffany here."

"Yeah. This place is too good for the likes of them."

Ryder carried three mugs back over to their table. "Here you go, ladies."

Pam took one and drank from it. "Not many catered weddings get sweet tea right. They always err on the side of unsweet, and that's just not right." Pam took another sip and set down the mason jar. "How long have you lived in Dalton Mill, Ryder?"

"My whole life."

Surprise registered on Pam's face. "Never wanted to live anywhere else?"

"Never, and I've been around. Horse shows, farm events, vacations. Always great to visit new places, but there's no place like the place you've planted your roots."

Pam said, "You'd get along with my husband. Bobby thinks the same thing. Me, on the other hand, I'd love to take off for a year or two and see stuff. Calling wherever we stop home for a few months before moving on again. Eventually we'd end up back home in Raleigh though."

"My parents are doing that right now."

She laughed. "It'll never happen. Just a dream I'll die with, I guess."

"I hope not," he said quietly.

Lorri caught the darkness clouding Ryder's eyes for a moment, but it was gone just as quickly. Her imagination, maybe.

"I'm going to let you two visit. I want to talk to Cody's mom before she leaves." Pam got up and left. "Fun chatting with you, Ryder."

"Great to meet you," he said. Pam walked off and Ryder turned to Lorri and smiled. "She's nice. I could see you being best friends."

"The best. My whole life, she's the one who has been there to help pull me through whatever life has tossed my way."

"You don't seem the type that needs that much support."

"Most of the time I'm not, but . . . well . . . sometimes I overestimate my strength." She shrugged. "So, under the commitment of not making assumptions about each other," she said.

He braced himself, wondering what was about to come.

"I heard the pastor mention your wife. You were married?"

He nodded slowly. "Yes." The word came out flat, but the way he winced, his eyes crinkling, there was more to the story.

"The end of a marriage is hard. Doesn't even matter who initiated the dissolution. It's hard on everyone."

"I agree. Completely." He lowered his gaze.

"You were married a long time?"

"Not as long as I would've liked." He exhaled a breath. "It's hard for me to talk about."

"Oh." She didn't really know what to make of that. Maybe it was still too soon. She knew how that felt. "Okay."

"Wait. No. I can't let you fill in the blanks on this one." He took a moment, swallowed, and then leaned back in his chair. "I was married. My wife . . . Valerie. An amazing woman."

Pain clouded his words. What could have possibly happened? She thought of how Craig had undermined her, breaking the most important thing, trust. But then she'd never claimed he was amazing. Craig had never been that invested. She knew that now.

Had Ryder's wife left for someone else? Something else? A career. She'd worked with women who'd left husbands who couldn't handle their commitment to their careers. She could see him standing firm here in his hometown, where he'd laid roots, rather than making a move. Ryder loved Dalton Mill.

"She was a wonderful wife. Always thoughtful. Creative. Full of life."

"You really loved her." He didn't have to say it. It was in every word. It hung in the air like Christmas. You knew what it was, even though you couldn't see it or touch it.

"She was lovely inside and out. Our son. Ronnie Dwayne. He looked just like her. Handsome little guy."

A child? The gravity of him being a father saddled her for a moment. She'd dreamed of being a mother but hadn't considered the possibility of him having a child. *We're just friends. It doesn't matter.*

He looked at her and drew in a breath. "They were my whole life."

"How long ago . . ." The question hung. She couldn't imagine that kind of love going ignored. How could she have left him?

"Seven years ago." The pause was long, becoming awkward.

"Car accident on a foggy Sunday morning. Trooper said there were no skid marks. They never saw the other car coming."

Her hand swept to her heart, as if holding it in place might keep the thought of that tragedy from crushing her. "Oh my gosh." It came out as a whisper. "Drunk driver?"

He nodded.

"The most unforgivable act." Her bitter past pulled her slightly off-balance. "I'm so sorry that happened to you."

"I guess seven years is a long time, but I'll tell you, it doesn't feel like even seven minutes ago some days." His lip twitched.

"I didn't know. I'm sorry I asked. I—"

"You deserve to know. It's my baggage. Part of who I am." His voice broke. "I carry it with me every day."

You got a whole steamer trunk full of it. How unfair. There were no words to convey how she felt, or anything she could say that might soothe that pain for him. Her heart ached for this good man who had so truly loved his family.

"Not a day goes by that I don't grieve over them. Not *for* them. I do know and believe they are in a good place. Doesn't keep me from wishing I'd been driving that day though."

"I can't imagine." She looked into his eyes. "I didn't expect this." *Perspective. All I've been through seems like nothing in comparison.* Most recently the bitterness she'd harbored looking around this gorgeous wedding venue and thinking that in just a couple of weeks Craig and Tiffany would be enjoying all of it. She'd owe that forget-about-it jar about twenty bucks before the night was over at this rate.

Ryder looked right into her eyes. "I cherish them every day. It hasn't been easy, and I'm not easy to be around sometimes."

She placed a hand on his arm. "I'm truly sorry for your loss. I hope you never lose a single memory. Only that the grief will fade from black to gray where you can at least live with it."

"Spending time with you has been real nice."

"I think so too. We all have our baggage, Ryder. It makes us who we are. Sometimes it comes out in more positive ways than others, but it's all according to His plan. It's hard to trust that sometimes."

"It sure is." The words drew out, edged with the reality of pain.

It was easier to say than to live that way. Who was she to be preaching like that? It wasn't her place to judge Jeff, and yet even now she clung to that anger toward him, so much so that it impacted her relationship with her parents. Jeff struggled with his demons. Addiction, and the lying and stealing. He'd hurt so many people.

When the day came, and they were told he was dead, it had shattered her parents. For her, she'd felt the loss of her brother years before that day. They just made it official.

"Some people's baggage is more like designer luggage," she said. "Mine's like a trash bag full of a mishmash of other people's problems I can't seem to let go of. I'm working on figuring out how to deal with that."

"You don't seem like you have a problem in the world," he said.

"For the record, you don't either. You're not hard to be around. I've really enjoyed getting to know you."

"You're a good listener." He stopped as if he had more to say. "I don't ever talk about this, but I'm glad you know. If I react in a way that doesn't make sense sometimes, maybe this will help you understand why."

She waited, not wanting to interrupt him, and not really knowing what to say even if he had finished. The thought of a loss that great tumbled in her mind, landing heavy on her heart. Other people's stories had a way of putting your own problems into perspective. When Jeff died, it tore her parents apart. Even now, all these years later, they were still broken. But losing a wife and a child at the same time?

He'd dropped his focus to the table. "It was . . ."

"Devastating," she said quietly.

"Yes." He lifted his gaze to hold hers. "You know in seven years' time I've had a lot of people say a lot of things when they find out about Valerie and Ronnie Dwayne, and never has it brought me any comfort, but yes, devastating is exactly what it was. You *do* understand."

"I'd never claim to understand that kind of loss." What more could she say? She knew drunk drivers killed. "That kind of accident is heartbreaking."

"It wasn't an accident." His jaw set. "An accident is an event that happens by chance. This was no accident. This was a wreck. It destroyed my entire life. I—" He raised his hand, stopping mid-sentence. "I'm sorry. I thought I could talk about this, but I . . ." He stood to leave.

"I'll be right here if you want to come back." Her heart ached for him.

His chest heaved, a pained smile pulling across his face. "You are really something. I mean that in the nicest way."

She could see his pain, feel it in her core. "We don't have to ever talk about this again."

He placed a gentle hand on her shoulder. She thought he might actually sit back down, but then he walked off.

How does someone ever find themselves again after something like that?

She'd been cheated on. It had felt like the end of the world. In contrast to what Ryder had been dealt, it was nothing. A blip on the radar. A zit on date night. Something that would heal.

Perspective.

She'd just received a heaping dose of it.

Chapter Twenty-two

Ryder barely slept the night following the Tuggle wedding. His dreams twisted the past and the present together in weird scenarios, but one thing he couldn't shake the next morning was the feeling he'd had when he heard about how and why Cody and Kasey had created the PT Foundation. He'd come home and gone online to research their story about how putting their attention on the foundation had changed their lives and helped others.

He sat out under the awning at the Rest Stop, realizing he'd been missing out on the peace that being near the creek brought over him. He thought more clearly down here.

He was antsy to talk to Diane, Reece, and Ross about what was consuming his thoughts since last night, but knew they deserved some extra sleep after all the work that had gone into the celebrity wedding. From here he'd heard the music playing late into the night.

Ryder tacked up Thunder and rode to the family cemetery.

There he knelt in grateful prayer for the love he'd shared with Valerie and Ronnie Dwayne, which still filled his heart.

The Tuggles were to have left last night after the reception, so he'd be back in his house sometime today. He wished now he hadn't made such a big deal of them cleaning the place up. Hopefully, it wouldn't take too long. He rode over to the barn to pass the time.

It was long after that Ryder's phone chirped with a text from Ross. *We're all at Mom's eating a late breakfast. Come on over.*

On the way, Ryder texted back.

He turned Thunder and loped across the fields to Diane's house. He could smell the bacon from down the hill. By the time he got there, his stomach was growling.

"Morning, Uncle Ryder," Reece said. She was in sweats and last night's makeup, with a messy bun on her head.

"You don't look like the girl I saw last night," he teased.

She stuck out her tongue. "Well, it's me. The wedding planner extraordinaire!"

"And her partner," Ross added.

"It looked picture perfect. Sounds like everyone was pleased," Ryder said.

Diane's grin showed how proud of them she was. She slid a plate of hot biscuits onto the table.

Ryder grabbed two and opened them up on his plate. Steam rose from the center. Diane grabbed his hand and the others took hold for the prayer.

"Amen," they said together.

"They were so happy, and they weren't upset about the

security leak. They were impressed with how we handled it," Ross said, continuing the pre-grace conversation.

"Excellent." He refrained from admitting he'd thought he'd been responsible for that leak. Boy, Lorri had been mad, but she'd forgiven quickly. Thank goodness.

He let them banter about every tiny detail of the week. They were proud of the accomplishment. He was proud of them.

Finally, with their stomachs full and exhaustion overtaking the euphoria of the success, things quieted.

"I have something I want to talk to y'all about," Ryder said.

"Is this about the beautiful lady you were dancing with at the reception?" Reece gave him a wicked smile. "Oh, I noticed. Y'all looked good together. I'd forgotten you were a great dancer."

He did get a little rush of excitement from the comment, but this was not about that. "No. It's about my beautiful bride. Your aunt and cousin."

Silence fell across the table.

"What is it, Ryder?" Diane's voice held concern. She and Reece exchanged a glance.

"I was really touched by the foundation Cody and Kasey started. Making something positive out of something bad. I was thinking we should start a scholarship fund in Valerie and Ronnie Dwayne's name." He swallowed. "I think it would be good."

Diane reached over and pressed her hand to Ryder's arm. Tears welled in her eyes. "That's beautiful."

"Uncle Ryder. Why didn't we think of that?" She bopped Ross on the shoulder. "We should definitely do this as a family. It's something we can start now and carry on for generations."

Ross said, "I don't know the ins and outs of how to set that up, but I can figure it out. We could have events to help raise additional money for the scholarship program, like a fund raiser so the whole town can get involved. Host events at The Wedding Ranch."

"Wait a minute." Reece rose in her seat. "We could even have a portion of our profits go back into the foundation. Mom! Wouldn't that be perfect?"

Ryder hitched a breath.

"We've just found the focus for this farm again. No more hesitating, Uncle Ryder. We live life to its fullest in their honor and work to have others live better ones because of the loss our family experienced." Reece sniffled. "My heart is pounding. I feel like everything is coming together."

Ross said, "I'll call Cody and get some tips on how to get started."

Ryder shook his head. "I take it you think it's a good idea. I didn't expect this big of a reaction. Thank you."

"Ryder, we all lost them. We all miss them every day, too. This is such a great thing to do. We're definitely behind you on this." Diane stood and took her dish to the sink. "It'll take time to put it together. We need a plan. We'll need a logo."

"Lorri can do all the branding. She did ours and it's amazing," Reece said. "And you did dance with her all night."

"Yes, I did." He didn't regret it. "But we might come up with something on our own. I'd rather invest in the scholarship than overhead costs."

"We're all in agreement on that. We should set a goal right now for when we want to hold the first event and get it on the calendar," Ross said.

"True, because our calendar is going to fill even quicker now." Reece pulled out her phone. "Is a year too long to wait, Uncle Ryder? We can get the branding going and start working on the awareness plan now."

"The sooner the better." Ryder stood. "Doesn't have to be fancy to get started. We could do something over the holidays. People are always in the giving mood then, and it would position us for a scholarship for this year's seniors."

"We won't waste a minute," Reece said.

Diane, Reece, and Ross gathered around Ryder, holding hands. Ryder said, with tears in his eyes, "Thank you. Really."

He turned and made a hasty exit. He wasn't one to cry in front of others. Thunder tossed his head when he saw Ryder come out of the house. Ryder hopped into the saddle, giving Thunder one swift kick, and took off back down to the creek, then back over the hill where Valerie and Ronnie Dwayne were buried.

He knelt there beneath that tree until, finally, peace fell over him.

Chapter Twenty-three

It was Labor Day and Lorri was glad for the extra day off after the long weekend of celebrating with Cody. There was nothing that made her feel more alive than spending time with old friends.

She worried about Ryder. He hadn't come back to the reception. She'd stayed longer than she normally would have just in case he returned.

Pam was a night owl. That girl had always had more party in her than Lorri back when they were in school, and that hadn't changed one bit.

It had been a long night though, and she was slow moving today for it.

She went up to the loft. All of the cuttings from the mat board and framing of Cody and Kasey's present were still on the floor. She swept them into the trash and put everything away.

Then she sifted through the large portfolios lined against the wall. Work in different stages had been neglected for so long that she didn't remember how they'd started.

She was anxious to see what she could create now with so many new beautiful things inspiring her.

Mister came upstairs, a little more clingy than usual after she'd been gone so much over the weekend. He laid on the floor and lifted a brow, as if to accuse her of being the one to make a mess this time.

"I did. You're right, and you were so good. I'm going to take you for an extra-long walk today. Maybe even a ride."

His head popped up. She'd have to take him for a ride now. He already had his hopes up.

With the mess cleaned up, she sat in her chair and pulled an easel in closer. Making long, sweeping motions with a charcoal pencil, she lightly sketched an outline. She was not even sure exactly what she was creating at first but it came together quickly. She abandoned the safety of the sketch process and started dipping her brushes into paint.

She worked for hours, stopping and stretching her arms up in the air, twisting from side to side. *I haven't used these muscles in a long time.* She took her phone from the corner of the easel and was shocked to see that the day was nearly gone.

"Mister, I owe you a walk." She dropped her brush into the cleaning jar and washed her hands in the hall powder room. "Come on, buddy. We haven't even eaten all day."

She made two sandwiches, one for her and one for Mister. She had a strict rule about sharing scraps with him, but that dog adored a good PB and J, and she loved treating him to one once in a while. For each bite she took, she tossed a piece of his sandwich to him. No matter how bad of a toss she made, Mister snagged it in one hungry bite.

"Last one."

Mister anxiously shifted on his paws, watching her. Instead of throwing it, she handed it to him, and he took it with all the grace of a child. Gentle and slow.

She rubbed him under the chin as he slopped the peanut butter around in his mouth.

He followed her to get the leash and then sat on command, waiting for her to connect it and lead the way outside.

She walked the neighborhood with new appreciation of what this land once represented. A thriving family business. Crops and cattle. Generations of habits and dreams. It was hard to imagine a time when none of this was here.

One day would all the small farms in America be gone, gobbled up by developers hoping to entice families into newer, trendier homes? Someday would these neighborhoods be bought and sold again? Perhaps demolished and turned to rubble only to be cleared away to let the soil again take control and grow crops or nourish livestock? It seemed doubtful, although only fair. Then again, maybe this type of community that Bloom had created was the best of both worlds. It could be if each of the homeowners took advantage of their acreage to grow food for the community, or at least themselves. Her neighbors had chickens; they brought her eggs once a month. A neighborly gesture. She supposed the hydroponic gardens and farmers market subsidized by the college also helped. Grown on the land and purchased at a fair price by the folks living here. It felt like an equalizer, although she doubted Ryder would ever agree on that point. She couldn't blame him really.

She counted the number of homes as she and Mister walked through the neighborhood. Lorri understood Ryder's misgivings, especially since he'd thought the property would remain in their family, but all in all it seemed like a really good compromise.

It was a long walk, and Mister had slowed considerably. "You're going to have to step it up, Mister. I can't carry you home."

He looked at her as if to say, "How much farther?"

"We'll take a rest, but just for a minute."

Mister sat and panted happily.

She imagined all of this area, the lay of the land, the way it rose and fell slightly, imagining it being nothing but green fields with cattle grazing against a backdrop of an old farmhouse. Old tobacco barns like the ones at The Wedding Ranch might have dotted the area too from years gone by when tobacco was the big cash crop here. She'd heard tearing down an old barn was bad luck; did Bloom know that?

She wondered if Bloom ever thought about the legacy of the land that he bought, changing its purpose as he escorted it into a new age and purpose.

He probably believed he was doing the right thing too.

Puzzles. Life is full of them.

If she hadn't been drawn by the advertisement about the new housing development and moved here, would she and Ryder have ever crossed paths? She was strangely connected to this man. In such a short time she trusted him, and although she kept telling herself they were friends, she knew this was something stronger. Something she wasn't looking for.

"Lorri!"

She turned to see Tinsley jogging toward them. "I recognized Mister a mile away."

"Not too many like this guy around."

"Special guys are hard to find," Tinsley said. "You're lucky."

Lorri glanced down at Mister, but her brain tossed Ryder's image in front of her mind too.

"How was your weekend?" Tinsley asked.

"It was really great. I visited with some old friends. Caught up." She purposely stayed vague, afraid she'd let it slip about Cody being in town, although that probably wasn't a big deal now.

"I was wondering if I could ask you a favor."

"Sure," Lorri said. "What can I do for you?"

Tinsley patted Mister on the head. "It involves this guy. The Animal Rescue Dog Walk is coming up. We'll be raising money for the animal shelter, and I'm putting together a team with some of the girls down at the vet clinic. Would you let Mister walk with us and be our mascot?"

"Of course. He'd love that."

"There's more." She pulled her shoulders up. "I was hoping you could help me design a T-shirt to sell. I've got someone who can take the artwork to screen-print format if you can create the design. I know shirts with Mister's face on them would really sell, and that would help so much. I'll pay you for your artwork, of course."

"I'd be happy to create a design for you, but at no charge. I owe you, and Mister will love the walk." Lorri's mind was already swirling with ideas. "What size are you thinking? A front-pocket design or shirt back? Are there any requirements, colors, or logos we need to include?"

"It's sort of up to us, but I'd think having the animal shelter logo on it would be helpful. I just think a picture of Mister would be great."

"I love this kind of job where I can get creative." Lorri thought about her already busy schedule. "When's the dog walk?"

"The second weekend in October, but I was hoping to get going on the T-shirts so we can sell a bunch early, that way we could reprint more with the profit from the first sales and sell them during the event too. Kind of doubling the investment."

"I like the way you think," Lorri said. "I'll put together a couple concepts this afternoon and email them over to you."

"I can't wait." Tinsley clapped her hands. "This is so great. Thank you." She let out a breath. "So, there's something else, and I know this is none of my business—"

"But you're going to ask anyway."

She giggled. "Yes. I am, because I'm dying to know if it's true."

Lorri braced herself. She was certain Tinsley was getting ready to ask about Cody.

"Well, word around town is that you went horseback riding with Ryder. Is that true?"

"Oh?" The question caught her completely off guard. "Well, yes. We've gotten together a couple of times since he rescued me at the fair. Did you see his truck here?"

"I still can't believe he stepped foot in this neighborhood. He swore he never would."

"How did you hear about the horseback riding?" She was certain no one had seen them, and she hadn't told anyone besides Pam.

"Dalton Mill is a small town. Everyone knows everything. I don't really know how, but it's just the way it is."

"When do I get to be in the loop on all of that?"

"I guess when everyone considers you one of us," Tinsley said, shrugging it off as common knowledge. "I already do, by the way."

"Well, thank you. It would have been nice to know about Ryder's wife before I asked. I didn't realize he'd been widowed. I felt terrible for asking."

"Oh yeah. Isn't it sad?" Her eyes darted as if wondering herself. "I should've told you. I guess it's old news, everyone kind of knows, and I didn't really think about it. Oh gosh. Sorry. It really tore him to pieces. People say he used to be so different. I didn't know him before it happened. I was still so young, but Mom says he was such a great guy before that happened."

"Seems like a great guy now."

Tinsley's brow arched. "Most of the time he's grumpy. They say he used to be warm and open, a wonderful father and husband. He turned inward after he lost them. People thought it would be temporary, you know, that he'd snap out of it at some point, but he's been on autopilot for a long time now."

"That sounds terribly lonely."

"He keeps to himself and his sister and her kids. His family is everything to him. I don't think it helped when his folks sold out and left town to see the country."

"Couldn't have made it any easier."

"This is just me speculating, but I think he carried a lot of guilt. I heard he was supposed to have driven his wife to Raleigh, but he'd been racing against the rain to get the hay up. His wife didn't want to put the trip off, so she decided to drive herself."

"That would be hard to shake."

"It was some guy high on drugs and alcohol who hit them. They say his blood alcohol level was so high it was a wonder he could even press the accelerator. Drunk, high, whatever it was—those who believe addiction only hurts the addict aren't seeing the whole picture."

"You're so right." Lorri's jaw ached. She'd mourned the strangers Jeff killed while under the influence, knowing there was a family somewhere that would never be the same. Just talking about the situation made her ache with guilt too. The what-ifs that may have changed that situation always assaulting her. "My brother was an addict. It's a terrible thing. It hurts so many other people and I don't know if he ever understood that." In her brother's case it wasn't so much the illness as it was his bad choices that had torn her family apart. Like dominoes, once they started falling, they took everything in their path down.

Lorri continued, "Ryder told me a little about the accident the other night. He didn't give me details though. No wonder it's so hard for him to talk about."

Tinsley's brows lifted. "I'm surprised he told you anything at all. He must really trust you."

She realized they had built a significant bond in the time they'd spent together. Genuine trust. "We've become good friends. He's a good guy. Funny." *He makes me laugh.* "He's easy to be around."

"Good. You could use some fun. Seems like the only person you spend your time with is this guy, and he's not human."

Mister barked.

"I'm not saying that's bad," Tinsley said. "Boy, he's so sensitive."

"I promised him a ride later, so I better get this walk over with. You want to come along with us?"

"No. I've got some stuff I have to do. Thanks for lending me Mister for the walk though. I was hoping you'd say yes."

"He'll love it. Thank you for asking me to help."

Tinsley raised her hand in a wave and began jogging in place. "Can't wait to see what you come up with."

Lorri watched her run off, ponytail bouncing from the back of her ball cap. "How about that, Mister. You're going to be a star."

He picked up the pace, apparently liking the sound of that.

Chapter Twenty-four

The next day, Lorri emailed Tinsley three design ideas and a wholesale contact for the shirts, hoping her price break might help. She printed out her favorite version and hung it on the tack strip next to the multiple sketches of the many faces of Mister in her studio.

Studio.

That sounded so official. Was it truly never too late to pursue a dream?

She went back downstairs and sat at her desk to check on her work projects and make sure they were all still on time. So much of her job these days didn't even require artistic talent. They had databases loaded with stock images, cutting design time into a smidgen of what it used to be. There were times when the days dragged on. Especially when she got stuck on long conference calls where she really was supposed to do nothing but listen.

She found new joy in those long, torturous calls by sketching while listening in. Letting her mind's eye go wild as she half paid attention, waiting for something pertinent to her part of the marketing package. At the end of the week, she had several sketches that she was actually proud of, just the way they were.

Inspired to spend more time creating, she ordered art supplies and spent her extra time rearranging and readying the space for their delivery.

A week later her studio was fully stocked. Canvas, mat board, paints, and all the little extras that a real artist would have already had on hand.

She also had the final approval from Tinsley on the artwork for the Animal Rescue Dog Walk shirts. The design was some of her best work. She'd started with a realistic painting, one with Mister as the subject with playful butterflies and bees.

This morning she awoke with an idea that had her excited. She left the original artwork unscathed, scanning it and then digitally coloring the image. It turned out bright and eye-catching and very pop-art-ish. The event lettering stood out against the colorful image in a fun way. She happily worked on the changes for a few hours, then emailed Tinsley to let her know it was done so she could take it over to her screen printer.

If it's a success, I'll offer to do an original shirt design for the fundraiser each year. Maybe she'd end up being their local artist of choice. *Artist. That sounded so good.* She didn't mind doing it for free for such a good cause. She'd drop the idea to Tinsley when she saw her.

What could possibly make this day any better?

The doorbell rang. Mister bounced to his feet letting out two big woofs on his way to the front door.

Tinsley must be as excited as I am.

Lorri carried the original artwork and the thumb drive with the digital files to the door with her. Swinging the door open with a knowing hello, she was surprised to not see Tinsley standing there.

"Ryder?" *This is the one thing that could make today even better.* "It's so good to see you."

"Yeah?" He stood there holding the handles of a large brown sack. "Hope it's okay I just dropped by."

"Definitely. Please come in."

He looked relieved. "What do you have there?"

She was wondering the same about what he was carrying. Lorri turned the drawing toward him. "I thought you were Tinsley coming to pick up the graphic I created for the Animal Rescue Dog Walk. Have you heard about it?"

"I have. Let me see." He took the drawing, his face brightening. "You're good." He looked at her square on. "Really good."

"I had a good model."

"He is a good-looking dog." His mouth twisted into a goofy grin. "Maybe I could be your model one day. Can you make me look that good?" He struck a pose, then laughed it off.

Little did he know that he'd already landed in several of her sketches, but she wasn't about to tell him that.

"They wanted something they could use for T-shirts for one of the teams. They're going to sell them early to build interest in the event, and then sell them for keepsakes after. Maybe give some away as raffle prizes."

"These will sell like crazy. I'll buy one."

"Thank you." She could picture his wide shoulders filling out the shirt.

"They're holding that event over at the property behind The Wedding Ranch," Ryder said.

"I didn't know that. You know all about this event then."

"Sure. The town has always done a silent auction to raise money for the animal rescue in the past, but it's dwindled to barely breaking even so they're trying something new. People are going to love those T-shirts. I knew you were a graphic artist, but I guess I hadn't really thought about you painting and doing stuff like this. I had no idea we had such a great artist in our midst."

"I'm not an artist. I mean, I used to dream of being a real artist, but a girl has to pay the bills. I was really excited Tinsley asked me to do it. Kind of made me feel more like part of the town."

"You're a good fit around here. Not like most city folk who decide to move out to the country."

"I'm taking that as a compliment. Why are we standing here at the door? Come on in." She led the way inside.

"I'm not interrupting, am I?"

"No. Of course not. Friends are always welcome." She met his smile. "Always."

He followed her into the living room and sat on the couch, placing the bag next to his feet. "You have a really beautiful home here. This is the first time I've really had a chance to see inside. It's nice."

"Thank you."

"It's not what I'd pictured in my mind."

"Really? How so?"

He looked hesitant to say. "Don't take this the wrong way, but it's really comfortable. I like how you brought the farmhouse look on the outside, inside."

She saw him look approvingly at the sliding barn doors that could be closed to cover the opening that led to the stairs to her loft. *My studio.*

"Those barn rails are the real deal," he said. "Where'd you find these?"

"Those. Yeah. They weren't easy to find. I found the vintage rails and cast iron wheels on eBay. They were reclaimed from a train station in a small town down in Georgia. They're stamped '1903.' They cost more to ship than what I paid for them because they were so heavy, but I love how they look." She'd stained the barn doors herself, taking the extra time to distress them, so that even though they had a high-gloss furniture finish they didn't look brand new.

He got up and walked over to them, checking them out closely. "Nice work."

"The guy I hired to do the installation thought I was flat-out nuts to hang these."

"He's wrong." He looked around, nodding with approval. "Like the desk too."

"I found that piece the year I graduated from college. I fell in love with it. It was so far out of my budget, but I was determined to get it. Finally, I talked the owner of the store into letting me work off part of the price. He held that desk, displayed in the window with a sold card on it, for eight months for me."

"That's a great story. He believed in you."

"I worked my butt off to earn that desk. It was a sweet reward. It's served me well."

"Not too many folks could fit a desk that size in a home office."

"Which is why it's in my living room."

He glanced at the papers on her desk and the drawings posted on the wooden presentation board on the left-hand side.

"You do beautiful work."

"Thank you."

He walked back over and sat down. "I had a really good time at the wedding reception."

"I did too."

"Thank you for not running me off after I accused you of being a wedding crasher and tried to kick you off the property."

A blush rose from her chest to her ears. "I thought you were kidding at first, but how would you have known any differently? We're still getting to know one another. It's fine."

"But," he held up his finger, "I won't make the mistake of jumping to conclusions again."

"I know. You already said that, and I know you're a man of your word."

"You are a very unique woman, my friend Lorri." He scooted the bag closer to her with the toe of his boot. "I brought you something."

A hint of smoke lingered. He pulled out a big chunk of something.

"What is that?"

Ryder cocked his head. "Whoops. It's a femur. This isn't for you. It's for you, Mister. Come here, boy."

Mister's ears perked. He slowly got up and tiptoed toward Ryder. His nose wiggled and bobbed, dewlaps huffing the whole way.

"That is the biggest bone I've ever seen," she said. "Probably better outside though."

"Definitely. I think he's going to appreciate it." But Mister was taking his time approaching the foreign object. "Eventually."

"He's impossibly slow sometimes." They laughed as he cautiously opened his mouth and then tugged the bone from Ryder's hand and started across the room.

Lorri got up from the couch and opened the back door. "Let's take that out back." Mister moved like a walker horse, rising each foot high with the pride of a show pony. "I believe you've made a forever friend."

When she turned back around, Ryder was standing with an armful of yellow roses wrapped in shimmery silver paper.

"I hope so." He extended them toward her.

She walked toward him filled with unexpected emotion. She'd received flowers lots of times over the years, but never like this.

"What are these for?"

"For you, my friend Lorri. You are appreciated, and special, and I'm really grateful we met."

She steadied herself, trying to keep her emotions in check. The divorce had been so ugly, and this . . . this was so nice and unexpected.

"Thank you, Ryder." She pressed her nose into the bouquet. "They smell so good. Yellow for friendship. They're perfect."

"I haven't stepped out of my little family circle for a long time. Lorri, I value this friendship. The time we've spent together here recently. It's been good, and I haven't danced like that in years."

"You could've fooled me. You were great, and it was magical

under the tent, with all the twinkle lights." Swept away. By him. By the whole night. She saw it in the reflection of his eyes too. Trying to maintain balance she quickly added, "Your niece and nephew have created something very special. I see why you're so proud of them."

"Very. One day they'll carry this farm on to the next generation. It'll change. It won't be like I had it all worked out in my head, but then I suppose I need to just focus on what I can do here and now and leave the future to them."

"It's hard to not let our visions expand further than our own lifespan. I know what you mean, but the here and now . . . that's what matters."

He took her hand in his, sweeping his thumb across the top. "With you around, I'm beginning to believe that."

Is he feeling the same pull that I am? "It's not easy to let life happen around us. It leaves us feeling out of control. It's uncomfortable." She sucked in a breath, then stepped back taking the flowers into the kitchen to fill a vase with water. She came back into the living room and arranged the flowers as they talked.

"But that's the thing. I believe and know we're *not* in control," Ryder said. "There's one big plan for all of our lives—we're just custodians of our time here, and yet I fight it every single day. I have no idea why."

She sat down on the couch catty-corner from him in the chair. "I've been working on that myself. Accepting what life is handing me and trying to see the new opportunities out of the obstacles. It's not easy. When I get irritated, I try to look at the situation from another perspective, but when it's personal . . . that's when it's really hard."

"Easy to say, hard to live. Mostly I leave that to my prayers when I ride the property each morning."

"That's something else I could use a refresher on." It had been a long time since she'd counted on prayer. Craig had never been much of a churchgoer to begin with, but once they got married it had completely faded away.

"I think it's harder where family is concerned, because I want to protect everyone. My sister, Reece, and Ross, they're my whole life. Have been since I lost Valerie and Ronnie Dwayne. Do you have any brothers or sisters?"

"Yes. A brother." What else could she say about him? She didn't mean to sound uncaring. There'd been a time when she loved Jeff so much it killed her to see him begin to self-implode.

"Does he live in Raleigh?"

"He's buried there." She dropped her chin. "He struggled for a long time."

"I'm sorry. Were you close?"

"It's complicated. He was such a good kid. Way smarter than I was. People thought we were twins. We were so close when we were young."

"Diane and I have always been close."

"It was different for us. Somewhere along the way, it was early—like before junior high, he got in with the wrong people. I don't really know how it all shifted, but he started drinking and getting into trouble. He never found his way. He didn't even finish school. He'd lie, cheat, and steal without a blink, living on a constant high." She pressed her hands together. "I don't know how we ended up so different. I'm sorry. I didn't mean to lay that all on you."

"You were close once."

"Inseparable, but when he got to the point that he stole from my parents, and so many lies. I just . . . it was like I'd lost my brother. I've tried to understand it, but I can't. When I got the phone call that he'd died, I didn't even cry. I'd written him off years before that."

"You lost him twice."

"Yeah. I guess I did. In my heart, he was still that sweet boy that let me play trucks with him in the sand pit, and one time he even dressed up in a tutu to have tea with me and my stuffed animals. He was a good big brother." She lowered her gaze. "Until he wasn't. So rather than deal with the awful truth, I shut him out and held on to the good parts."

Ryder chuckled at that. "Got to cling to the happy memories. I'd have killed Diane if she tried to make me wear a tutu."

"He didn't like it much. I tried for so long to help him," she admitted. "We had the exact same upbringing and yet I had this intense drive to succeed and he was just in neutral. He had no faith that he was good enough. No faith at all. Wouldn't go to church. Not even with the family on Christmas. The drugs were all he lived for. He never had a real relationship that I know of."

"That's hard to imagine, isn't it?"

"It is. He had a very sad life. A constant struggle, and it was hard on all of us. I wonder, if we had quit focusing on the substance abuse and gotten him psychiatric help, if he may have had a chance. I think there was more at play than the addiction."

"Root cause," Ryder said. "You can't fix a problem by addressing the symptoms. Never works."

"Right. So why didn't we see that soon enough?"

"It's hard to dig down to the root cause. It's in the rotten underbelly of everything we see. It takes patience and in this microwavin', drive-thru, instant gratification age, it's nearly impossible to see things for what they are. Don't beat yourself up over it."

"Easy to say for someone else, isn't it?"

"Yes. We both need to live in the future, and put the past behind us." His words were soft, understanding.

"I've been trying."

"Haven't ever met anyone quite like you before."

"Is that good?" She eyed him playfully, trying to lighten up the moment. Why had she told him all that?

"Yes. It's very good, my friend Lorri. Troubling at the same time. I'm a little out of my element here. I haven't made a new friend in a long, long time."

She pushed her hair back from her face. "All my baggage hasn't scared you away, has it? Still friends?"

He stretched his hand out. "You will forever be considered my friend Lorri."

My friend Lorri. Those words tickled her heart. "I really like it when you say that."

"Then I'll say it more often."

Chapter Twenty-five

It was the morning of Craig's wedding and Lorri couldn't shake the black mood that hung over her. It had seemed so far off, and now it was here. Agitated with Craig and Tiffany for getting married here in her town, she couldn't help but feel like it was a personal attack.

Her phone rang, breaking the obsession for a moment, but for the first time since the day she'd given Ryder her phone number, she let it go to voice mail when he called.

The next phone call was Pam, but Lorri wasn't up to admitting the emotions or being consoled for them so she let voice mail get that one too.

Lorri was overwhelmed by her mood. The thought of the friends she and Craig had spent so many years socializing with rejoicing in his happiness with someone else practically in her own backyard was eating away at her.

Why is this bothering me so much?

Even Mister's silly antics couldn't shake Lorri from the foul mood.

She went to her purse and pulled out all the cash she had and stuffed it into the forget-about-it jar. "That should cover me for the whole doggone day."

She forced herself to go upstairs to the loft and work on the painting of the mill that she'd started, but nothing came to her. She'd sat there with paint on the tip of her brush so long that it became tacky. She dabbed one spot on the canvas, then got up to wash out the brush. She went back to her bedroom and closed the door. Mister whimpered from the hallway as she crawled into bed.

Tears over the marriage that was behind her now continued to fall. She couldn't make sense of the sorrow she was feeling. *This is what I wanted.*

She woke up an hour later, feeling sorry for herself.

She dragged the box she'd tucked on the top shelf of her closet down and sat on the bed with it. It held all kinds of memorabilia that she hadn't been able to part with. From the corsage Craig had given to her for homecoming, to their old marriage license, almost too faded to read.

My wedding day had been no more special than paying the water bill downtown.

They'd driven to the courthouse. Craig had refused to wear a suit, instead wearing khakis and a purple polo shirt. She wore a flowered dress she usually saved for special occasions. They hadn't even taken the whole day off work, instead meeting on their lunch hour that Friday afternoon. But she'd been happy with it then. She still remembered how her excitement had pushed her up the steep city building steps as she clung to Craig's hand. All she wanted was to be out of her parents' house, away from the drama that pulled all the attention onto Jeff. That marriage license had been her ticket out.

Their wedding day had been a nonevent. Not horrible, just not special. Her relationship with Craig had been more like roommates than a marriage. There had never been any fireworks. No special thoughtful gestures just because, but Craig had been there when she needed him. He'd comforted her when things went wrong and he'd been there through the worst of times. Maybe some of that was because their relationship had started so young. Each other's first, and both desperate to grow up and have freedom.

It had rained earlier. Shamefully she'd hoped for a hurricane to dampen Craig and Tiffany's day, but of course that hadn't happened. It was a beautiful blue-sky afternoon.

She wondered if Craig would wear a tux. Would there be lots of guests? Would she know most of them? How many tiers would the cake have?

Did we even have a cake to celebrate our wedding? Certainly we must have.

Something happened while those questions rolled through her head.

The need to know consumed her.

She'd been to Ryder's often enough now she knew how to get to The Wedding Ranch the back way. He'd accused her of crashing Cody's wedding, so certainly crashing this wedding shouldn't be that hard. There wouldn't even be security.

It wasn't like she planned to stand up and object to the wedding. She just wanted a little peek. What was wrong with that?

She didn't have much time though. Lorri leapt into action, showering and putting on makeup, fluffing her hair. She slipped into a simple buckskin-colored dress, black belt at the waist, and black shoes.

She twisted in front of the full-length mirror. Tasteful, she thought. Subtle enough to blend into the background, which is exactly what she planned to do. Five more bucks in the forget-about-it jar was not going to cover this.

The whole drive to the back entrance of Ryder's property Lorri told herself this was a bad idea, but that didn't stop her. She parked and started walking toward the venue.

Hopefully, no one noticed her tromping through the field. Leaves had started to fall from the trees, and there wasn't near the coverage there had been when Cody and Kasey got married here.

She stepped out of her shoes, carrying them before she broke an ankle. That would be awful. She could see it now. The ambulance four-wheeling through the hayfield to get to her. Way worse than almost being run over by a runaway steer. At least there'd been a silver lining in that. If it hadn't been for that crazy cow, she might not have ever met Ryder.

What am I doing here?

But she'd already come this far. Satisfying her dying curiosity wouldn't take but a few minutes.

She quick-stepped between two buildings, and tucked herself inside the tall tobacco barn. There were no benches set up outside like there had been at Cody and Kasey's wedding. She remembered Tinsley talking about how creative the twins were, switching up the venue to make each event unique. Today the venue had an enormous amount of pink.

She turned, and standing only a few feet away from her was the bride with her back to her. She'd recognize her a mile away even if that little Yorkie hadn't been dancing along the edges of her lacy train.

Lorri skirted back outside, almost sick to her stomach. Tiffany's wedding gown was beautiful. Soft off-white, simple, and elegant. Even though summer was over, Tiffany's body was still as tan as if she'd walked off the beach under the tropical sun yesterday.

Leave. Just leave.

But her feet had other ideas. Crouching slightly, she walked around to the other side of the tobacco barn. Her heart pounded so loud she was certain anyone within three yards could hear it.

She slipped her shoes back on, and tried to look like she belonged as caterers rushed past her carrying covered pans into the old barn.

Standing off to the side, she recognized a lot of the guests, laughing and enjoying themselves. Her eyes hopped from one couple to the next. She knew the majority of the guests. Stacy and Carmen and their husbands stood talking to another couple. Embarrassment flooded over her. *What am I doing? What did I expect?*

Her breath caught in her throat when she heard someone call out her name from behind her.

She turned in that direction.

Ryder? He was walking toward her wearing a huge smile.

She glanced at the surrounding people. Everyone was so busy with their own conversations no one else seemed to have noticed, thank goodness, but figuring out how to explain what she was doing here to Ryder after the big deal she made about him accusing her of crashing Cody's wedding, that wasn't going to be elegant at all.

"Hey, you look beautiful. I didn't know you were coming today."

She couldn't lie to him. "Surprise." She backed into the building. Thankfully he followed without her having to tug him in like it was a kidnapping.

"Friend of the bride?" he asked.

"Definitely not. She's marrying my ex-husband."

Ryder's neck lurched forward. "What?"

"I shouldn't be here." She grabbed his hands. "I was just so nosy, and was going to take a little peek, and now here I am—how am I supposed to get out of here without them seeing me?"

He laughed. "No way. You really are crashing this wedding."

She peeked around Ryder and saw Craig walking in her direction. "It's not funny. It's horrible and I'm humiliated to have to admit it to you, but now my ex is coming this way." She pulled in close to Ryder's chest. "Please don't let him see me."

She could feel Ryder's breath on her forehead.

"That's the guy who cheated on you?" Ryder's jaw pulsed. "Doesn't surprise me."

"Shh. He's coming." She ducked, pulling herself closer to Ryder, all the while wishing to disappear.

Craig's voice carried over the noise. "Lorri? Is that you?"

She tensed, dreading the next moment when Craig got close enough to confront her.

A gentle hand tipped her chin. Ryder pressed his lips to hers.

It was doubtful that even holding her breath, bracing herself for the worst, could leave her this dizzied. She responded to his kiss, relishing the way his strong hands moved her so effortlessly, and with just the brush of his lips, her heart beat twice as fast.

He walked her into the shadow of the building out of sight, but then didn't waste a second. "Come on." He grabbed her hand and broke into a run.

Unsteady from that kiss, she let Ryder whisk her away and then out through the bushes. Cars were double and triple parked all around them.

She followed behind him as he zigged, then zagged, and finally darted between two vehicles heading for a merlot-colored gangster-style car in the middle of the driveway.

"Go. Get in," he said, swinging her past him into the bushes next to the car.

"What? I can't steal someone's car."

"Jump in the passenger seat and hunker down. I'll be there in a minute."

She hesitated, but she didn't have much choice. Hoping for the best, she waited until the valet walked off to park another car. She darted out and jumped into the front passenger seat of the fancy ride.

Collapsing into a puddle on the floorboard she wished she could wiggle her nose and disappear. If anyone discovered her, she didn't know how she'd talk her way out of this one.

The door handle clicked, and the driver's-side door opened. She heard the jingle of keys and the engine turned over. She opened her eyes, relieved to see the familiar leather cowboy boots mash the gas pedal.

"Stay down," he whispered. The car swerved to the left and then to the right, then sped along for a ways before it halted. "Come on, my friend Lorri. You can get up. The coast is clear."

She scrambled to get her legs up under her, and turned to sit in the seat. "Oh my gosh. I'm so sorry. This is so not like me."

He kept laughing. "I've never driven a getaway car before."

As mortified as she was, she had to laugh too.

"You were seriously married to that guy?"

"I was."

"Well, those two are a piece of work. They deserve each other. They have been a huge pain for the twins. Bridezilla and that little dog, and your ex, well, he is about the biggest blow-hard I've ever met."

"That's him."

"You deserve better."

"Thank you." She took in a big breath. "Cody's wedding was so beautiful, and we had such a wonderful night. The thought of Craig and that woman getting married there, experiencing that, it gnawed at me."

"It shouldn't."

"I just couldn't let it go. I had to see for myself, and I was so relieved that although it was way nicer than my wedding to Craig, it was nothing like the night we were there."

His eyes were soft, his voice kind. "I think that had more to do with the company than the venue."

Her mouth grew cottony. She touched her lips. "It was a night I'll never forget."

"Me either."

"Then why can't I let this go? I don't want to be with Craig. I'm very happy. So why did I do that?"

"You're asking the wrong person. I've been trying to figure out how to move on for years. The past is what we know. The future . . . it's uncharted territory."

"It is." She pressed her fingers to her face. "I'm so embarrassed."

"Well, no one knows but you and me. Let's pretend it didn't happen."

"How am I supposed to do that?"

"You're dressed real pretty. Let's turn this around. A do-over. I just picked you up for an afternoon date."

"A date?" *Is he kidding?* "A real date?"

He nodded.

She took in the fine interior of the vehicle. "This *is* a really nice car."

"A '34 Ford five-window coupe. It belonged to my great-grandfather. He bought it new. When he died he handed it down to my grandfather. My dad was never the car guy I was, so when my grandfather died no one was surprised when he left it to me. Pop-Pop and I would tinker on this thing for hours." He lovingly patted the steering wheel. "I always feel close to him when I'm driving this."

"That's so special."

"I was supposed to drive the bride and groom away today."

"What? Oh my gosh. You've got to get back."

"Nope." He shook his head. "They don't deserve to enjoy it. I texted Ross. He is over the two of them, too. He said he'll play dumb and blame the vendor."

"Leave them stranded?"

"They won't be stranded. There are a hundred cars in that

lot. Besides I was just driving them around the block to where the jackass groom parked his car so they could drive themselves to the airport. He was too cheap to book the whole excursion."

"He must be paying for it. He's much freer with other people's money."

"He's a winner. I can't picture the two of you together. Not at all."

"We were young." There was really no other explanation, except that sometimes you needed distance to see the real picture. She'd gotten oodles of advice over the years, plenty of folks telling her he was no good. "In my imagination, I saw him for who I wanted him to be. Not who he really was."

Am I doing that now with Ryder?

"I have to ask you something." She pulled her feet up into the seat of the car and faced him. Almost afraid to hear the truth . . . she had to know. "About that kiss? Was that my imagination too? Is there really any way that two people who've known each other for such a short time could—"

Ryder pulled off to the side of the road, leaned over, and put his hand behind her neck, kissing her again, only there was no rush.

And this time she had no question what it meant, as she tried to catch her breath.

He sat back.

She touched her lips. "This is real, isn't it?"

"So real. I was afraid to say it out loud else it might disappear, but this—you and me—this isn't going anywhere."

"Oh my gosh." She held her hands to her heart, as a tear slipped down her cheek.

Chapter Twenty-six

Ryder got back on the road and drove three towns over to a small inn with a diner known for its home-style cooking. "It's not fancy, but it's a date."

He got out of the car and walked to the other side to let her out. He took her hand and guided her to the door, one hand on the small of her back.

"Two for an early dinner, please."

The silver-haired woman had sparkling blue eyes. "My pleasure. Will you two follow me?"

They did, and as he pulled out Lorri's chair, the woman said, "Today is special for the two of you, isn't it?"

Lorri nodded, and Ryder said, "Very much."

"May I have the pleasure of choosing your menu for you today?"

They looked at each other. "Can't say anyone has ever offered before. That sounds lovely." Ryder reached across the table and took Lorri's hand in his.

He liked showing her around Dalton Mill, telling her the history about things, and surprising her. She reacted with enthusiasm at the smallest of things. She could afford any of it on her own, yet she was so humble and appreciative. Even something so small as presenting her with her own brush for Dottie. Something that would stay on his farm, but she was as delighted as if it had been jewelry.

The more he got to know Lorri, the more he wanted to know and the more he wanted to share with her.

It made him feel special to lift her up with those little kindnesses, but sitting here with her today he realized there was even more about her that was precious to him.

They were served a beautiful pastry-wrapped chicken dish with fresh collards and carrots. "The presentation is lovely," Lorri said.

"I hope you two enjoy it."

"We will." He watched as the woman disappeared into the kitchen. With it being so early in the afternoon, they were the only two in the restaurant. "I'd enjoy a peanut butter sandwich right now. Who knew driving the getaway car worked up such an appetite?"

"I'm hungry too."

They ate the special entrée and celebrated with a slice of chocolate cake.

"One piece, two forks," Ryder had said.

Lorri fought him for the last bite, and he liked that about her.

"Are you ready to get back to town?"

"I hope the party is over."

He pulled out his phone and texted someone. "They are cleaning up. You're home free."

He settled the bill with the woman, then walked Lorri back out to the car. "How did you get to The Wedding Ranch this morning?"

"I took the back road. The way we went when we went horseback riding."

"Aren't you clever. You walked through that field? That's a hike."

"I was determined."

"Was it worth it?"

"Not really. No, I take that back. If that's the humbling road I needed to take to get us to here . . . I'm glad I did it."

"Me too. Plus, I kind of like this adventurous side of you."

"It's new."

He drove her to her car. "It was a good day."

"It was. I guess now I can remember this day as our day, not his."

"Me too. Mind if I come by tomorrow evening? I want to take you to dinner."

"I'd like that."

He watched her drive off, then sat down in the grass, listening to the creek in the distance and letting nature happen around him. It was nearly dark by the time he got into the old car and put it back in the garage.

The next day he drove over to Lorri's. He planned to clarify some of those early vague answers he'd given her before. He rapped on the wood door next to the colorful fall wreath she'd recently hung. He wasn't usually a fan of that girly kind of stuff, but this wreath was void of ribbons and ruffles. Vivid maple leaves in a range of colors swirled around a twig base, and wheat, cotton pods, and even dried soybeans filled the circle. All it lacked were a few golden tobacco leaves; maybe he'd bring her a couple, or ask her to make him one.

"You're early. I love that about you."

"Dad always said if you're going to be late don't even bother. I guess he drove that into me."

"A good habit, but I think I'd rather have you late than not at all. Come on in. I'll let Mister out and we can leave."

"You don't need to do that."

"I thought we were going to dinner?"

"Yes, we are, but I'm cooking for you. At my house, and Mister is invited."

"Well, how about that, Mister?" Her mouth dropped, surprised, but pleased. "He'll love it."

He'd let her think he lived down at the creek; this was one of those vague pieces of information he needed to correct. "Yeah, about the Rest Stop. That's not where I live."

"No?"

He shook his head. "That's my hideaway. The kids needed my place for your friends to stay while they were in town."

"Cody and Kasey?"

"And their son, yes. So I stayed down there for the week while they used my place."

"You really *are* a good sport."

"Family. It was really a minor imposition. I used to hang out down at the creek all the time. I'm glad the situation forced me to do it again."

"Me too, else I may have never experienced that. I'd love to go now that the leaves are in their full color. I know it's gorgeous."

"It is."

"You'd do anything for Reece and Ross. I like that about you."

"When I agreed to let them lease those few acres to start The Wedding Ranch, I promised I'd do whatever I could to help them make it work. It's not exactly my kind of thing, but they both believe in it so much."

"That's really neat."

"Well, I didn't think that through very well. I've been kicked out of my house, driven horse and buggies, even chauffeured people from the airport in my pickup truck. People want these authentic country, farm, or western weddings, and they are paying big-time for it. My old tractor has spent more time on photo shoots than in the fields the last year."

"I think it's nice." She grabbed a light jacket. "So where do you live then?"

"Not far. Just up the road. Y'all ready?"

"Absolutely." Lorri grabbed Mister's leash, but didn't put it on him.

He jumped right into Ryder's truck, hanging his head between the seats as Ryder drove out of the neighborhood to the main road. Instead of left toward the venue, he took a right and followed the road around two sharp curves. There was nothing but farmland out in this direction, and she'd only been this way a time or two. He slowed to turn into a driveway between tall stacked stone pillars. Fancy wooden gates parted. As they drove forward they went under a huge timber that spanned the whole driveway. Black iron plates connected them like one of those old Texas ranch entrances.

"It's like Southfork," she said, referring to the fancy estate on the show *Dallas* she'd seen in reruns.

"Hardly. This is rough-cut timbers and working solutions, no high society."

"It's beautiful just the same."

"Thank you."

The old farmhouse with a wraparound porch stood out bright white against the land. Wooden barns in the hues that only weather and age can create looked warm below the shiny metal roofs.

"You look surprised," he said.

"Well, I am. I thought you lived at the Rest Stop. Nothing wrong with that, but it's a far cry from this."

"My sister, your veterinarian, lives just over there." He pointed toward a more modern brick home sitting up on the rise. He got out and walked around to her side.

When he opened the door, Mister bounded to the ground. A chicken clucked and called out a frantic squawk as Mister took a leap toward it.

"Mister!" Lorri hopped out and raced in that direction. "No. Bad dog."

Ryder stood there laughing. "Don't worry. He'll figure it out."

Hopefully, I will too.

Lorri came back out of breath. "I'm so sorry. If he catches one, I promise to replace it."

"The chickens can get back in the coop if they're scared. They've been chased by far more adept hunters than your house pet. We've got coyotes and fox out here. I'm not worried about them in the slightest."

She seemed to calm down. He ushered her inside and straight into the kitchen. The brick floor told of days gone by, especially in places where it was worn smooth. He liked the history that held. Although the appliances were all brand new, the big fireplace at the far end was his favorite part. Old and reliable. He'd started the fire earlier and the coals glowed hot. He planned to treat Lorri to his famous cast iron cooking tonight.

"The fire is nice," she said.

"I'm cooking our dinner there. Old cowboy style. Cast iron and Dutch ovens."

"What's on our menu?"

He leaned against the kitchen island, gripping the hefty butcher block in his palms, and crossing one boot over the other. "Steaks, and I'm hoping you like them rare."

"I do."

"I knew I liked you. Most city folk seem to want to cook the life out of a steak, or smother it in marinade and sauces. Not me. Let's see, also have some sweet potatoes, broccoli, and my famous fire-roasted cornbread."

"Famous?"

"Famous around here, and apple cobbler."

"Oh my gosh. You really *can* cook. I don't know how I can

help, but you tell me what to do, and I'll try my best. I'm good at following directions."

"I don't mind being the cook around here."

"I don't mind that either."

He put his arm around her waist. "I'm really glad you're here."

He handed her an apron, then put one over his head and tied it behind his back. Standing there in her green and white apron, she looked cute and completely uncomfortable, but being with her just got easier and easier.

He placed a bowl of mushrooms on the island in front of her. "You can handle this. Slice them into smaller pieces and toss them in this bowl." He plucked the stem from one of the bigger mushrooms. "Just pull the stems like this. We won't use that part."

She did as he showed her while he worked on getting his cast iron pieces in place and seasoning the steaks. Then he mixed the cornbread recipe.

She leaned over the skillet looking at the soupy mixture. "That's going to turn into bread?" She shook her head. "I'm no cook, but I'm pretty sure that's impossible."

He put the pan on the coals and covered it with the heavy lid.

"Trust the process, my friend Lorri."

It struck his happy button, the way she giggled when he called her that.

Smells mingled with the hickory he'd just added to the fire, a sweet and savory mix. Ryder turned on some music, and they settled in the chairs in the keeping room on the other side of the fireplace. Comfortable conversation stole the time, and when he glanced at his watch it was past the time he'd meant to check on things.

He used heavy gloves and tongs to lift the lids.

"Dinner is ready." He carried the dutch oven to the counter to slice the steaks into narrow strips, pulling all the fatty edges off and piling them into a bowl.

"Those steaks are massive!"

"Mister. Dinner's ready." He leaned close. "I knew I had that guy to feed."

"Oh my gosh," Lorri said. "He'll never eat dog food again."

"Sure he will."

Mister gobbled the dish of beef, then sprawled out on the floor. Ryder pulled the Dutch oven off the fire. He fixed their plates in the kitchen, then they went into the dining room.

He pulled out a heavily upholstered chair for Lorri. The flower arrangement looked like he was trying too hard, but it was truly just a happy accident.

"My niece cleans my house," he explained as he took his seat. "She does stuff like that." He twisted the pumpkin-shaped vase to the side, so he could see Lorri better. "Didn't want you to think that was my doing. Flowers aren't my thing, although I do like them."

"I like it."

"Me too. Makes it feel homier. You deserve them. I just didn't want to take the credit."

"Thank you."

"Dig in while it's hot."

They ate, not bothering with a lot of small talk. He gave her a few cooking pointers and promised to cook for her again.

"I'm stuffed," she said, placing her napkin on the table. "That was a five-star meal."

"I'm glad you liked it. I'll pack up some leftovers for you. I always cook too much. I can't seem to remedy that."

"My lucky day." She pushed her chair back. "I'll help you clean up."

"No. Let me do it, please? Make yourself at home."

"You don't mind?"

"No. It won't take me but a few minutes. I've got a system. Then we'll eat cobbler on the patio."

"Okay, but no cobbler for Mister. I put my foot down on sweets."

"Fine. You're the boss." He cleaned up and dished dessert into two small oval dishes. He used a melon scooper to put ice cream on each and then drizzled a thin line of dark chocolate across the top.

He walked out of the kitchen with the dessert, looking for Lorri. He saw her in the study standing at Valerie's secretary, a piece her mom had found at an auction in Virginia. Lorri's hand shook as she lifted the picture of Valerie and Ronnie Dwayne.

The silver frame had been a wedding present. Ornate and heavy. The black and white photo had been taken in the hayfield the summer before the wreck. He could still hear their laughter when he looked at it.

He wondered what she heard.

He watched her trembling fingers move from the picture

to the article that had run in the local paper. He wished he'd thought to put it away. His insides screamed for her to move away from it.

She did and he breathed a sigh.

Lorri must've heard him exhale. Her hands retreated to her sides.

With a forced smile she said, "You collect butterflies," nodding toward the collection displayed in the glass shadow box hanging on the wall. "That's how you knew that yellow one was a lisa that day when we were riding."

"I don't. My sister, Diane, used to collect them. She's always loved them. I learned from her." He walked over to a shelf. "Me? I collected rocks."

"Rocks?"

"Mm-hmm. Still do sort of. When I was young, I could entertain myself all day long sifting through the gravel they brought for the driveway. It was a private road back then. I just knew I was going to find rubies and emeralds. As I got older, I learned about the gemstones that could be found here in North Carolina. I have a ton of them. This isn't even half of them." He pulled out small square drawers, one at a time. "Emeralds, jasper, rubies—"

"That's not a ruby. Rubies are red." She raised her hand, flaunting the ruby and diamond band on her right hand. "I know. They're my birthstone."

"It might not look like much in its raw form, but I assure you those are rubies. Come here." He led her to his desk on the other side of the long room. He'd made it from a jeweler's display case, using big chunky wooden legs from a table that had seen better days, and the glass case as the top. Beneath that glass were all kinds of gems, some polished, others just piles of dusty rock, rough stones and cut ones, gold and silver clasps and catches. Projects in process lay sprawled in a collage. On top, his tools lay scattered on the leather mat.

He reached into the case and withdrew a single bluish-gray feather. "I found this while I was working one day. From the color and length, I think it might be from a blue heron. I'm not sure, but I thought it would make a pretty hat feather." He handed it to her.

Her eyes lit. He'd attached tiny red gemstones somehow to the thick sturdy vein running down the center of the feather. "Are those rubies?"

"They are."

"This is really neat. Where did you get the idea?"

"It just came to me one day. A way to put two things from nature together. I've always worn feathers in my cowboy hats, and this seemed like a nice way for a lady to do the same by making it prettier with the stones I'd collected."

"You should sell these."

"I just do it for fun. My sister has one. I made Reece a white one with pink quartz down the center. It turned out real nice. She says she gets compliments from customers all the time."

"I'm sure she does. I'd love to see that one. Not that I wear hats, but I bet this would make a beautiful lapel pin or pendant on a long necklace."

He lifted his hat from a hook on the wall and placed it on her head. He stepped back. "You look great in a hat."

"Really?" She self-consciously reached up for it.

"Yeah. I like it. A lot."

"Thanks. Who knows, maybe there's a little cowgirl in me?" She playfully shrugged.

"Oh, I think there is. I saw you sit that horse."

"It's so interesting to me that a manly man with rough edges—well, not rough, but you know what I mean. An outdoorsman. An expert of land and livestock. Cooking the old-fashioned way even. This collection, the artistry of the jewelry and feathers is nice. You're a multifaceted man."

She closed her eyes for a second.

"Ryder, I saw the look on your face when you came into the room. We can't ignore that. I'm talking a mile a minute because I'm uncomfortable. I know you were too."

"I was."

"I'm sorry. You're upset. I didn't realize . . ." She stepped back. "I—it just caught my eye. I should've asked before I came in here. I can see it's personal."

"No. I told you to make yourself at home. How could you have known? I didn't." He walked over and put the article in a drawer. "Some things are still so present."

"I'm sure." She ran her hand along the top of the glass-topped desk. "How long were you two married?" She hitched a breath. "No. You don't have to answer that."

"That's a fair question. We were married for six years. Doesn't sound that long, but we dated forever. Local girl. It was hard on the whole town when I lost her."

Lorri's lips parted, but she remained silent.

"Our son, Ronnie Dwayne, was the spitting image of her. He was four. They'd gone up to Raleigh to visit a friend. I was going to drive them, but rain had messed up my schedule. She didn't want to reschedule. It was one night away. They'd planned to be home early on Sunday so we could go to church together."

He watched her swallow, her eyes glistening.

"They didn't know what hit them. The man who broadsided them had been drinking all night, and who knows what else. He didn't even realize what he'd done. He was staggering in the street screaming because my wife wouldn't get out of the car and talk to him when the police arrested him."

Lorri stood there shaking her head.

"She was already gone." He walked a step or two. "These were her things. Most of them. The feathers, the rocks, those are mine, but everything else in here was Valerie's with the exception of Diane's old butterfly collections." His throat tightened. "This room is full of things I loved. Everyone loved Valerie."

"You must miss them so deeply."

"I do."

"It's yours to hold close."

He turned his back to her, trying to keep his emotion in check.

She placed a hand on his shoulder, her touch light, but so soothing. "If there's something I can do, or just listen . . . please let me. I can just be here and not talk at all."

She would. He believed that. He turned to her. "We're a pair, aren't we? Battle scars and all."

"Yes. We kind of are. Emotional baggage," she said.

"Whatever name you put to it. It hurts."

"Right. Why we both just wanted to be friends, for example, and maybe why it seems like so much more already."

"Doesn't make much sense from the outside looking in. Might even look downright stupid, but a person has their reasons."

"I'm so sorry I touched a nerve being in here. I'd never want to make you uncomfortable, much less hurt you."

"I know that."

"Should I leave?"

He hesitated, but as much as those old feelings had crashed over him when he saw her holding Valerie and Ronnie Dwayne's picture, the comfort in having her here was just as big.

"No. I don't want you to leave, and I thank you for understanding." He placed his hand on the small of her back and guided her to the door. "Let's go on the porch and eat this cobbler before it gets cold."

Chapter Twenty-seven

Under the moonlight, they enjoyed the apple cobbler Ryder had cooked cowboy-style over the fire. She had no idea how something on and under the coals could produce this kind of delicate dessert. The sweet crunchy topping mingling with the fresh-picked apples was a pleasing combination that set off the meal just right. As she savored her last bite, she was sorry the evening was coming to an end. Darkness had fallen over them, cloaking them in darkness except for the light from the fire.

The embers sparkled much like those gemstones Ryder collected. He too had an artist's eye. He just hadn't realized it yet.

The words from her childhood pastor flooded back. God doesn't give us anything just for our own benefit. She'd always considered painting her gift. Maybe that's why she was now being so drawn to it again. There was more she needed to do with her gifts.

"You all done?" Ryder asked.

"Yeah. Sorry, I was kind of daydreaming."

"I noticed. Something good?"

Lorri placed her fork in her bowl. "Yeah. I was thinking about this town. How it inspires me."

"It'll do that. You know, I've been talking to the family, well, Diane, Reece, and Ross, about starting a scholarship fund in Valerie and Ronnie Dwayne's memory."

"That's beautiful."

"Thank you. I want to figure out how to shift my thoughts to something positive so the memories won't be as painful. I think Valerie would love this idea, and I know she wouldn't be proud of the way I've stalled without her here."

"Well, don't beat yourself up on that. If it takes twenty years for you to heal, it's no one else's timeline but your own. Don't forget that, but it's such a wonderful gesture."

He nodded.

"I could do the branding for you. Any idea what you'll call it? Bolt Memorial Scholarship maybe?"

"No. Something simple and generic. I'm not looking for recognition for it. The mission behind it is personal, but others don't need to know that it's a memorial scholarship. Maybe just Dalton Mill Scholarship, or since I'd like it to be awarded to students with an eye toward agriculture in some way, maybe we'll tie that in."

"Good idea. Maybe something as simple as the Ranch Scholarship."

"I like that. I really like that a lot, and since The Wedding Ranch is pooling a percentage of all of their profits into the fund too, it's a cool tie-in." Then Ryder turned to Lorri. "Or we could call it the Lisa Scholarship. You know, like the butterfly.

Diane always said the yellow ones were symbols of hope and guidance toward positive change."

"Then I think that's the one to go with." Design ideas were already fluttering in her mind.

"I agree. It's a good change. Diane will like it too." He pressed his hand to her leg. "Thank you."

She couldn't deny the feelings that came over her when they touched. She leaned into him. *Will being just friends really be enough?* If he kissed her now, she wouldn't stop him. She might not leave at all. She lowered her gaze, wishing he'd tip up her chin and kiss her.

"Reece and Ross are going to set up some events to raise money. I've got Ronnie Dwayne's college fund. I never stopped paying into it since the day he was born. Nice chunk of change to seed the account."

"I'd be happy to design shirts, or maybe offer a painting if that would help."

"That would be great."

"You should put up a few of those beautiful feathers with the stones on them. Maybe even turn one into a necklace?"

"So you can bid on it," he teased.

"I would." She hoped he'd say yes. "Reece and Ross are smart. They could figure out how to take it online to expand the reach. I think some unique and one-of-a-kind things are important."

"I don't want people knowing I make those feathers. I do it for the joy of it. It would ruin that."

"People love you, that would drive the price right up!"

"No. I feel funny about that."

"Well, then put them up without any information on the art-ist. No rule against that. Whatever I can do, you let me know. I could work on any branding you might need." She stood and held up her plate, looking around for a trash can. "Where do you want me to put this?" Lorri reached her hand out to him. "I can take yours too."

"Best thing about all of these plates and the cutlery is you can toss them in the fire. Totally disposable."

She lifted the wooden utensils from the bowl. "These too?"

"Completely. Ross is all into that zero-footprint thing. He gave them to me for Christmas a couple of years ago and I'm hooked. Go ahead. Throw them in."

Hesitant, she waited to see if he was going to stop her, but he didn't. As soon as they hit the coals the flames licked the edges of the bowls making them disappear into curling smoke. Embers sparkled along the edges of the utensils, burning them quickly to nothing but ash. "I don't mind doing dishes as much as I thought," she teased.

"It's kind of liberating, isn't it?"

"It sure is." She brushed her hands together as she watched Ryder push dirt over the fire and secure the area.

"You ready to go?"

"Guess so." But that wasn't entirely true. It was hard to leave, and it was getting harder to say goodbye to him.

Ryder drove her and Mister home, walked her to the door, and kissed her lightly on the cheek. "Thank you for a wonder-ful evening." There was something more in his voice that she couldn't put her finger on.

She and Mister went inside. She got undressed and showered.

So much had happened between her and Ryder in the short time they'd known one another. Something real. She felt it when they were apart. Needed it when they were together.

In her bedroom she lifted the blinds, wanting to sleep beneath those twinkling stars. Lorri slipped under the covers and lay there looking out at the sky. The moon was a sliver. Mister laid beneath the window, exhausted from their busy day.

The next morning, she resisted the urge to call Ryder and thank him again for the night.

It's an excuse. I already said thank you last night.

She had plenty to do, and even though she thought of Ryder often throughout the day she didn't call.

Her calendar was full of meetings, and two new proposals to work on. One was for a bookstore chain slated to open twelve locations in closed movie theatres in major cities across the country. It would take the bookstore experience to a venue where booklovers could gather for live hosted events or via satellite on the big screens. It was a great concept. The other was annual updates to the Ford automotive materials. She'd been in charge of those for over six years now. It was a huge amount of work, but they were never looking for anything very different, preferring the vehicles to be the draw, so it was more project housekeeping than creativity.

At the end of her workday, she was satisfied with all she'd achieved, but disappointed that Ryder hadn't reached out.

She fed Mister then let him out back, taking her laptop with her. A bird fluttered from a branch to the new birdhouse, making it sway under his weight.

Mister took off across the yard after a squirrel who'd already scaled a tree and hopped to another before he ever made it over. He stood there looking a bit defeated.

The bird squawked, as if warning Mister, or maybe he was making fun of him. Poor Mister. He wasn't the hunting type. No, he was slow even at full speed; only the length of his legs gave him the advantage to make it anywhere in a hurry.

His nose to the ground, he traced the curling trail of some animal that must have crossed the yard recently.

She opened her laptop and searched for the article she'd seen in Ryder's study. She'd only had a moment to scan the details.

She typed in Ryder's name first. A long list of agriculture boards, hay for sale, even an article about The Wedding Ranch filled her screen. Apparently, he'd been the prize pitcher of the Dalton Mill High School baseball team, setting records and even being scouted for the minors. He'd tried to stop the land sale between Bloom and his parents to no avail.

There were no pictures of him playing baseball, but she did run across one of his house before the porch and shutters were added. There was also an aerial of the entire spread. The best she could tell, she was situated just below where his parents' house had once been. Maybe in their old front yard. *That must be weird for him. Small world.*

She continued her search trying other keywords. Finally, by searching the name of the local paper, then going through the archives from seven years ago, she was finally able to track down the article.

She took her time reading through it word for word this

time. There weren't many facts about the accident itself. It was more of a local interest story telling about why Valerie had been in Raleigh that morning, and the loss it was to the community. She'd driven to visit a former Dalton Mill resident, Agnes Dewey, who'd been moved to an assisted living center to be closer to her daughter. Valerie and her four-year-old son spent the afternoon and evening with Mrs. Dewey, bringing her Valerie's homemade strawberry preserves. They'd worked on a puzzle made from a photograph of butterflies taken on the family's farm that summer.

The journalist clearly understood the little things mattered the most. The mention of the homemade preserves and the puzzle seemed so familiar that she felt connected to the people in the story.

Valerie must've been a special woman. She could see Ryder having wanted to drive them himself, but he'd never have told her not to go. That would have been selfish, and Lorri knew there was nothing selfish in that man's spirit.

The last line of the article was vague, mentioning the driver of the other car had been convicted of two prior DUIs.

Familiar anger settled in Lorri's chest. The kind that stole her breath. She'd lived through this emotion before.

What makes people so reckless?

It's one thing to abuse yourself, but when you let that abuse drive irrational thinking that takes another life—unforgivable.

Her brother had well-greased this pipeline of emotion over the years.

She couldn't imagine the pain Ryder experienced. Losing a spouse was hard; losing a child had to have been agony—

especially without his spouse there to share the burden of that loss. She'd do anything to help him survive that sorrow.

A shiver ran through her.

She printed out a copy of the article, reading it one more time.

Only this time the similarities struck her in a different way. Her heart sunk and her hand began to tremble. She hopped up and ran upstairs to her studio where she'd tucked the personal box of Jeff's things in the attic. Scrambling, she pushed the other things that had been shoved in front of it since then and dragged the box into the room.

She dug to the bottom where the court records were. Flipping through the papers she stopped and slowly reread the details of the accident. This time she was reading it with a new perspective.

Please don't let it have been Valerie and Ronnie Dwayne.

Her heart pounded. A tear slipping down her cheek as she tried to focus on the words on the page. *Where is it?*

She found what she was looking for. Her hand to her mouth she whispered, "No." She stared at it, reading the names over and over again.

"No. Please wake me up and tell me I'm dreaming. It can't be. This isn't fair."

God be with Ryder, and help him live his life with their love in his heart.

She'd be no comfort now. *My fault.* Not directly, but by way of not finding a way to stop Jeff's self-destructing behavior from destroying Ryder's family.

She walked downstairs, numb with despair.

She tucked the article into the top drawer of her desk. She'd probably never read it again, but it seemed only right that there be some sort of reminder of this woman and child who had meant so much to Ryder.

Ryder called the following morning, but she let it go to voice mail. He left a message inviting her out on a short trail ride. She couldn't face him. Not yet, maybe never.

On Thursday night Lorri's doorbell rang, but when she opened the door there was no one there. Puzzled, she started to close it when she noticed a tote bag on the mat.

She carried the bag inside. A delicious smell rose from the top. In the kitchen she unpacked three containers. Heaping servings of meatloaf, mashed potatoes and gravy, and greens. She folded the bag, and a small card fluttered to the ground. She knelt down and picked it up.

The back of Ryder's business card read, *Hope you enjoy dinner. Call me when you've got some free time.—Ryder*

Lorri stood there at her kitchen counter looking at all that food. Her stomach grumbled. She hadn't eaten much the last few days.

She made a plate for herself and took it to the table. Mister sniffed the air. She poured a little gravy over his food, then sat back down. Sitting there eating alone, her mind drifted to her brother, Jeff.

Lorri brushed her hand against her damp skin as she remembered her mother clinging to her that day they got the news. She'd been frantic over his injuries, praying that this would be the catalyst that would set him straight. It wasn't until the next day that they learned of the full scope of the accident, and that there'd been fatalities.

I can't keep this from Ryder.

She got in bed, and tossed and turned until sunrise. She took Mister out for his morning walk early, hoping to avoid interacting with anyone. She just wasn't up to it.

They walked over to the farmers market through the shortcut in her back fence. The market was busy with commuters stopping for coffee. They gave the residents a discount on coffee in their neighborhood mugs. It looked like she must be the only one who didn't take advantage of that deal on a regular basis.

She waited in line and ordered a cup of tea. She and Mister sat at a table and people-watched while she scanned her phone messages.

A post on social media caught her eye. She scrolled back up. The headline read, "Finding True Peace in Past Disappointments." She clicked on it. Internet service this side of the building was spotty sometimes though, and the connection timed out.

Probably for the best. "Come on, Mister. I've got a meeting in twenty minutes anyway. We'd better hurry."

As soon as they walked through the gate, Mister sat waiting to be unleashed. She unhooked the leash and let him take off on his own.

She got back to her desk just in time to dial in to the meeting. Feeling restless today, she spun her chair to one side then the other. She jotted down a few notes, then marked off the completed sections of the itinerary as the call progressed. She didn't even have a report out for this meeting. She was simply listening in case she needed to participate.

She grabbed a green colored pencil and started scribbling on the desk pad.

Pam texted her during the meeting.

Pam: Checking in.

Lorri: Busy with conf calls today. Ugh.

Pam: Hate those days.

Lorri: Me too. Plus I was up all night.

Pam: What the heck?

Lorri: A bunch of things. Ryder. Jeff.

Pam: Anniversary of Jeff's death is next Tuesday. I was wondering if you were okay.

Lorri: I'll call you. You good?

Pam: Great.

The conference call droned on for another twenty minutes. By the time she hung up she had several drafts branding the Lisa Scholarship. Some of them were pretty good.

She got up and fixed another cup of tea, then sat down and worked all day on her favorite designs. She put together a full packet, just like she would for a paying customer. There were four different designs and color layouts, but she had a clear favorite.

She wondered which ones Reece, Ross, and Diane would like best. She'd become so close to all of them. To think she was falling for the one man that it would be impossible to have a relationship with weighed on her.

She emailed the whole package to Ross at The Wedding Ranch email from their website, wishing them well on the project with a note that said they were welcome to use any or all of the designs gratis, but not to feel bad if they had something else in mind.

That weekend Mother Nature delivered true fall-like temperatures. She'd missed several calls from Ryder that week, and he had to be wondering why she was avoiding him.

The next time he called, she forced herself to answer.

"How's my friend Lorri this morning?"

"Hi, thank you for the dinner. That was so thoughtful."

"Didn't wake you, did I?" he asked.

"No."

"You don't sound good. Are you okay?"

How was she supposed to respond to that? "Not feeling so great lately."

"I'm sorry about that. I wanted to see if you'd spend the day with me over here at the house? We can exercise the horses and enjoy the change of season. I'll cook something if you're up to it."

"I'd love that, but I don't think I should."

"Have you been outside? It's a brisk morning." He seemed delighted by the cooler temperatures. "I love this time of year. Can't wait to experience fall with you."

With me? You won't be thinking that when I tell you what I know. Things in her life were changing. She'd never had anyone ask her to enjoy the change of season before. If only she could un-know what she knew about the accident.

"Please come. I bet you'll feel better after being out in the fresh air."

She couldn't sit on this information. Each day she didn't tell him was one more that she lied to him, and she wasn't a liar. "I'll be there. Give me an hour. Can I bring anything?"

"Just your smile. See you when you get here."

Any other day that would have made her heart bubble. Today it only hurt to know that she was about to reopen old wounds that hadn't yet healed.

Dressed in leggings under jeans and layers on top too, she pulled the tags off of a hip-length jacket she'd bought on sale while in Denver on business. It had been too cute and too good of a deal to pass up, but she'd never had the chance to wear it in the four years she'd owned it. This seemed like the perfect opportunity.

Her phone rang. "Pam? Hi."

"I tried to call you earlier," Pam said. "Did you get my message?"

"I did. Sorry." Truth was she was distracted. "I was going to call you."

"Did something happen? You sound strange."

Lorri told Pam every gut-wrenching detail. How fond she was growing of Ryder. The way he made her feel. The hope in her heart about being a part of things with him, and then what she'd discovered about the accident. And that Jeff had been the one at the wheel of that other car that stole Ryder's perfect family from him.

"Lorri, I can't believe this."

"I'm on my way to tell him."

"I don't know. Maybe you should just keep it to yourself. I mean, would you want to know? Does it matter?"

"I don't think I'd want to know, but I'd deserve to. Wouldn't it be the ultimate betrayal to not tell him?" Lorri hated to think how bad that would hurt him.

"Look. You said so yourself it's taken him seven years to begin to break out of that grief. Why drag him back under? Just relax and enjoy his company. Maybe it's going to be nothing more than friends anyway."

"That's possible," Lorri said.

"Then it wouldn't matter anyway. I mean, if he doesn't know you're Jeff's sister now, it's highly unlikely he'd find out. And you like spending time with him. You're both so happy and doing so well. Don't ruin it."

In exactly an hour Lorri pulled into Ryder's driveway still considering everything Pam had said. Maybe she had a good point. She'd just be sure they were nothing more than friends and then everyone would be happy. *I don't know if I can do this.*

She drove around to where Ryder had the horses tacked up at the hitching post, parked, and walked over to meet him.

"I think it's even colder over here, where the land is open with nothing to break the wind." She huddled into her jacket, running toward him to keep warm.

"Might be. Don't you love fall?" he said as she got closer.

"I love pumpkin spiced lattes. Is that the same thing?"

He shook his head. "Not at all. And if you gourmet coffee gals stopped to consider it, you'd realize you could get a nice slice of pie with all the pumpkin spice you'd like and real coffee for less calories and a whole lot more satisfaction." He tightened the cinch on Dottie. "If you ask me, there's never a good reason to ruin a decent cup of coffee."

"Well, I tell you what. If you serve me an honest-to-goodness slice of homemade pumpkin pie with my coffee, I promise to drink it straight. Deal?"

"Deal." He walked over toward the barn. "Come here. I've got something for you."

She followed him inside to the tack room. It smelled of leather. Saddles were stacked on individual racks four high along the short wall. On the outside wall, halters and reins and all sorts of equipment hung side by side, but instead of hooks, a thick tree branch with the bark still on it had been cut into two-inch-thick slices. The four-inch diameter of the branch was perfect for hanging the leads and leather neatly over them.

A wooden plaque with the word HEADQUARTERS hung over a Dutch door. He walked into that room.

"This is your office?" she asked.

"Yep." He stepped around the heavy wooden desk and plopped into a red leather chair with cowhide accents on it. "You like it?"

"I do. It looks like you." *Rugged. Colorful. Quiet. Manly. Very much a cowboy style.*

He turned and picked up a large box from the credenza behind him. "I hope you like this."

Her heart fluttered much like a little girl on Christmas morning. She hadn't expected a present. "For me?" *Why? I shouldn't accept this.*

"It is." He didn't wait for her to open it. He lifted the top from the box, then took out a stunning cowboy hat. Cocoa brown, the leather was cut out under the brim letting turquoise felt show through. "Let's see how it fits."

She leaned forward.

"Pull your hair back from your face," he said quietly.

She pushed her fingers through her hair, and he placed the hat on her head.

Ryder let out an approving sound. "Perfect fit. Oh, you look good."

She pressed the guilt behind her, but his kindness made it even harder. How could she be falling in love with this man, after what happened?

"No mirror out here," he said. "You'll just have to trust me."

The comment had been playful, but it hit home. "I trust you." She hadn't meant it to come out so serious, but there it was.

The left corner of his lip pulled. "I'm happy to hear that, because I trust you too, my friend Lorrie." He came around the desk and grabbed a scarf and gloves from the coat tree next to the door. "Here." He slung the wool scarf around her neck. "Get it up around your neck."

She adjusted the scarf and slid on the gloves.

"I think we're ready to roll." He clapped his gloved hands together and led the way back out to the horses.

Lorri checked all the saddle riggings like he'd taught her, although it seemed a waste of time to do so behind him when he was clearly the expert. She put her foot in the stirrup and lifted herself. Ryder was right there spotting her, but she was able to get herself to the saddle this time.

They rode the perimeter fences, him telling her how he and Pop-Pop had used to do this together.

It was as if they'd drifted back in time, when things were simpler, and his grandfather could've been riding with them.

Ryder had a million stories. His life had been so full. Her life felt small in comparison. From the back of Dottie looking out across the landscape, where the trees were green before now, dry leaves were beginning to pile against the fence line. She was thankful to experience this side of nature's artwork. The colors were richer. Her mind's eye was mixing colors trying to match them.

"I'm so thankful you're sharing all of this with me," she said.

"Me too." He loped off, and she let Dottie have the freedom to keep up.

The exhilaration of being on horseback running across a field side by side and trusting that her bottom wasn't going to leave that saddle had to have been the bravest thing she'd done in her life.

That night as she was leaving, Ryder stood in the open door of her SUV as he said, "Lorri, thank you for coming. I enjoyed every minute with you."

"Oh . . ." She stopped short of turning the key. "Ryder, I can't leave without telling you something."

"What's wrong?"

"This has been a wonderful day. You are . . . a good man."

Ryder pushed his hat back. "Then why do you look like you're going to cry?"

"Ryder, I don't know why I didn't put this together sooner."

She lifted her hands to her face in an attempt to hide the tears that were beginning to fall.

"Hey now. It can't be that bad. Slow down."

She dropped her hands in her lap. "It's worse than bad."

"Here's your hat back." Lorri took it off and handed it to him through the window, sweeping at her tears.

"I bought that for you. Please, keep it."

"I don't deserve it." She pushed it away. "Please. Ryder. Take it. You have to listen to me."

He took the hat. "Fine. What's going on, gal?"

"After I saw the article in your office . . ." She turned her back to him. "I . . ."

"It's okay. I didn't know it was a boundary. Well, it's not. It was just a pinch. A little obstacle and we're already over it."

"No. It's more than that. There were so many coincidences. I didn't think it could be."

"I don't understand what you're trying to say."

She turned and looked at him. "Ryder. That drunk driver. That wreck. Everything that tore your life apart. It was Jeff."

"Jeff Pike. Right. I know that."

"My brother. Walker is my married name. My whole career has been under that name, so I didn't change it in the divorce."

"He was your brother?" He shook his head. "No. How can . . . ? Did you track me down? Is this some kind of sick guilt trip you're on?"

"No. I didn't know before." The words tumbled out in a rush. The situation was bad enough without something like that heaped on top. "Meeting you was purely random. I swear."

Ryder stared, as though he was looking right through her.

"His name wasn't in the article that I saw, but when I read the details and they were so similar to what had happened with Jeff, I looked up the report from his records." She gasped for a breath. "It was him. I'm so sorry." The last words came out in a sob. "I'm so, so, so sorry."

"I think you'd better leave."

She sucked in a stuttered breath and twisted the key in the ignition.

He backed away from the truck.

His lips pulled into a thin line, as if he might explode. She pulled off and drove straight home.

He kicked the dirt, then jumped in his truck and pressed his foot on the accelerator, sending the motor roaring like a hungry bear on a rampage in the opposite direction.

He drove for an hour, bleary-eyed and unable to even utter a prayer.

His jaw ached. *Of all the things you could lay on me, Lord.*

At mile marker 150 Ryder veered off to the side of the road. His headlights flooded over the grass and weeds there. The forged steel cross he'd made in his workshop rose from the bank. No one else would probably ever notice it, and nothing without some very specific effort could take it down. He'd planted it deep, and it was made of heavy metal.

It wasn't fancy. It hadn't been for anyone but him, and his family.

He stared at the homemade landmark. The promise that he'd never forget her or their son. The apology for not having made the time to drive them himself.

Why hadn't I been driving? Either outcome was better, either they'd have all said their last goodbye to this life together, or the accident might never have happened.

He was a good driver. Not easily distracted. Ronnie Dwayne was a burst of energy in the mornings; he probably babbled nonstop the whole way. Maybe that was good. Maybe. There were a hundred maybes, and he'd never know what happened. How or why.

Oh, Valerie. Please help me.

He knelt in the damp grass.

He'd opened his heart a tiny bit, and who snuck in but someone connected to the fool who had taken every precious thing from him.

On one knee he pressed his fingers to his forehead, leaning forward, caring not one bit about the cars speeding past on the highway. He cried, deep painful sobs from within, until he huffed and panted, trying to catch his breath.

He opened his eyes and rested his hand on the arm of the cross.

A feather drifted, landing on the ground right next to his boot.

He looked up but didn't see anything. He lifted the feather, holding it between his fingers.

"What are you trying to tell me, Valerie?"

He sat there for a long time not knowing what he expected, until he began to walk back to the truck. "I needed one more goodbye. I miss you both."

He drove home in complete silence.

Chapter Twenty-eight

Lorri packed her things to go spend time with her parents on this anniversary of Jeff's death. Unsure if she'd stay the night or not, she packed Mister up and took him with her. He was a comfort to have nearby, and he was good in the car. He usually laid in the back, but today she spread a sheet in the passenger seat and let him sit up front with her. He didn't look all that comfortable. He was so big that he sat hunched over. After his chin bumped the dash a couple of times, he climbed onto the floorboard with his body leaning over the seat and chin on the center console.

With one hand on the wheel and the other on Mister's head, she turned on the cruise control.

Mom and Dad weren't expecting her. They'd begged her to come spend time with them on this anniversary every year since Jeff died, but she'd never seen the point. It was so hard to watch her parents so broken over something Jeff brought on himself.

It was different this year though. Compassion for Jeff came

easy today. Jeff was their son. Their grief was real, and for the first time she really understood and acknowledged their feelings. They still loved Jeff. Seeing and understanding Ryder's grief had changed her perspective. Losing a child had to be the worst trauma a parent could ever experience. No matter how or why that loss occurred, the pain lingered.

Even though the short time she'd spent with Ryder had all turned into one big mess, she learned a lot of things about herself while they were together.

She headed north on the highway, thinking about how different she felt about this day than she had last year. *I've been selfish. The next time I stand in judgment of something or someone, I pray I recognize it and can find empathy and compassion.*

At Jeff's funeral she'd been so angry with him she could barely speak to anyone. She held Mom as she wept, but Lorri's heart hadn't been there for her.

Lorri had never forgiven Jeff for all the things he'd put their family through, and she had held on to that grudge. Her folks couldn't even express their sorrow without her throwing her two cents in.

She blinked away a tear. *I'm so sorry.*

Ashamed, she didn't know how she'd make it up to Mom and Dad, but she'd find a way. She pulled into the driveway, prepared to somehow do that. This house was much smaller than their house in Raleigh, but it was updated and charming. Today the special wreath that Mom had made in Jeff's honor hung on the door.

Her parents had clung to hope. Each thing that happened, the next arrest, injury, or episode they thought might be what could help Jeff find his way again, but that tomorrow never happened. Even when Jeff hocked Dad's irreplaceable collection of pocket watches, they'd recovered the few that could be tracked down and spent more money keeping him out of jail and sending him to rehab.

Dad had been so hurt. One of those watches had belonged to his grandfather, another had been left to him by his best friend. They'd served in the army together. You couldn't replace those things.

There came a point when her parents quit telling her about the trouble he was in, knowing her response wouldn't be what they wanted to hear.

But on this visit, she held kindness in her heart. She couldn't have a special friendship with Ryder, but she could repair the strain that she'd caused in her family.

She stood on the porch ready to knock, but something made her pause. Every flower and piece of greenery in that wreath had been lovingly tied into place. *Jeff, I loved you. You were my brother. I'm sorry your life was so hard. I wish there'd been something I could have done to change that for you.*

Tears fell, almost taking her breath. In the years since his death, she hadn't shed a tear for him. Now they came in waves. She sat on the porch step. Her hands over her face, she leaned forward sobbing.

The door behind her opened. "I thought I heard a car." Mom sounded so cheerful. "I'm so glad you came."

She couldn't stop crying.

"Lorri?" Mom stepped outside and sat next to her. "Honey, what's the matter?"

Mister pushed his nose to Lorri's shoulder.

Lorri turned into her mom's warm embrace.

"I'm here for you." Mom pushed Lorri's hair back from her face. "It's okay. I have no idea what this is all about, but that doesn't matter. This family gets through everything."

That only turned the squeeze on Lorri's heart tighter. She hadn't been a very positive part of this family for a long time. *And here I was judging Jeff.* "Mom. I've been selfish. I'm so sorry."

"What do you think you've done?"

Lorri sniffled back the tears, wiping them from her cheeks with her fingers. She heard the screen door open. "There you are. Aren't y'all chilly? Why are you—"

"Honey, we'll be right in." Mom pulled her closer.

Dad groaned. "Oh no. Tears?"

That made Lorri smile. Dad had never been good with tears. That had always been Mom's department. "We're coming in now, Daddy." She squeezed Mom's hands. "I love you so much."

"And we both love you, darling."

She climbed to her feet, and Mister jumped up too. She walked inside and slapped her hand against her hip for Mister to follow.

He waited for the command to come through the doorway, then she told him to sit.

Mister sat, his eyes on her waiting for the next command.

"Rest."

He laid down and put his chin on his paws.

"He's so well behaved, but man, he's gotten big," Dad said.

"I barely notice that anymore."

"That was a lot of tears. Did somebody break my little girl's heart?" he asked. "We could sic Mister on him."

"No, Daddy. This isn't about me." She reached for his hand, and then Mom's. "Or maybe it's all about me and what I've done wrong. I know Jeff's struggles had to be heart-wrenching for you both. I'm sorry I didn't make it any easier up to or after he died. I'm really sorry."

Her father's head tilted gently. "Oh, Lorri. We have always loved you both more than you can ever imagine. We hurt when you hurt. Every heartache is one for us too. Thank you for recognizing our pain, but honey, you had to deal with those things your way. There is no good way to get through it. Come here." He held her, rocking her and dropping a kiss on the top of her head.

It had been years since he'd done that. She was fifteen again, crying over Donnie Humphries. Her first broken heart.

"I don't know where all this is coming from, but Lorri, I am glad you're able to finally grieve for Jeff. He loved you. He loved us all. Sometimes it's hard to love people when you know they are self-destructing, but that's what we have to do. When you have a child of your own one day, you'll understand that."

"No more apologies about this, Lorri," Dad said. "Here's the thing. Everyone handles things differently, and your anger didn't make you wrong. Okay?"

"I feel awful about it."

"I think you're about to find real peace in your heart. I know you've given me some," Mom said.

"I don't know how you can forgive me."

"You're our daughter."

"Can't be that simple."

"It most certainly is," Mom said.

She noticed the dining room table was already set. Mom had started the tradition of making Jeff's favorite foods on this day.

"You hungry?" Dad rubbed his belly. "I'm starving. I've been having to smell all this stuff since breakfast this morning."

"Pure torture, right?" Lorri placed her hand on his back. "I'll help Mom get everything served up."

She'd never really thought about it before, how Mom was such a good cook, and yet she hadn't ever learned. Lorri had been in such a hurry to move out of the house by then that she never had the chance. "Maybe next year I can help you cook everything. You could teach me the recipes."

"I'd love that."

Lorri hadn't seen such delight in Mom's smile in a long time.

"Then, let's count on that."

"I'll teach you some of your favorite dishes too, so someday you can pass them on to your daughter." Mom came over and hugged her again. "I hope you never felt slighted."

"Never. We were lucky to have such wonderful parents always there for us."

Mom handed her a bowl of potato salad. On the top, deviled egg halves made the center of two flowers with chive stems and red bacon bit petals.

"Remember how you and Jeff would fight for the flowers? That used to make me laugh, because there were always two. One for each of you."

"I can't believe we never realized that." They'd practically come to blows to dig out the first portion. Lorri carried the bowl and set it on the table.

Mom carried a chicken pot pie and a basket of rolls. The menu was a real hodgepodge, fried pork chops, pizza, home-made potato chips, ham, baked beans, and enchilada casserole. Each dish held memories. Welcome ones.

Dad blessed the food and said a few words about Jeff and expressed his thanks for the rest of the family being together to remember Jeff.

"I feel like I need a nap after all that food," Lorri said after the meal was finished.

Mister laid down in the doorway, looking hopeful they might get to take a nap.

"You can lay down in the guest room if you want." Mom picked up the empty plates and started moving them to the kitchen.

"No. Let me clear the table. Maybe you could find the old family albums. Let's look through them. Can we?"

Mom and Dad exchanged a glance, then a smile. "I know exactly where they are." She hustled off.

"You're making your mother a very happy woman today."

"I never realized—"

"Don't explain. I was serious when I said no more apologies about this. It's life. There's no instruction booklet, and Lord knows it isn't easy. Are you happy in Dalton Mill?"

"I am. I think I'm finally figuring out who I am. It's funny how you can kind of lose yourself when you're married. It's been a year of discovery. Some good. Some bad."

"It's not always a bad thing. You have to be aware enough

to hold on to the real parts of yourself, and then you mesh and learn from each other. Growing in positive ways. I don't think you and Craig really did that," Dad said. "You outgrew him, and he kind of stayed the same."

"Yeah. You might be right."

Mom came into the room carrying three large albums. "Here we go!" She plopped down in the middle of the couch. Dad sat on one side and Lorri grabbed her glass of tea from the table and went to sit on the other side, tucking her feet beneath her.

Mom flipped open the first book. "We can skip to the back of this one. Mostly wedding pictures of me and your dad."

"No! Let's look at them too."

Mom looked pleased. She placed her hand on the picture of her and Dad in front of the church.

Lorri had forgotten how young they looked in these pictures. Or maybe she hadn't really noticed before. "Your gown was so elegant. Look how long that train is."

"I had no idea how heavy it would make the dress. It was like pulling an anchor behind me."

Her dad laughed. "And the girls had to keep running behind her and straightening it out."

"It was a pain, but that was my dream wedding gown. Each one of those pearls on the bodice were hand-sewn."

Dad leaned closer to Mom. "You were the prettiest bride in the world. I still can see you when you stepped into view at the end of the aisle. Took my breath away."

Mom blushed. She flipped forward to the baby pictures of Lorri. There were a ton, and lots of her and Jeff together.

They spent hours going through old family photo albums,

taking a break for dessert. German chocolate cake and banana pudding.

There were a few pictures from the shows she and Jeff used to perform on the patio. Magic shows, tumbling, and there was that one time they did turtle races. Her turtle refused to come out of his shell. Jeff had painted a number three like Dale Earnhardt on his turtle's shell after that.

"Here's when we were teaching Jeff to ride a bike. Look at you, Lorri. You loved those streamers on the handlebars of that pink bike."

"I remember that bike."

So many precious memories. Decorating eggs at Easter, and they were never your average dunk-in-a-paper-cup-of-dye variety. There were feathers, glue, paint, and wax involved. And come Halloween the pumpkin carving went from simple knives and spoons to power tools. Her creativity had been in full gear from a very young age, and Jeff had fueled it with his competitiveness.

"You were always artistic," Mom said.

"Jeff could never outshine you in that area," Dad said. "But he could definitely play sports better."

Lorri laughed. She never could throw or catch, as much as she'd tried. It used to drive Jeff crazy. He'd accuse her of not trying, but she just didn't have the skill.

Lorri and her mom and dad all cried over the sweet boy he'd been, still unsure of what changed to set his life on such a hard path.

As they talked about the latter years, she withheld her harsh opinions. They'd heard them all before. Instead, she listened and really tried to understand and offer comfort. There were more incidents than she'd even realized. He'd been under house arrest for a year for driving drunk. She remembered that but didn't know about all the times he'd been in jail following that.

Lorri said, "Mom, do you remember the box of stuff you gave me? The one marked 'Personal'?"

"I do."

"I never realized it wasn't my stuff. Probably just as well, else I might have thrown it away back then. I went through that box not too long ago."

"Your brother had such a time. Bless his heart, he just couldn't find his way."

Dad got up and took their dessert plates into the kitchen. Mister followed him, hopeful for a scrap or two, no doubt.

"He really did have a heart of gold. His letters were sweet. He never meant to cause so much trouble. And after that accident it was all he could do to get through the days." Mom's lip trembled.

The brother Lorri loved had done awful things. She'd convinced herself that he was really no longer the same person, but in those letters he wrote to Mom from a cold cot in a cell somewhere in North Carolina, he was. He was trying, and the more he tried the more he felt as if he were being sucked down into something dark and wrong.

"It was so sad." Lorri hugged her mother's arm. "I'm sorry, Mom. I'm supposed to be here comforting you, and I'm a complete wreck."

Mom pulled her close, kissing her. "You never mourned his

loss. You've held this in for a long time. It was bound to happen at some point."

"I was so mad at him."

"I know. It's okay."

She raised her head, gulping for air between sobs. Mom's eyes looked so blue although they were red from crying. Jeff had her blue eyes.

"It's been an emotional day," Dad said. "Let me fix us something to eat."

"No, Daddy. All we've done is eat."

He stood, filling the doorway. "There's some Watergate salad in the fridge. Your mom forgot to put it out earlier."

"Okay, but just a little scoop," Lorri conceded. Dad still knew how to make her feel better.

Dad walked back out of the room, and Mom inched closer. "Some of the stuff that happened, even your Daddy never knew."

"Oh, Mom. You shouldn't have tried to take that on for everyone."

"I did what I thought Jeff needed me to. I know I made mistakes. Enabling him. It's easier to look back and see it, but at the time, there was hope. I felt hope."

"You needed to feel that. You're the best mother. You always believed in us no matter what. Thank you, Mom." She'd wondered about that last day of Jeff's life, but had never had the courage to ask. "Mom, do you think he crashed the car on purpose that day?"

"No. I have to believe he had some kind of seizure or something. He never would have taken his life without leaving me a note."

Lorri thought of the stack of letters Jeff had written to her mother. "You're right. He'd never do anything like that." They'd never know for sure though.

"Go get some sleep. It's been a long and tiring day. A good one, but we all need some rest," Mom said.

She hugged her mom good night.

"You dream of all the wonderful days ahead of you, darling. You've found forgiveness in your heart. You will be amazed at the things that will come your way now. Be ready, sweet girl."

How she hoped that was true. She did feel more at peace today than she had in years. In her prayers that night she prayed for Ryder and his family, and for Jeff too. *I hope you found peace.*

Chapter Twenty-nine

The next morning, Lorri sat with her mom on the back porch sipping coffee.

"Thank you for this wonderful time together, Lorri."

"I'm glad I came. This was really nice."

"And overdue. I'm happy we had such a good visit."

"I'd love for you to see my place. It's not that far, but if you don't want to drive it, I'll even come and get you."

"I think we can make it down there. Have you made some friends?"

"Yeah, I have, and I know all my neighbors too."

"Any *special* friends?" Mom's eyes were full of hope and speculation.

Lorri thought not to mention Ryder, but she had a feeling Pam may have already mentioned him to Mom. "I thought so. Just friends, but it was refreshing to do something with a man who wasn't pushing his own agenda. Really sweet guy, a gentleman, even cooked for me."

"He sounds perfect. Does he dance?"

Pam had definitely mentioned him. She shouldn't be surprised. Her parents treated Pam like another daughter. "Yeah. We danced. He's an amazing dancer, but it'll never work. I'm not even sure we can be friends."

"If he's a good man why are you so sure?"

"He was widowed seven years ago. Lost his wife and son in a car accident." She wondered if Mom would put it together more quickly than she had. It took a moment, then her eyes widened. She figured it out. Lorri shook her head. "I know. What are the odds? Mom, he's the husband of the—"

"Don't even say it. Oh my gosh. I can't believe it."

Lorri's hands shook. "It took me a long time to figure it out. I don't know how I didn't realize it sooner. He must hate me."

"No. Lorri. You are not responsible for Jeff's mistakes. You've forgiven Jeff finally. Now you need to forgive yourself, too. I have no idea what Ryder's journey is. He may or may not let you in, but I know if you two were brought together in such a strange way, then there's a reason. Don't be afraid to leave the past where it is."

"I don't know how to do that."

"Well, it's simple. You pray. You put one foot in front of the other. You get up every morning and make it a good day. Trust that it will be okay and when you slip back into the past, stop yourself. Take another step forward and keep going."

"I'll try." She hugged Mom and Dad walked into the room with Mister. "You're just in time, Dad. I'm getting ready to go home."

"I'll walk you out."

"Bye, Mom."

"Call me if you need a pep talk. You're going to be fine. I never had to worry about you, honey."

Dad said, "That's one big dog. What was Craig thinking buying that thing?"

"He's a good dog, and I never worry about my safety."

"Since you refuse to get a gun, I guess he's a good option to keep my little girl safe."

"Thanks, Daddy."

"Lorri, thank you for coming," Dad said. "We needed this, but don't think I didn't notice that you didn't mention your new friend. Pam told us about Ryder. He sounds more like a man who deserves a girl as special as you."

I knew it.

"I always wanted better than Craig for you. If you two ever become more than friends I expect to meet him."

Dad could still make her feel like his little girl. "I promise, Daddy."

"Are you driving straight home?"

"Pretty much. Just a couple short stops on the way back, but they won't take long. I'll call and let you know when I get there."

She pulled away from the curb and headed south. She wished she could turn back time and have been there for Mom and Dad before. This visit had been way overdue.

She drove around the block, driving without a real plan. Then she turned into the parking lot of a supermarket, and went inside. She must've stood there trying to decide what kind of flowers to buy for a good five minutes. Finally, she grabbed a handful of red Gerbera daisies and took them to the self-checkout.

The flowers made Jeff being gone seem real for the first time. She started her car and began driving. Her mind was full of the stories and pictures she and her parents had shared last night, but she was alone now, with her own emotions, as she drove to where Jeff had been buried.

She entered the gates and drove to the back where the tall building with the cremated remains of bodies were stacked like Legos. More buildings had been added since she'd been here. So many lives. Gone. Across the way, a woman sobbed into a hankie, dabbing at her eyes.

"You stay here, Mister." She lowered the windows halfway, then got out and walked to where Jeff's remains had been stored in a wall that looked so utilitarian. Every square marked with an engraved bronze plaque in the exact same design. No difference. No way of knowing any information about the loved one there. She lifted the flowers and dropped them into the cylinder beside Jeff's name.

"I'm sorry it's taken me so long. I know your life was hard. I hope where you are now only good things are happening. That you're never cold, or hungry. Never faced with difficult choices. Knowing that you will always be loved."

She glanced over as a silver-haired man and young daughter walked by.

"I picked those flowers for a reason," she said quietly. "Do you remember that day?" She waited, but there was no answer. No feeling that he was listening. She didn't deserve it. Not yet.

"You were right about Craig. You always were a good judge of character. What happened to you? I wish I could understand it. You were the smart one between us. The talented one. I don't know how this happened to your life. It seems so unfair that yours was so hard. Why would God let that happen?"

She stood waiting for the father and daughter to leave. "Remember junior prom? I had bought my dress and every-thing. Craig called and canceled on me the day before saying he was sick. Later I found out that he'd taken someone else to the dance." She swept a tear away. "You brought me Gerbera daisies. You said they were happy flowers and I deserved to be happy. You also told me Craig would never be good enough for me. I wish I'd listened."

Closing her eyes, she whispered, "I love you, Jeff. I miss the brother that always had my back. I'm tired of being mad at you." She walked up to the columbarium and placed her hand on Jeff's name. "I'm sorry it took me so long."

She turned and headed back to her car. Mister had his head hung out the side window. With her hands in her pockets, she walked along, paying little attention to anything when her foot turned on the sidewalk. As she stumbled, a yellow butterfly flew over and paused for a moment, then flitted from one side of her to the other.

"Little lisa." Eurema lisa, *like the one that almost landed right in my hand that day with Ryder.* Like the beautiful design she'd created for Ryder's scholarship initiative.

The butterfly rose higher, then swirled back toward her nearly brushing her cheek, then flew away.

Mister spotted her and let out a woof. The SUV rocked from

the weight of him lunging side to side. "That took longer than expected. You're a good boy." She reached into the glove box and grabbed a dog treat. "Here you go." He chomped on it, immediately forgiving her.

She drove home thinking of that butterfly. The visit with her parents had been uplifting.

As they got closer to home, Mister recognized the neighborhood, standing and pressing his nose to the glass.

"We're home," she said as she pulled into the garage. She let Mister jump down from the truck, then they went inside and she called Dad so he wouldn't worry. He answered on the first ring.

"I made it home." She put a scoop of dog food in Mister's bowl. He nudged the kibble around, never one to be fast about anything.

"Thanks for letting us know," Dad said, speaking for them both. "We really enjoyed the visit."

"Me too." She adjusted the thermostat.

Dad said, "Please come for Thanksgiving. We'd love that. Your aunt and uncle are coming to town too. It should be nice."

"Sounds like a plan." She hung up and checked her emails and messages.

Mister came over and rested his damp chin on her thigh. The older he got the droolier he was. She grabbed a couple of tissues and dabbed at his jowls. Like a child, he twisted out of her reach.

She let Mister out back.

Lorri went upstairs to her studio and turned on the lights. She raised the blinds one by one, sunlight filling the room, then sat in front of the painting she'd been working on.

She closed her eyes, letting her mind slow. She was sorry she'd found it so easy to judge Jeff for the way he spent his life. She still hadn't figured out what she was supposed to really do with hers. Yes, she tried to be kind and considerate. Worked hard and didn't create drama. And now she was here in this small town. Running from the conflict. At first anyway, but she didn't regret the move. Not for a moment.

She missed spending time with Ryder. Wished it could've been different. They spoke honestly, even when the conversations were difficult.

Was that because of Ryder, or had she changed?

"Does it matter?" She stared at the painting of Ryder's property. All those colors they'd enjoyed the other day.

Her dream had been to create art that was thought-provoking and hope-filled. Something that would tickle a memory or make someone take a trip to see what she'd painted for them, or for those limited to travel, a way to share what they may have never had the opportunity to experience otherwise.

She was ready to experience that. To trust her gift and give it her all. The graphics for work were directed by hungry account execs looking for ways to manipulate or sway the purchasing public into seeing things their way. Harboring the keeping-up-with-the-Joneses attitude, dreaming bigger than their pocketbooks could comfortably afford. It paid her bills, had done so for years now.

This painting, it filled her heart rather than her bank account. She now understood the heart and soul needed to be full too.

She'd done exactly what her Dad had told her she should do.

But for all those financially comfortable years, she'd sacrificed attention to the things that were important to her. To top it off the one person she did all of that for, Craig, hadn't cared enough to even honor their vows. The lesson there was clear. *Do what matters to me. It's my journey. My purpose. I'll touch the right people.*

She spread a few colors and made soft purposeful dabs. The new brushes Pam had given her felt good in her hand.

The images took shape with each pull of her brush.

There was more in this landscape than the trees, creek, and mill. There were memories, laughs, and whimsy. The tiny butterfly, little lisa, floating along the top of the seed heads between the tall blades of grass, zigging and zagging haphazardly as if the act of taking flight had made it dizzy, like the one that day when Lorri went horseback riding with Ryder, and maybe a distant relative of the butterfly that had practically kissed her cheek when she left Jeff today with less anger in her heart.

Chapter Thirty

Ryder dialed Lorri, but it went to voice mail again. He was beginning to think she'd blocked his number.

He unfolded the *Leafland Ledger News* to read the headlines. As
he turned the page, a swirl of color caught his eye. He recognized the image, but it took him a minute to remember where
he'd seen it before.

On Lorri's desk. It was just as eye-catching in thumbnail size as
it had been printed on a full sheet of paper.

A tick of aggravation gnawed at him as he made the connection. She'd created the logo for Bloom. The crooked man
who'd swayed his father out of his land.

"Good morning, Ryder." Diane walked in the back door carrying a glossy envelope. She poured herself a cup of coffee.
"Oh. What's that face for?"

"Nothing. What?"

She tossed the envelope on the table and pulled out the chair across from him. "You look out of sorts. Haven't seen that snarl lately." She nudged him jokingly as she sat.

He pointed at the graphic. "Lorri made that."

She nodded, then her mouth formed an *O*. "Oh, Bloom?"

"Mm-hmm."

"Well, it's still a nice logo."

He inhaled as he shook his head.

"What?" Diane stared at him. "You can't be pissed at Bloom. Or her for being connected to him. That's misplaced anger. Bloom didn't cheat Dad out of our land. He paid a fair price."

"More than fair. Dad couldn't say no." Ryder closed the paper. They'd had this argument before.

"When are you going to let that go? Not having that acreage hasn't changed our lives one bit. If Dad was still farming it, we wouldn't have it either."

"I know."

"Wh—what?" Diane straightened. "Okay. I didn't expect that."

"You're right."

"Of course I am, but this is the first time you've said that." Diane sat up straighter, showing off a toothy smile. "I do like to hear you say it. Can you repeat it one more time?" She leaned forward, pressing her hand to the back of her ear. "Please?"

"You're. Right."

"It really has such a good ring to it." She wrapped her hands around her coffee mug. "You know, you are much easier to be around these days."

A slow smile replaced the quit-giving-me-a-hard-time look. "It's easier *being* me these days."

"She's nice," Diane said.

He nodded his head slowly. "She sure is." They both knew they were talking about Lorri.

"And you're not going to hold this Bloom connection against her. Are you?"

"It may have bugged me for a nanosecond, but no. It's a lovely graphic, and it's her job. She's good at it."

"Very. You know, she sent a whole packet of graphics over for the scholarship. Did you decide on the Lisa Scholarship as the name of it?"

"She and I talked about it. I like it."

"I do too," Diane said. "The logo is gorgeous."

"I knew you would appreciate the symbolism. You always said the *eurema lisa* sightings meant good change was coming. A symbol of hope. It's perfect," he said.

"Just like she seems to be for you." Diane's brow arched.

"There's no such thing as perfection. You know that," he said.

"No, but you've been your old self. Even the kids have been talking about it. We're happy for you, Ryder. Don't fight it."

"We're friends. Or we were."

"You mean maybe more than friends?"

"It's complicated, Diane. More so than you could imagine."

"Then uncomplicate it."

He looked at his sister. She'd been just as broken by all of this. For a split second he considered not telling her, but she deserved to know. "Lorri's brother was the one driving the car that morning in Raleigh."

She cocked her head. "Jeff Pike?"

"Yes. She said she'd put it together and had to tell me."

She held her hand to her mouth, then let out the breath she was holding. "I can't believe it. I bet you were stunned. I am."

"Honestly, I wish she'd never told me," he said. "It changes things."

"It doesn't have to, Ryder. *She* didn't do it." Diane folded her arms across her chest. "Just like you not driving didn't allow it to happen."

It had taken him a long time to accept that. Still felt guilty for it some days.

Diane went on. "We don't have to figure out the past. There aren't answers. We know that."

She wasn't wrong about that. He got up and dumped his coffee in the sink. "I'm not really comfortable with this conversation."

"Well, too bad. I'm your sister and you can't just stick your head in the sand. Look, this whole family was broken-hearted when we lost Valerie and Ronnie Dwayne, and you know what . . . that is never, ever going to change. Even if you fall into complete and utter happiness it doesn't erase a thing from the past. It's okay. No one is keeping score. Forgive yourself. Forgive Jeff. Make Lorri forgive herself and Jeff too. Live, Ryder. You're almost back. I love it. It makes my heart so happy."

He saw the hope in his sister's eyes. "I missed her. Lorri, I mean. In a good way." It felt wrong even saying it.

"That's the healthiest thing I've heard you say in a long, long time."

"What would people think?"

"They'd never know, and who cares. It wasn't their loss to deal with."

"It scares me to death." He walked back over and sat at the table. "I can't go through that kind of grief again."

"I know." She placed her hand on top of his. "It's okay. We're moving forward. On all of it. The past . . . well, it was part of the journey. It wasn't our final destination. No telling where the future turns will take us." She cleared her throat and tapped the envelope she'd placed on the table. "I brought something to show you."

"That it?" He glanced up. "Was wondering what that was."

"It's perfect timing actually." She slid the thick stack of paper out of the envelope then swept the first few pages from the top and set the others aside. "These are a few pictures from the Tuggle wedding."

"Oh yeah." He reached for them, but she tugged them back.

"Before you look at these—it's not your imagination, Ryder. What you think you're feeling with Lorri. There's something to the two of you together. Everyone saw it that night on the dance floor."

The words hung there between them.

Finally, he took the glossy sheets from her.

Diane leaned in. "Reece brought these pictures over late last night so I could help her pick out the whittled-down set to share with the bride and groom in their keepsake album. She was so excited to show me these. Not for the couple, but for us. You look so happy. I couldn't wait to bring them over."

He looked at the striking black and white photography. At first it didn't even register that it was him in the picture with the beautiful woman. She was all he could see. Her face glowing in the twinkle lights. His hand balancing hers. Her hands were so soft. Her body warm as they swayed to the music in unison. As delicate as a breeze.

"That's joy, Ryder. In both of your faces. Look at how relaxed you two are, your hands, posture, the tilt of her jaw and lift in your smile. There's something there that no one can deny."

He pulled the picture closer, then stood, turning away from his sister as he studied it. The song played in his mind. Reliving the rush of his heart, his palms dampened.

All the feelings came rushing back.

Ryder looked at Diane. "Right before this was taken, I'd accused her of crashing the wedding, and tried to kick her off the property." He snickered.

"You were jealous." She was enjoying teasing him about that.

"I was not."

"Yes, you were."

"Maybe," he conceded, "but honestly I think the motivation was more that I thought she'd broken a confidence. She knew how important the event was to the kids. You know I'd die before I'd let Reece and Ross down. I can't believe I told her about it."

"That's not like you at all, but it turned out fine."

"Thank goodness. I couldn't have forgiven myself if I'd done something to ruin everything they've worked so hard on."

"Don't worry about them. They'll make it on hard work and gumption. It's in our Bolt DNA."

"We do have that."

"Welcome back, little brother. Your heart is doing more than just pumping blood. You're appreciating life again."

"Stop being dramatic."

"No. *You* stop." She snatched the picture from him with her fingertips. "You can't tell me there's not something to this. Those two people are not fighting."

"It resolved quickly."

"Because there's something good there holding you two together. All I'm saying is, don't let this slip away. It's been seven years. I miss you. We will never know why God called Valerie and Ronnie Dwayne back when he did, nor is there any promise that we'll ever understand the gravity of it all, but it's not for us to figure out. You've mourned. You survived for a reason. I'm so thankful for the father figure you are to Reece and Ross. I'm so proud of them, and your help has been a positive influence. That's something I can't repay you for, but I want my happy brother back. If I can help you make that happen we'll be even."

"It's family. There's no being even."

"You've done more than I could have ever dreamed of. It's your turn to dream a little, Ryder. Look at this again." She held a different picture up this time.

Lorri was laughing in the picture, and he remembered what was going through his mind at that moment. That he could live like this forever with her.

"Dream," Diane said. "About her. About possibilities. Even if it hurts."

He reached for the photo. "Can I have this?"

"Of course. Why don't you invite her to Sunday supper? The kids are both gonna be here."

"She wouldn't come. I'm not sure she's comfortable with us

being friends after the other night. She was so upset when she left."

"That's for you to fix, and if it's so you are just friends, that's fine too."

"Thank you."

"You know what they say about love. When you're not looking is when you walk right smack into it."

"Diane, go easy on me here. I'm trying. She's got her own scars to heal too, and they aren't seven years old."

"Okay, okay. I'll try to stay neutral. A little."

His sister left and he sat there for a good long while in contemplation.

A part of Ryder couldn't stop living in the moment of those pictures, and yet it terrified him too. He missed her when she was out of town, and it was almost the end of the day and he still hadn't heard from her. He called, but again there was no answer. It was possible she had meetings stacked up today. That wasn't unusual. He hung up, choosing not to leave a message.

By four o'clock though, he was getting antsy and finally texted her.

Just checking in on my friend Lorri ☺

She hadn't responded by dinner time. She had to eat, and he knew she didn't cook. What she needed was comfort food. She needed Mom's chicken and dumplings, and he had that recipe down pat.

It was close to seven when he dropped off a casserole dish to his sister's, then headed to Lorri's house with one to try to talk to her.

He stood at the door, nerves racing as if he'd downed a vat

of coffee. He knocked, and Mister let out a woof, but she didn't answer.

He knocked again, and this time Mister woofed until she came to the door and peeked outside.

Her hair was a mess, and her eyes were red and swollen.

"Can we talk?" he asked.

"I'm not feeling well."

"I made you chicken and dumplings. It cures just about anything."

"I don't think there's a cure for this," she said.

It hurt seeing her like this. "Can I at least set this down on the counter for you? It's still hot."

"Yeah. Sure." She backed away from the door.

He walked straight to the kitchen. Mister greeted him happily, and Ryder reciprocated with a head rub. He placed his hand on Lorri's arm.

She hitched a breath, tensing beneath his touch.

"When you told me you were Jeff's sister, it was a shock."

Shivering slightly, she nodded.

"Our stories are complicated. Individually and together. But we're good for each other. Don't you agree?"

"Every time you look at me, you'll think of it. It's too much to overcome."

"Lorri, let me decide what's too much for me."

"I would never want to hurt you."

"*You* didn't." How could he convince her? "I'm here by my choice. I missed you when you were out of town. I . . . I'm not saying I can snap my finger and forgive Jeff, but I can tell you that I know I need to."

"Forgiveness can be hard."

"I'm aware of that. It's taken me a long time to forgive myself, and some days I still forget. I want to live in the present, and the future. We said we'd help each other with that."

She walked to the living room and sat on the couch. He sat next to her and noticed her trembling.

"Wait a second, I know exactly what you need." He ran to the door, letting Mister follow along. He grabbed a large bag from his truck and jogged back to the house.

Lorri hadn't moved.

He stood there in front of her holding a big black trash bag.

She managed a laugh. "What is that? Is this some kind of metaphor about my baggage?"

"No, although you did say it was like a trash bag, didn't you?" He laughed. "No. That Sunday after the steer incident at the fair, I thought you were going to go back and I might see you again."

"To buy the quilt. Yeah, and I didn't make it back."

He handed her the bag. "I've been waiting for just the right time. I think this is it." He wanted more than anything to sweep her into his arms and take care of her.

Lorri reached into the plastic bag, and lifted the thick fabric corner. "It's the quilt." She looked surprised. "You bought it for me?"

"I did." He sat down on the couch. "Coming to see you is the first time I'd set foot on this land since the day my father sold it. That might not mean much to you, but it was a big step for me."

"I know, and then I let you down."

"No. You didn't let me down. Things have moved fast—like an undertow."

"It has."

"Whatever this is here between you and me, it's powerful, and honestly I don't want it to stop."

"We both have a lot of baggage, and we don't know much about each other."

"Tell me something I don't know," he said.

"I was pivotal in the new material for Bloom." She watched him for a reaction.

"I know."

"You do?"

"Admired the draft on your desk, then saw it in the paper. Put two and two together." He shrugged. "Tell me something else I should know. Your hopes and dreams. Your favorite flavor of ice cream? I don't know. Start anywhere."

"I love homemade strawberry ice cream. Hands down it's my favorite. My grandfather would make it for us."

"Mine's chocolate, but I'll make strawberry for you just like he did."

"Well, he made us hand crank it. That wasn't all that much fun."

"I'll make the ice cream. You can just enjoy it. It's Diane's favorite too."

"Were you and Diane always close?"

"We fought tooth and nail as kids sometimes, but at the end of the day we were over it. As adults, we couldn't be closer."

"And at the end of the day . . . Jeff and I weren't." Her bottom lip trembled. "I could never forgive him, but I have now." She let out a breath. "I have to."

He pulled her close. "I get it. You're right. People let us down. Things happen we have no control over. We don't have to understand it to survive it, but we might not get through it alone. I think you and I can survive this together. I want you in my life."

"I'm afraid you'll hate me for what Jeff did, and I'm afraid I'll get my heart broken."

"Don't be afraid." He took her hands in his.

"I need some time to think."

He kissed her on the forehead. "I'm going to give you some time to think, but please don't leave me hanging. Trust that what we have is something special, and that we can figure that out together." He stood and took a step toward the door. "I'm coming back in the morning. Okay?"

"Okay." She pulled her feet beneath her, hugging her knees.

She looked tiny and fragile sitting there alone as he walked out.

Chapter Thirty-one

The next morning, when Lorri didn't come to the door, Ryder tried the handle, which was unlocked, and let himself in. Mister didn't even bark.

Ryder stood there, not really understanding why two wounded souls should find each other in this way, but not questioning it.

He gave Mister a pat on the head as he walked by. Lorri still lay where he'd left her last night.

Her eyes fluttered open, then filled with tears.

He took the feather from his pocket and pressed it into her hand.

She looked at it, then curled her fingers around it. "I guess this is goodbye?"

"No. It's not. You are more than my friend Lorri. You gave me a reason to laugh again. We've both been through a lot, but there's no reason those things need to keep us apart. I know I don't want to live my life without you in it."

"But—"

Ryder wrapped his hand around hers. "Like that feather. Our life will change in the wind. We're going to land in situations we don't expect. We'll lose things. Find new ones. That feather drifted to my feet as I faced what life without you in it might be. I don't want to ever experience that."

"But can we? Ryder, this is the worst situation."

"It's not. It sounds like it, but it's what we make it, and I know one thing for certain. I can't say goodbye to you," he said. "I need you in my life."

She pushed herself up on the couch. "How can you look at me . . . knowing?"

"The same way I've looked at you since the day I met you. There's something special about you, Lorri, and I won't question it, and I'll never put it at risk. Please, please trust me with your heart." His pounded wildly.

"I do." She wrapped her arms around his neck, sobbing softly. "I've fallen in love with you."

He held her. "We'll respect our pasts and focus on our future. We'll say grateful prayers and not question the blessings. I want to enjoy every sunrise with you and snuggle every sunset."

"I'm going to paint them all, so we never forget how beautiful they are."

"I'll hang one right over the fireplace."

Epilogue

❧

Christmas in Dalton Mill was magical. Lorri and Ryder cut a Christmas tree down right there on his property. Turned out when Ryder was nine he'd had the idea of having his own Christmas tree farm. Pop-Pop had helped him plant a row of twelve Virginia pines to get started, teaching him how to shape them throughout the year. To this day, Ryder still planted a dozen pines each year to keep enough fresh trees for family and friends. That Christmas, the towering tree in the town square was one of Ryder's too.

They worked on the scholarship together—everyone in the family had a role—and Lorri felt like a part of the family already. She made time in her schedule for what she loved most. Ryder, painting, and Mister, of course.

By the time the Lisa Scholarship event took place she and Ryder had put every concern from their pasts behind them, fully embracing the gift that came from that day at the fair when Billy Ray Helms's steer got loose and their lives collided.

"Welcome to our inaugural fund raiser for the Lisa Scholarship," Reece announced from the podium at the front of the big barn.

The Wedding Ranch was decorated in lovely yellows and blues, setting off the logo that Lorri had designed with the butterfly on it that now hung as a backdrop on the stage. This may have been the largest sample of her work she'd ever seen.

Reece spoke eloquently. "Our family is so excited to launch this special scholarship helping our next generations garner the education needed to keep Dalton Mill sustainable by awarding graduates in the fields of animal science or agriculture."

It was standing room only and everyone had dressed for the elegant affair. Lorri stood near the stage in the same emerald-green dress she'd been wearing the day Ryder had accused her of crashing Cody and Kasey's wedding. She reached over and squeezed his hand. "You sure do clean up nice, cowboy," she whispered.

"Got to look my best on this special day." He adjusted the cavalry knot in the scarf tucked into his western jacket.

Lorri scanned the room. Twelve of her paintings had been hung gallery style, with lighting and all, along one wall. In glass trophy cubes they'd displayed the feathers that Ryder had created on black velvet jewelry stands. They were exquisite. Bob Timberlake, a local artist who had become quite famous, had even donated some original pieces.

Cody sat with Kasey and Jake at a table at the edge of the stage. This concert and sale had drawn a crowd.

"Bidding is open on all of the items around the room. Can everyone join me in a round of applause for our generous donations?" Reece lifted her hands to clap, and the guests responded in a ruckus that rolled like thunder. "Kiosks are available at each corner, or you can download our app if you haven't already. We have a scrumptious dinner which will be served as soon as I get off this stage, and I know everyone is chomping at the bit for Cody Tuggle to play for us tonight."

The crowd cheered even louder with a few shrill whistles this time.

"We have one more piece of business standing between you and dinner. Ryder, it's all yours."

Lorri cocked her head. "What?"

His smile was bright. "I *can* keep a secret."

She laughed, remembering how he'd bragged about Cody coming to get married at The Wedding Ranch. He was a man of his word. She knew that now.

Someone touched her shoulder as Ryder walked up on stage. She turned. "Mom? Dad?"

Ryder took the mic. "I didn't figure you'd mind one little song before dinner. I won't be doing the singing, but my friend over here has put some words to music for me."

Cody stood and ambled to the stage carrying his guitar. He waved, flashing that big Nashville grin he was known for.

"Lorri, will you join me up here?" Ryder requested.

"What is going on?" She glanced at Mom, who looked like she was having the time of her life standing there in a beautiful dress and Dad in his Sunday suit. Mom nudged her toward the stage.

Cody started singing while she made her way through the

crowd to the stage. In a flurry of excitement, she crossed behind Cody and took Ryder's hand.

She'd only half heard the words to the song in all the confusion, but when he sang the chorus again they spoke to only her.

"I love you," Ryder said. "You are my happiness."

Cody finished the song to a huge round of applause. "Thank you," he said. "Ryder wrote that for my dear friend Lorri. We've known each other since high school. Girl, I have never known you to be happier than you are with this guy, and he's a good one."

She swept tears that wouldn't stop.

Ryder dropped to one knee. "My friend Lorri, you make me as joyful as the morning sun. I'd be so honored to have you be my wife. Will you marry me?"

She gasped for a breath.

Cody stood there grinning and nodding. She looked to where her parents had been standing, and beside them Pam was crying too and giving her a thumbs-up.

"Yes, Ryder. Yes, I'll marry you!"

He took her shaking hand and slid a ring on her finger. A simple wide gold band with a feather etched across the front and a perfect row of rubies running down the center.

Cody strummed his guitar and everyone clapped. The commotion swirled as fast as her beating heart. Ryder stood, hugged her, and then picked her up, kissing her full on the mouth and turning three hundred and sixty degrees before putting her down.

Reece's voice came over the crowd. "Well, I guess we know

who will be getting married at The Wedding Ranch next! And now, dinner is being served. Bon appétit."

"I've never been so happy in my life," Lorri said.

"Hey, look." Ryder motioned over to where Diane stood much closer than usual to Mark. Her arm hugging Mark's biceps, she waved to Ryder and Lorri and blew them a kiss.

Mark gave him a thumbs-up.

"Is it just me or do you think there's a spark there?" Ryder said, barely moving his lips as he waved back.

"Oh, that is most definitely a spark." Lorri's smile widened. "Seems to be a lot of that going around tonight."

Acknowledgments

I am grateful to the team of professionals who've helped me bring this story from my heart to the book now in your hands.

Thank you to my agent, Steve Laube, for a seamless transition and for being supportive, personally and professionally, through the writing process.

To my editors, Eileen Rothschild and Lisa Bonvissuto, and the entire SMP team, I am honored to work with such a wonderful group of people. Eileen, we've brought so many Christmas stories to life together, and they've changed my life. I'm beyond thrilled to bring my first women's fiction with St. Martin's Press to publication with you and Lisa. Thank you for this wonderful opportunity. I've enjoyed the chance to dig deeper, shine brighter, and bring these characters and complex families to light in a story of forgiveness and love.

And heartfelt gratitude to my family and friends who give me strength, wisdom, and support every day.

About the Author

Adam Sanner

USA Today bestselling author NANCY NAIGLE whips up small-town love stories with a dash of suspense and a whole lot of heart. Now happily retired, she devotes her time to writing, antiquing, and the occasional spa day with friends. A native of Virginia Beach, she currently calls the Blue Ridge Mountains home. Nancy is the author of *Christmas Joy* and *Hope at Christmas*, both of which have been turned into films for the Hallmark Channel.